ANCIENT

A Search for the Lost City of the Mayas

Book Two in the
Brian Sadler Archaeological Mystery Series

Bill Thompson

*Published by
Ascendente Books
Dallas, Texas*

This is a work of fiction. The events and characters described herein are imaginary and any reference to specific places or living persons is incidental. The opinions expressed in this manuscript are solely the opinions of the author. The author has represented and warranted full ownership and/or legal rights to publish all the materials in this book.
Ancient: A Search for the Lost City of the Mayas
All Rights Reserved
Copyright © 2013, 2015
V.2.0
This book may not be reproduced, transmitted or stored in whole or in part by any means, including graphic, electronic or mechanical without the express written consent of the author except in the case of brief quotations embodied in critical articles and reviews.
Published by Ascendente Books
ISBN 978-0996181662
Printed in the United States of America

*This book is affectionately dedicated
to my real-life young explorer,
Captain Jack Thompson.
May your life be filled with great adventures.*

Love, Abuelo

ACKNOWLEDGEMENTS
Many thanks to former Assistant District Attorney Nancy Shew for help on ensuring the law enforcement and judicial scenes were correct and to my sons Ryan and Jeff and to Margie for proofreading and offering valuable feedback and suggestions.

ANCIENT

17 April 1540
His Excellency Carlos V
King of The Spanish Monarchy
Holy Roman Emperor
Savior of the New World

Your Excellency, your subject Pedro de Alvarado y Contreras writes to you from New Spain, from my post as Governor of the Kingdoms of Honduras and Guatemala, which were bestowed upon me by the grace of your Majesty.

I write to inform you of a discovery made many years ago, which resides today in the realm that I govern. It is my belief that you should have been made aware of this long ago but it was the order of my leader, Hernan Cortes, that he alone would inform you of the discovery he and I made, and that I never speak of it. I have learned only recently that Cortes is deceased, and I am concerned that it is likely he did not inform you, his King, of the existence of this important discovery, as I would have expected to receive instructions from you had you known of it. It is therefore with sincere apology that I now do so, and I am your humble servant should you wish to chastise me for my failure to previously bring this to the attention of Your Excellency.

As you are aware, in 1519 my leader Hernan Cortes and I led an expedition to conquer the once mighty natives known as Aztecs in New Spain, or Mexico as the natives refer to it. Between 1523 and 1527 I obeyed the commands of my leader and conquered the Cakchiquel in Guatemala. Following orders, I had many of the heathens killed in the name of our Lord and Savior when they refused to convert to Christianity. Others were enslaved.

One heathen who was brought to salvation through our Lord Jesus Christ was handed over to me after the conquest of the Quiche' nation in the name of your Excellency. That was in the year 1527. This man was literate in the language of his people, whom they call the Maya. He had been a scribe. I am certain many of the blasphemous books which we burned during those times were written by this man himself and a few others like him.

My leader Hernan Cortes and I interviewed this scribe to determine if there were yet more books we should destroy to promote the salvation of these savages. He told us of a building, part of a citadel high upon a mountaintop a few days' ride from the capital here in Santiago de los Caballeros de Guatemala, which as you recall was also the capital in 1527.

I remember well that Cortes and I, accompanied by troops for our safety and security, rode with the scribe to the foot of a mountain. With great difficulty our men created a pathway for my leader and the rest of us to reach the summit of the peak. At this time, the scribe told me that he would show us a prize hidden at the top of a broad rock staircase, through a narrow passageway between two high cliffs. Cortes told our men to remain behind and stay on alert in case it was an ambush. The two of us then went with the scribe up the expansive stairway, which was at least ten varas wide and thirty high. At the top was the narrow aperture and on the other

ANCIENT

side was a small plaza with one building, a heathen temple which he called Templo del Santuario – the Temple of the Sanctuary. He told us this temple building had once been covered by sheets of gold so that it shone to the heavens during the day. He said the sheets had been removed and transported far away by his people when our victorious Spanish forces came into this land.

Walking through enormous statues of jaguars, one on each side of the doorway, we entered the pagan temple and found that it consisted of several rooms, each with walls covered in shelves from floor to ceiling. Each shelf held books in the form of bound codices, held together in long stitched sheets. There were so many it was not possible to count them. Truly I believe there must have been a thousand or more. There were crude tables and chairs in the middle of each room, where the scribe said the priests used to sit and study the books. In the very rear of the structure was another room with a sealed door. The door contained inscriptions and strange writings carved into the seals around it. The native with us said this room was accessible only by the high priest and was said to contain gold, but it was also full of danger. I wanted to tear open the door but Cortes held up his hand to indicate I should be patient. Upon seeing that I wanted to open the door, the native commenced shaking uncontrollably and was obviously terrified. He fell to the ground as though possessed by a demon, jumped up suddenly, ran outside and would not enter again.

BILL THOMPSON

I said to Cortes that we should get our men to light torches and burn the books. He advised that since the location was remote and forbidding, he would leave the building as it was and seek the advice of your Majesty. Perhaps you would want to have a history of these heathen people or to see with your own eyes the blasphemies they wrote. Cortes also said he would return with mules and men to remove and transport the gold if that were your command.

I was surprised, my sovereign Majesty, that my leader then removed his sword and suddenly executed the native who had brought us here. We left his body on the table in that room. I feared for my own life as well for a time, since one knows not of the avarice in the heart of a man faced with temptation, but I was never in danger.

After our departure from the mountain I said nothing more about the matter, having been told directly by Cortes that I was never to speak of it again. I did however make a map in case I was ordered to return. I enclose it with this letter.

Over the years I heard tales that Hernan Cortes had returned to the place and taken the gold for himself. Sworn to secrecy, I chose not to investigate those rumors. I can only trust that Cortes was an honorable man and that your Majesty knows of the hidden gold.

Although all of this has come to mind frequently over the years, it was only recently that it returned to my consciousness, upon my learning of the death of Cortes. I felt it imperative that I inform

ANCIENT

you of the existence of this place, if only that you might direct me to examine the closed room, destroy the entire building, or to send some of the blasphemous books to your Majesty for your perusal. Command me and I will obey.

Further, if you wish me to enquire as to the movement of sheets of gold from Guatemala to a place far to the north by the Maya or the rumors that Cortes himself took gold from the sealed room, I shall await your orders on that subject as well.

I am your loyal subject, awaiting your direction.

Your obedient servant,
Pedro de Alvarado
Governor of the Kingdoms of Honduras and Guatemala

BILL THOMPSON

ANCIENT

BOOK ONE

BILL THOMPSON

ANCIENT

CHAPTER ONE

Near the border between Belize and Guatemala

Brian Sadler sat in total darkness seven hundred feet below the surface of the ground. He could hear nothing – the sounds of the rest of his party had long since disappeared and he felt totally alone. He had been left with a backpack, his iPhone and a promise they would return for him in less than two hours. They were now way over an hour late and his mind was racing, playing tricks on him in the absolute blackness. He sat on a rock, occasionally turning on his headlamp but mostly keeping it off to conserve the battery. If anything happened to the others and they failed to return, he would need light to find his way out . . . if he could make it back up at all.

The initial descent into the recently discovered cave had proven uneventful. There were three others in the group: Alfredo, a local guide and the man who had found the cave; Brian's girlfriend Nicole Farber; and Sam Adams, Brian's old friend who owned the San Ignacio Inn, a hotel in Belize where Brian and Nicole were staying. Sam had introduced Brian to Alfredo, remarking that he had explored caves all over the Cayo District in western Belize but had never found a new one before.

Sam came along just to see what secrets this new cave might hold. He was always looking for something different to introduce to his guests when they asked for adventure off the beaten path. A previously unknown cavern, especially one with Mayan pottery and even a body, might prove interesting.

The trip to this cave wasn't part of Brian's itinerary in Belize and Guatemala. He had important work to do and not much time to do it in. But this was Sunday and there were a few days to kill before he left on his mission. At the last minute Brian had decided to take Alfredo up on his offer. It would be exciting to view something the public hadn't seen. A new, unexplored cave. Who knew what secrets might lie beyond the next turn? And Brian, ever the adventurer, couldn't resist a side trip. This would be a little diversion before his real mission in Guatemala began. But look what this Sunday afternoon expedition had turned into.

Brian wasn't even certain what country he was in. They could have crossed over into Guatemala for all he knew. Like so much of the jungle here, this area was virtually unexplored and the border between the two countries snaked through dense jungle with no boundary or marker. The countryside contained a vast, buried wealth of Mayan temples, tombs, house mounds and artifacts, but limited resources in these small, relatively poor countries allowed only a fraction of the sites to be explored. That meant that new finds like the cave where Brian sat were always exciting. There was no way to know what one might find. Alfredo had done limited exploring on the three visits he'd made since

ANCIENT

he found the hole while hunting with his dog. He knew there were Mayan pots and a skeleton in the cave, because he had seen them. He had no idea what else might be in there.

The few caves in Belize that were open to the public had been rendered accessible – they were cleaned up and had handrails, lights, ropes and ladders installed – and they were fairly easy to navigate. This one was different because it was new. There were no amenities to help – the descent started out easy but they soon had come to a ten-foot drop down a slick rock. A rope attached to a carabiner was dangling there - Alfredo explained he had installed it on his first visit and all they had to do was basically slide down the rope. It sounded simple and everyone managed it fine by using gloves Alfredo had given them. Brian asked if they would be coming back this way; Alfredo laughed and said, "No, climbing this rope would be difficult for all of you, I think. I know you are in good shape, but rock climbing is a tough sport!" He said they would continue through the cave and exit through another means he'd discovered on his last visit.

After they descended a hundred feet and made a number of turns, the only light at all came from their headlamps. There were bats and the occasional lizard for a while, but by the time they were several hundred feet down it was far too cold for those creatures to live comfortably.

The descent itself had gone uneventfully. Four hours ago they were deep inside the cave. Alfredo, the guide, had turned to the group and said, "This last part ahead will take us into the lowest part of the cave I've found so far. This is the chamber where you will see Mayan pots and a skeleton lying in a niche in the cave wall. At that point we will be about seven hundred feet below the surface. Watch your steps, amigos. The rocks are very slippery here."

The guide went first, holding on to small outcroppings from the rocks on the side of him, as he slid partially on his feet, partially on his butt, down a large rock and landed on the sand floor. He turned and his light shone on the rest. "Who's next?" he said.

Nicole volunteered, and she navigated the short drop without incident. Brian's friend Sam did the same. As Brian sat on the top of the large rock he needed to go down, he began to slide before he was ready and he struggled to grab a handhold to stop himself. He couldn't find a good grip and slid faster, turning partially on his right side as he moved down the slippery rock. Where the rock ended he hit his right shoulder hard on an outcropping. At the same instant he fell about three feet onto the sandy floor. No one was looking his way; they all had their eyes on the Mayan skeleton that lay in a niche in the opposite wall.

Brian stood up, massaging his shoulder. The guide looked around and said, "OK. We are ready to go ahead. The rest of the way will be trickier. There are many twists and turns. When I was last here two weeks ago, I dug rocks, moved some rubble and found another way back to the top. It involves a lot of climbing, but it's a faster and easier way out than coming back through here." Alfredo noticed Brian moving his arm around. He asked, "Are you OK?"

"I hit my shoulder on the way down. Lost my footing, dammit."

The guide told Brian to come with him to the other end of the room where they stood. "Try

ANCIENT

to go through this small opening. The rest of the trip will be like this, and you must move through tricky holes, plus climb a rope."

As Brian knelt to twist into the tight hole, his right arm began to throb. He tried to make a fist and realized he couldn't grip. "I'm not sure that I can do the rest," he admitted, angry at himself and incredibly disappointed that he wouldn't be able to explore the winding cave tunnels.

"OK, that's it then," Alfredo said. "We go back now."

"No. Can't you come back here and get me after you take the others to the top?"

"Probably, but that's not how I do it. If one person can't go on, we all go back. That's the only safe way."

Brian insisted that the others go ahead. Nicole looked at him and said, "I'll stay with you if you want, but I have to tell you I'm not comfortable sitting here with this skeleton in absolute darkness."

"No, everyone's going on," Brian replied. "Alfredo, take the others on through and come back down with a rope to help me get back up the same way we came down. How long do you think you'll be gone?"

"Senor, if everything goes smoothly, I would be gone one and a half hours. But every time I come into this cave, things are different. Rocks fall. Things get slippery, just like where you fell. If we go ahead and find we can't go further, I will need to backtrack. That is why I do not recommend we leave you. I am certain I will return, but what if something happened?"

Brian managed a laugh, hoping for Nicole's sake it sounded sincere. "Nothing's going to happen. If you get to the surface and can't get back down, just go get help." As he spoke, he recalled the three-hour trip from their hotel in San Ignacio to this site, much of it on unpaved, deeply rutted roads. At one point they had had to use machetes to cut their way through the underbrush, continuing on what was nothing more than a wide path. If they had not had an ATV, the trek would have been impossible. And the last mile or two was uphill on foot. If the guide couldn't return to rescue him, it would probably be a day before they could make the round trip to get help and return. Which meant Brian would be spending the night seven hundred feet below the surface.

"Senor, I strongly suggest this is not a good idea."

Nicole said, "Brian, I insist. We have to stop now and all go up. We will figure out how to pull you up as we go."

"Actually, Senorita," Alfredo said, "I have more ropes in the other pack I left in the ATV. We will have a difficult time bringing Senor Brian to the surface from here. It would probably be better for me to go up myself and get the ropes."

"OK, that settles it," Brian said. "I stay, you all go. Come back with the ropes when you all reach the top and I'll see you then."

Reluctantly accepting, Alfredo told Brian he must stay exactly in this place until the guide returned. "You may decide later that you feel well enough to attempt your own rescue, or to try to meet me halfway. I must tell you that would be foolish beyond imagination. This cave has many side paths, and I had to lay a rope behind me from the surface when I descended the first time. If I had not done that, I could easily have taken a wrong turn and been lost forever. I cannot say enough that you must

ANCIENT

stay here. I know where you are right now, and this is where I will come to find you."

And so Nicole, Sam and the guide Alfredo left. At first Brian could hear their voices getting fainter and fainter as they moved away from the place where he sat on a rock, then he heard nothing at all. Although the room was large, maybe nine feet square with a ceiling over twenty feet tall, Brian found it claustrophobic when he turned off his light. He remembered his phone and found a little solace in reading a book he had downloaded. It was nothing more than a way to pass the time, and he worried about running down the phone's battery. There was a slim chance the guide might not return for a long time – Brian might need the dim light from the phone if that happened.

How stupid and selfish of me to jeopardize the safety of all these people, he said to himself. *Why did I even think about taking an outing for the hell of it, just to see a damned cave before the public was allowed to explore it?*

At one point he switched on his headlamp for a few minutes and examined the three large Mayan pots lying on the ground across the room. He also walked to the niche in the cavern wall and glanced at the skeleton. It was intact, just where the body had been placed hundreds of years ago. Being alone in the dark with this ancient Mayan didn't worry Brian, but he did think a little about if God protected this body, that hopefully He didn't care if Brian waited awhile until his friends returned.

He also had a backpack – each of them had been given one to carry by the guide. One contained ropes, another had rappelling gear and a third had food for today's lunch. Brian didn't know which one he had been given, so he busied himself by opening the pack. He was pleased to discover that he had all the sandwiches, five beers and some water. Enough to last several days, he figured. And an incentive for the others to push Alfredo to hurry back down and get him, if they got to the top and were hungry for lunch. But what if they didn't make it back up? What if they got stranded themselves – by a rock slide, or a guide who lost his way, or something worse? What if one of them was hurt too? As the time passed, Brian glanced more and more often at the luminous dial of his watch and his concern grew. He worried more that Nicole might not make it back to the surface than he did about himself. *What an idiot,* he thought. *Why in hell did I even think about bringing her down here? She didn't even want to come. She was just being a trouper.*

Another hour came and went with no sign of the guide who'd promised to rescue him. Brian looked at his watch – it was early afternoon and the group had been gone four hours. He switched on his headlamp. It glowed steadily, then flickered. The battery was dying. He turned it off quickly, sat on a rock, and held his head in his hands. For the first time in a long time, he began to pray.

ANCIENT

CHAPTER TWO

New York City
Three months earlier

Brian Sadler stood in the front window of Bijan Rarities, watching the March shower steadily increase in intensity. It pelted the sidewalk along Fifth Avenue, turning New York streets into a sluggish stream of traffic. An hour ago he had debated arranging a car for the short ride to the Monument Club, where he was scheduled to have lunch, but he decided the light showers were manageable on foot. Now it was a different story, but also too late to change his plans. A taxi was also out of the question on a rainy weekday at noon in Manhattan.

As he had done for several months, Brian spent this morning on the upcoming sale of a collection purchased by a Wall Street hedge fund manager thirty years ago. It contained over two hundred ancient artifacts from Mexico City. In the 1400s the Aztecs built Tenochtitlan. It became the capital of their empire and was a vast complex of temples, buildings and homes. In around 1521

BILL THOMPSON

Hernan Cortes laid siege to the city. His victory brought down not only the capital but the entire Aztec civilization itself. As the Spanish so often did, Cortes built a cathedral on the site where a major temple once stood, and eventually the entire area became the bustling metropolis of Mexico City, one of the world's most densely populated cities. The Aztec capital was known to have existed somewhere, but it was largely forgotten.

In 1978 workers building the bus and subway system unearthed a massive disc of stone that led them to a stairway and the huge Temple of Tenochtitlan. Archaeologists from the University of Mexico descended upon the site and made an intelligent decision – they called in colleagues from around the world. This project was far too vast, and Mexico was too poor, to provide the massive resources required to quickly examine the enormous area. Most significantly, time was short – the metro system had to be completed so the government was not willing to allow years to do an archaeological dig as it should be done. One thing led to another and, as happens so often, time constraints caused priceless artifacts to be removed from the places they had lain for centuries, ending up in the hands of a collector willing to pay a staggering sum to own them.

Brian had been pleased when the owner and his wife called Bijan Rarities to handle the sale of the artifacts. "The reputation of your gallery and its previous owner, Darius Nazir, are unprecedented, Mr. Sadler," the owner had said when they first met over drinks at the 21 Club a year ago. The owner had heard of the fabulous Inkharaton sale of Egyptian artifacts Bijan Rarities had handled some time back, and had watched the program that had broadcast

ANCIENT

the auction live and simultaneously from Egypt and New York. Brian had been present at Bijan that day as an observer, but had had no idea that through a bizarre turn of events, he would end up owning the gallery himself not long afterwards.

"Yes, the Inkharaton sale certainly gave us vast publicity," Brian had responded to the collector. "And your sale will too."

There had been a world of issues with the Aztec Commission, as the trove had come to be named. Primary to the difficulty had been the fact that only a dozen of the nearly fifty items owned by the couple were actually in the United States. Those had been legally exported from Mexico in the 1990s, but until now the government had refused to allow the other items to be shipped out of the country. Brian found no fault with this – he felt it was a shame when great museums nabbed ancient items from third world countries who couldn't afford to excavate or exhibit them and whisked them away to Berlin, or London, or New York. There they remained for decades, on view to many but not accessible to the people of their home country. Therefore, if Bijan Rarities were to successfully sell the antiquities Brian had to overcome the problem of location. It was one thing to own a piece of civilization; it was another thing altogether to get permission to export it from the country where the priceless artifacts had been unearthed.

For the past several weeks Brian had been working on arranging another worldwide broadcast – this time on *History*, the New York-based network previously known as the History Channel – which would provide an hour of history about Tenochtitlan and its creation by the Aztecs, and two further hours showing the artifacts themselves, with renowned archaeologist Dr. Pablo Nunez of the Mexican Museum of Antiquities as the narrator. The involvement of Dr. Nunez had been a concession in getting the artifacts released, but Brian was glad to have his expertise regardless. Brian planned to create the show along the lines of *Antiques Roadshow*, showing an artifact while Dr. Nunez discussed it. Brian would then provide an auction estimate. The items would easily bring many millions of dollars, Brian figured, as most of them were priceless and were unique examples of art, pottery and inscriptions which had never before been discovered.

The show would be taped in advance, unlike the live Egyptian show on Discovery that Bijan Rarities had previously orchestrated. Two weeks after the show aired the sale of the Aztec relics would occur. That auction would not be televised for public viewing but instead would be simulcast from three places: Bijan's New York headquarters, its new gallery on Old Bond Street in London and the Tenochtitlan site in Mexico City. It was certain to create a major stir, fueled by publicity from the show itself, Bijan's substantial marketing efforts, and the intense interest from the collector and museum community for the items being offered.

This morning Brian's work specifically focused on finishing a major key to the entire sale - ensuring the new owners could actually take possession of their auction items, since so many of the artifacts were physically in Mexico. Thanks to the network of people known to the late Darius Nazir, who had previously owned Bijan Rarities, Brian had access to help from very high places. And it had taken a deputy ambassador's call to the director of antiquities in Mexico City to get approval for the

ANCIENT

successful bidders to be permitted to export the artifacts to their home countries. Brian had received a fax with official authorization for the removal of the items from Mexico once the auction was completed. Now he could wrap this project up.

History network had come back to him yesterday. The show's layout had been determined, a crew had been in Mexico for weeks filming both the artifacts and the ancient site where they were discovered, and the show's director at History was ready to meet with Brian to put the finishing touches on the event and set a date. It appeared that within a few months, almost a year's worth of effort would come to fruition. The Aztec Commission had become overwhelming to Brian – it was almost the only thing he had worked on for months, and he was finding himself wishing there were something else to distract him, especially now that most of the task list was the network's, in final preparation and filming. Brian's personal involvement was almost finished.

Turning from the rain outside Bijan Rarities' Fifth Avenue showroom windows, Brian spoke to Collette Conning, who sat at a desk at the rear of the gallery doing paperwork.

"I'm heading out to lunch with Lord Borland, and I have no idea when I'll be back. This could be another wild goose chase, but you never know."

She replied, "From his call Arthur Borland seems just the opposite of a wild goose chase. He's a British lord, for goodness sake. We're pretty proud of that lot, overall. He sounds like a man with both feet on the ground to me. Stay dry out there, or at least don't get drenched. And keep your mobile turned on in case I need you." It made him smile when she used British words for things Americans termed differently.

BILL THOMPSON

Brian felt in his pocket for his cell phone. Donning rubber boots and a trench coat he stepped through the front entrance to the sidewalk, raised his black umbrella and started to walk toward Madison Avenue.

I hope Lord Borland shows up after all this effort, Brian thought to himself as he made his way along the sidewalk, seemingly hitting every puddle that existed. A car struck a pothole in the street, throwing water Brian's way and causing him to lose his footing. He almost fell into the throng of pedestrians maneuvering around him.

Brian turned onto Madison Avenue, wishing there were an easy way to have taken the subway to the Club from his office. Given the layout of the underground train system and where Brian was headed, that was impossible. So he trudged along in the driving rain, walking north until he came to 75th Street and the building occupied by the Monument Club. The Victorian era structure was an imposing four stories high, marked by nothing more than a brass plaque bearing the club's address.

Brian always enjoyed coming to this place. It was founded in London in 1890 by a group of archaeologists, professional and amateur. Today the Monument Club was a place where members, mostly men with a smattering of women, gathered to read, study, discuss and contemplate history. The latest archaeological finds were always a key topic, and rumors of new discoveries were eagerly dissected by a group of fanatics who loved the subjects of ancient cities, artifacts and digs.

Not long after he assumed ownership of Bijan Rarities, Brian had inquired as to how he could become a member of the Monument Club. Learning that he must be sponsored, he had called his friend

ANCIENT

Oscar Carrington, owner of a prestigious London antiques gallery, to see if Carrington had a connection.

The response was perfect. "Since I'm a member myself, I'm your man. I'll be happy to sponsor you and I promise you'll be glad you joined. The Monument Club is a fabulous place to learn. And the original club's right here in London. I'll wager you don't know that about sixty thousand volumes are in its major archaeological library on the third floor. Even more than in the club you Yanks have!"

Brian was hooked at that point and soon was a regular at the club, getting to know some of the members and joining in discussions about this artifact or that, upcoming digs or whispers of lost cities. He dealt in antiquities every day but his fascination for archaeology and artifacts never waned. And now that Brian recently had opened the London gallery for Bijan Rarities, he hoped to find himself more often in that venue he loved.

Reaching the entrance, Brian rang the bell. Instantly the door opened and a uniformed porter said, "Good afternoon, Mr. Sadler. Particularly nasty weather today, sir. Let me take your topcoat and umbrella." He then pointed Brian to a nearby chair where he sat and took off his wet boots. Other than sodden pant legs, Brian was pleased to find himself relatively presentable.

"Your guest is waiting in the dining room, sir."

Brian walked into the dark-paneled room where a handful of men were having lunch. A waiter at the door greeted Brian and led him to the table he liked most, next to expansive windows overlooking Madison Avenue. Glancing outside, Brian saw that today the view consisted of nothing more than dark skies, fog and pouring rain. He couldn't even see Central Park just down the street.

A tall man dressed in a pinstripe suit was seated at Brian's table. "Mr. Sadler?" the man said, rising and extending his hand. "I'm Arthur Borland."

"My Lord. It's very nice to meet you."

A waiter appeared at Brian's side and set a glass of wine on the table in front of him.

"Would you care for a Sancerre, Lord Borland, or something else to drink?" Brian asked.

"Call me Arthur, please. And yes, I rather think I would enjoy a glass of wine."

"My condolences at the loss of your father. I regret that I didn't have the pleasure of meeting him."

"Although it's been months since his disappearance, something inside me still holds out hope he will turn up someday. So when people offer condolences, I correct them. I don't accept that he's gone. To me, he's away on another of his adventures . . . just MIA for now. Some of my friends say I'm bonkers for clinging to the thread of hope he could still be alive, but I know Father. Whatever may have happened, he wouldn't have gone peacefully to his grave."

The men settled into the comfortable armchairs and ordered lunch. The club was a warm, inviting place in normal circumstances. Today Brian found it even more so – thunder rumbled incessantly, logs popped in a huge stone fireplace and the flames danced, flickering off the dark mahogany walls of the room. He loved a rainy day – something he got from his mother, he reflected – and this was turning into one for the record books.

They made small talk, discussing Arthur Borland's flight from London to New York. It turned

ANCIENT

out Borland was here frequently, handling his family's business. "I make the trip across the pond so often," he said, "it really isn't difficult at all. Flying's not what it used to be but business class on British Airways serves me well and I have a lot of frequent flyer miles to help on the fare. I can eat, drink and get some work done." Frankly, Borland's agreeing to meet in New York had been great for Brian, who was tied down here with the Aztec Commission project.

Brian observed Lord Borland as they talked. He was a nervous man, unable to sit still for long. He moved his fingers and hands frequently as they talked.

"How are you coming along on the Aztec exhibition and auction?" Borland asked. "The wonderful publicity you've received in the London papers indicates it's going to be something really special."

Brian filled him in on where things stood and Borland replied, "I'm sure it's a headache with all the 'behind the scenes' work you're having to do. It all seems so easy when one sees a television show in its final form."

The waiter removed plates and asked if either of them would like coffee. "I don't know your preference, Brian," Arthur replied, "but I think I'll have another glass of this wonderful Sancerre."

Agreeing, Brian asked the waiter to serve them in the bar. The men rose from the table. Lord Borland retrieved a valise he had stashed by his chair. The men moved down the hall into another elegantly paneled area, its floor-to-ceiling windows framing the famous avenue, a room that sported an even larger, older and grander fireplace. A few tables were occupied. Some men played cards in a corner of the room. Another read *Archaeology* magazine; still others seemed content merely to be alone with a drink, reflecting, on a dark dreary day. Brian and his guest took a table near the hearth.

Arthur said, "If you have some time I'd like to tell you a story about my father's last expedition in Belize and Guatemala. Although it's enigmatic, I promise it's also exciting. And I'll tell you why we've never had a funeral for Father. Why I think he may turn up someday. All this will tie together with the reason I called you – I promise!"

Lord Borland reached down, opened the valise next to him and took out a small wooden box wrapped in cloth. Removing the wrapping, he set the box on the table. "We'll discuss this little keepsake later," Borland said, smiling. Brian saw his hands shaking almost uncontrollably. Arthur noticed his glance and immediately put his hands in his lap.

Brian looked at the box then gestured to the window. The rain was intensifying and the sky growing ever darker. He smiled and replied, "I have all the time in the world. On a day like this, I can think of nothing I'd rather do than sit by the fire in good company, with an adventure unfolding before me."

He settled back into his chair, sipping his Sancerre as the story began.

ANCIENT

CHAPTER THREE

As people of vast wealth often can, the family was able to take advantage of opportunities most people couldn't imagine. At lunch with Queen Elizabeth one day in the sixties, Jack's father had mentioned his son's interest in Central America, particularly in the Mayan regions.

"There's a position open in British Honduras," the Queen had casually remarked. "If Jack wanted to spend some time with the Maya I think he could find himself with more than he could ever imagine."

British Honduras became Belize in 1973, but not before Jack Borland was Governor-General of the colony, the Queen's own representative to this small country. Using the power vested in him as its leader, he kept a close eye on the archaeological excavations that occurred from time to time.

The colony was poor and Britain wasn't interested in funding excavations, so it was left to one university or another to pay for an expedition. Jack ensured all of these expeditions received their permits - he was widely known as a great friend to the archaeologists, using his resources as the colony's leader to pull strings and smooth out the hiccups that inevitably happened. In return he was kept informed about every interesting find, every exciting discovery. When a major dig was underway, it was not unusual to see the Governor-General himself on horseback at the site, watching the progress with his own eyes.

In this manner Jack Borland learned much about the Maya and their history. Once an excavation was underway Jack was always full of questions. Sometimes things were found which were puzzling, enigmatic and that somehow didn't fit with previous thinking. Jack loved those situations. His mind was open to every possibility – he didn't know, for instance, how the primitive Mayans managed to lift fifty-ton blocks a hundred feet in the air to top off a temple in the jungle. And he wouldn't have been any more surprised to find out the Mayan kings knew the mystery of levitation than he would to learn they had complicated pulley-and-block systems. He loved the mystery as much as the solution. Perhaps more.

"Now I'll tell you about my father's most recent expedition," Arthur continued. Nearly two years ago, Captain Jack and a party of six men had left San Ignacio, Belize, a town close to the border with Guatemala. The group headed west, crossed the border and went into the Guatemalan jungle on a quest to locate a priceless hoard – the fabled library of the Maya. Jack Borland had headed dozens of forays into the forbidding terrain before but this one would turn out differently. The party ultimately vanished without a trace.

San Ignacio is a village of around ten thousand people that sits on the banks of the Macal River and serves as the capital of the Cayo District. Tourists who arrive here are mostly passing through,

ANCIENT

visiting the ancient Mayan ruin of Xunantunich or heading to the Guatemalan border for a day trip to Tikal, one of the best known and most well excavated Mayan sites. They may stop in town to have lunch but not a lot of tourists stay overnight in San Ignacio. The ones who do stand out. No one was better known, or better liked in this small town, than Captain Jack. For the former Governor-General, this place had been the starting point for a succession of ultimately fruitless expeditions over the last few years.

It takes very little time for information to spread in a place where everyone knows everyone else. Every time Borland showed up in town he was ecstatic about yet another possibility - a piece of information, a shred of parchment, a tale passed from one generation to the next. So far Captain Jack Borland had had no success but the townspeople welcomed his arrival. He was always excited, enthusiastic and willing to bolster the local economy by purchasing provisions and hiring men to accompany his expeditions. Never mind that they always returned empty-handed. They all knew Captain Jack would show up again someday, excited about yet another adventure.

This time Jack Borland seemed more enthused about the quest than ever. During the week that he interviewed and hired three local men to accompany him into the jungle, rumors circulated that this time was different - Borland was on the verge of a major discovery. Everyone knew that for years Captain Jack had been searching for the legendary library of the Mayas, their version of the fabled Library of Alexandria, Egypt, a storehouse of written information about a civilization that had otherwise left very little in writing to allow understanding of them. Some scholars and historians believed that the ancient library had housed not just written records but also the richest artifacts of this once-great culture, including massive troves of gold objects hidden hundreds of years ago by Mayan kings.

Others, including most archaeologists familiar with these people, believed that the Mayan library was a myth, that this civilization never had extensive written records of their history and never amassed a storehouse of treasure. Others thought if anything ever had existed, the Spaniards had appropriated or destroyed it much as they did in other so-called heathen societies, which they endeavored to "civilize". The Spaniards believed they were the only civilized people in a strange land of barely human Indians. It was typical for them to scourge the area, kill the people, burn their "heathen" books and records and steal anything of value in the name of the King. Hernan Cortes and his band of Spanish conquerors dealt with the Maya in this fashion, almost totally obliterating any written records of the people and their past.

Thankfully for history, a few records survived. Many citizens of San Ignacio thought Jack Borland had seen them. Rumor had it that when Jack had been Governor-General of the colony of British Honduras fifty years ago, he witnessed the opening of a cave containing books. The cave later disappeared.

Some people said Borland had gone to the archives in Seville, Spain, looking at journals written by various scribes, the most literate members of the Spanish entourages that swept the Maya countryside in the sixteenth and seventeenth centuries. Others mentioned rumors of an ancient map on parchment, covered in strange symbols – a map that roughly

ANCIENT

corresponded to the area of the jungle where they were headed this time. So the story went, it was a secret document Jack had located while he was Governor. He managed to keep it for himself once the country became independent.

Not all the theories were as believable as these rumors. One of the weirdest was that the storehouse Borland was seeking was far, far older than the Maya themselves, maybe older than the pyramids of Egypt. No one knew anything for sure.

For many days Jack worked to assemble his team and supplies. The evenings found him in one bar or another, buying rounds of drinks and regaling everyone with fantastic stories. Everyone loved him – although they enjoyed his company, no one got information out of him, even when he lapsed into one of his frequent drunken binges.

This time when departure day came there was a noticeable air of excitement in the village. It was Saturday and the local market was underway. But on this day practically the entire town gathered not at the market but a block away by a small caravan of vehicles, to see off Captain Jack and his men. There were six in all – Jack and his team of three explorers plus two men who would drive the SUVs back when the others entered the rain forest on foot. The group had spent days assembling and packing equipment and provisions. A priest blessed the men, sprinkling holy water on each of them. It was a festive time as the team headed off, moving westward to the border, then across into the Guatemalan jungle.

Every Saturday brought communication from the expedition by satellite phone. The solar powered phone was the way Borland kept in touch and he allowed his men to talk briefly to their families. On the first call Captain Jack advised they were ready to move into the jungle on foot. There were Jack, three Belizean natives and a load of equipment and provisions.

The last call they'd received was from deep in the Guatemalan jungle. The team, following Captain Jack's directions, was slowly climbing up a mountain. The men were following a crude trail that had seen little activity in months – they were frequently forced to cut swaths out of the dense jungle to make any progress. It was grueling work, made more difficult by oppressive heat, humidity and torrential downpours for ten or fifteen minutes every afternoon.

Below the canopy of trees and plants, down on the jungle floor where the men trod, it was steamy and damp all the time. Clothes stuck to your body. Insects constantly buzzed around every exposed piece of skin. The native men were exhausted after only an hour or so of work and frequently they had to stop for water and insect repellent. But they were making progress uphill, according to Captain Jack's optimistic report that day.

Then one Saturday came and went with no phone call. Then another. A month passed with no contact, then a second and third. The team had vanished.

ANCIENT

CHAPTER FOUR

The rain intensified as Brian sipped on his wine, captivated as Arthur continued the story.

"Three months after they left I flew from London to Belize City, drove to San Ignacio and hired two men to help me locate Father's expedition." One of the guides whom Arthur hired spoke a few words of English and had a vested interest in finding the missing men. His brother was on Captain Jack's expedition and was now missing. The other guide had driven Jack to the drop-off point in Guatemala and therefore he knew the exact place at which Borland had entered into the jungle on foot. He said the beginning was just off the highway, marked by a crude sign with an arrow pointing into the air, inscribed with a lighthearted message - *Jaguar's Call. Food and Lodging. 1000 meters straight up.*

"I'd never heard of Jaguar's Call," Arthur continued. The guides said it was a retreat high on the mountain run by a white man, a place to which many would-be treasure hunters found their ways. Perhaps Jack had made it there. If so, the proprietor could give them information.

BILL THOMPSON

Arthur Borland and his two guides found the spot where Captain Jack's expedition had entered the jungle. They walked over a mile - at times the trail was barely visible, obscured by vines and undergrowth. Soon one of the natives yelled, "Senor Arthur, come!" The man had found a campsite, long abandoned, and a rock into which was etched "Borland 2011." An arrow pointed the direction in which the expedition started up the mountain.

Until now they had been ascending slowly but suddenly things changed. The real climb was about to begin - over eight thousand feet of mountain, covered with almost impenetrable undergrowth, stood dauntingly before them.

With little more to guide them than the knowledge that the group would have been moving upwards, the Belizeans pointed out a rough trail leading away from the rock they had found. The group moved into the forest using machetes to cut undergrowth from the makeshift trail they were on. In the months since Captain Jack was here it had become quickly overgrown but it was still a recognizable trail.

They moved slowly upwards, every exhausting day ending with the setting up of camp and preparation of a meal. They set up a perimeter, kept a fire going and took turns guarding throughout the night while the others slept. They would be no match for the predators which inhabited this jungle if they were caught unawares.

Arthur and his team had three thousand feet of climbing left before they'd find the Jaguar's Call, a collection of shabby buildings its owner jokingly called a "jungle resort." The truth was, no tourists ever ventured this far into the rain forest. You faced a grueling climb in a dangerous jungle to get to a

ANCIENT

'resort' totally lacking in creature comforts. No one ever came here for fun. This was a stopping point for people with a mission.

The Jaguar's Call was a destination for travelers of a different kind – people who were seeking treasure or archaeologically significant artifacts. This particular mountain, one of the highest in the area at nearly nine thousand feet, was the subject of countless fables. Some said there were mines from which the Maya had retrieved tons of gold. Others wove tales of intricately carved temples merely waiting to be rescued from the undergrowth – buildings jutting from the trees like ancient skyscrapers, which would give their discoverers instant fame and recognition. Some thought these buildings contained wealth or the secrets of the Mayan civilization so many people yearned to know. Maybe there were clues as to why the entire culture suddenly abandoned everything they had created.

Like Captain Jack, some who arrived at Jaguar's Call had maps. The one Jack currently believed in indicated that this mountain was the site of the fabled Mayan library – a place that could reveal the secrets about this major civilization. Atop this mountain, above the tree line but still hidden in the jungle growth, lay a city hidden for hundreds, maybe thousands of years. At least Jack's map said so. And Captain Jack Borland was convinced this time, just as he had been so many times before.

The proprietor of Jaguar's Call was Ralph Alvin Buncombe, a man who bore a striking resemblance to the actor Sean Connery. He'd come to Central America from the United States fifteen years ago. Like many other expatriates in remote places worldwide, he was running away from something. In Ralph's particular case it was a little problem with the police in Laredo, Texas over a Mexican girl Ralph insisted had told him she was twenty years old. After Child Protective Services of Texas got involved it turned out she was fifteen, and although she was stunning, worldly and totally willing to be Ralph's partner, Ralph was facing up to ten years in the state penitentiary. Out on bail prior to his trial, he chose one day to withdraw his nest egg and drive his Jeep to Belize, a place he'd always wanted to visit. He didn't plan on coming back.

Ralph ended up in San Ignacio, less than fifteen minutes from Belize's western border and a long, long way from the authorities in Texas. One thing led to another and Ralph himself got caught up in the treasure frenzy. He heard stories in the local bars. He saw an "authentic" map with his own eyes. It looked very old and very worn. Just like they all did. Unfortunately Ralph didn't know that it was just another of many available for sale to unsuspecting foreigners. He paid several hundred dollars for it, much to the delight of its previous owner.

Long story short, Ralph himself made the same trip so many others had made. He crossed the border into Guatemala and headed for fame and fortune. There was no path up the mountain in those days so he and his men stopped where the map said to begin their ascent and they cut a swath through the jungle. It took weeks of grueling labor to get to the top, and after six more weeks of exploring he had nothing at all to show for it.

As Ralph Buncombe's small party headed down the mountain they encountered a group of Brits on the way up. These men also had a map – apparently a different one from Ralph's – and they were secretive about it. Like all the others, they were certain they had *the* map that would lead them to the

ANCIENT

treasure, or the mine, or the city, or whatever it was they sought.

That chance encounter gave Ralph an idea. He went back to San Ignacio, withdrew the rest of his cash and hired a crew to go back into the jungle, back to the same trail where he had earlier climbed the mountain. He went halfway up and built a camp to accommodate those feckless men who sought treasure on this mountain. Ralph's men cut trees and created four buildings: a bunkhouse with some really basic plumbing for a toilet and shower, a dining hall and bar, a combination office, general store and owner's quarters, and a secure storage structure. The latter would allow adventurers to leave cumbersome gear while they climbed the last five thousand feet to reach the summit.

Ralph eventually acquired the nickname "Lucky" because he was the first to turn the mountain into something at least marginally profitable. So Lucky Buncombe became the proprietor of the Jaguar's Call, a place about as far from the police in Laredo, Texas as Lucky could get. And that was fine with him. Every gringo in Central America who came and stayed had a past. Ralph Buncombe left his past and hoped for a lucky future free from prison.

Over the years Lucky added amenities to the Jaguar's Call. He bought an old generator so he could have electricity and he hauled an ancient refrigerator, kind of an icebox actually, up the hill so he could keep things reasonably cold. He and a couple of guys who sometimes worked for him made most of the furniture and he bought crude mattresses and linens in town, hauling them up the mountain. So the camp became a somewhat decent albeit really basic halfway point to regroup and prepare for the rest of the climb up the mountain.

People walked into the camp at the Jaguar's Call without prior notice. Word of mouth was Lucky's marketing plan: most guides coming to this mountain knew it was there. Reservations would have been impossible anyway, since there was no communication other than an old satellite phone that he had stuck in a drawer. He kept it for emergencies only and in fifteen years he had never had occasion to use it. In the odd moment when he thought about it, he figured it didn't work by now anyway. The technology had changed so much but Lucky had never switched to a cell phone, figuring he'd rather remain anonymous than start handing out his personal information to anybody who might use it to find him after all these years.

Lucky was puttering around his office when he heard sounds in the jungle. "Someone's coming," he said out loud, standing up and glancing in a small mirror he'd picked up in town ages ago. "Glad I shaved yesterday."

Lucky hadn't had a visitor in over a month. He wondered if this was another group of treasure hunters or maybe naturalists or archaeologists on a trek up the peak. Whoever they were, he was anxious to see them, hungry for conversation and word of what was going on in the outside world he had left so abruptly many years back. He also hoped they spoke English. His Spanish was good, his French passable, but he far preferred to converse in his native tongue when possible.

As the group drew closer he could hear snippets of conversation and Lucky smiled as he heard someone say, "Senor, camp ahead." If the

ANCIENT

guides were speaking even pidgin English, there must be at least one gringo in the group.

In a few minutes three men emerged. Two were short and dark, clearly locals who undoubtedly were the guides. Lucky thought he recognized one of them, either from seeing him in Belize or maybe the man had guided a previous treasure hunter up the hill. A third man, tall and fair-skinned, walked behind them.

"Good morning!" Lucky said in English, raising his hand. "Welcome to Jaguar's Call."

"Good morning to you," the white man said, his British accent unmistakable. "My name is Arthur Borland. I hope you have accommodations for three for a night or two."

The surprise at hearing Lord Borland's name was unmistakable on Lucky's face. "No problem whatsoever. You're my only guests. And may I ask, are you the son of Captain Jack?"

Arthur was thrilled! He quickly confirmed his identity. "I hope and pray that you know my father from having met him here, when he was on his way up this mountain."

"That's exactly right. Where is the old bastard?"

Arthur told Lucky that Jack had been missing for several months and that he hoped Lucky might have information to help in Arthur's search.

Lucky was genuinely concerned. "I had no idea that he hadn't come back down. Lots of guys who go up this mountain one way figure out a different way to get back, and I wasn't terribly surprised not to see him again after he came through here." He looked at Arthur. "You probably know your dad better than anyone. He's tough. I bet money he's still alive up there somewhere." Lucky pointed in the direction of the mountaintop that loomed thousands of feet above them. "Your dad is a brave man. He's seen it all. If anyone could survive whatever's up there, he could. I'll tell you everything I know. Let's get you situated with a bunk and a place to stash your gear."

Lucky motioned to a shady spot with a couple of chairs under a tree. He and Arthur sat as the guides took small pipes from their pockets, filled them with tobacco and smoked contentedly.

"Care for a beer?" Arthur asked. "I brought a couple."

"That'd be great. I haven't had a beer in awhile."

"They're warm, I'm afraid. You'll have to drink it the British way."

"Tell me what you know about my father."

ANCIENT

CHAPTER FIVE

Lucky Buncombe told Arthur about the day over four months ago when Captain Jack and his group had walked into the campsite at Jaguar's Call. "I'd known Jack for awhile. He came here once before and this last time we talked before he continued his trip up the hill. He only decided recently that this mountain was most likely the site he's been searching for all these years. But you probably know all that."

Lucky smiled as he and Arthur talked about his father. Like everyone else, he had found Captain Jack extremely entertaining from the minute he laid eyes on him. When the entourage arrived, Jack had stepped into the clearing first. "My good man," Jack had beamed at Lucky. "You're a sight for sore eyes and that's for sure. I feel as though I've been climbing this mountain for a month, and now we get to the famous Jaguar's Call . . . our rest haven on the way to success!"

"We sat in these same chairs under this very tree," Lucky said. He recalled that Jack put his rucksack down and sat while his men set about dropping packs, unloading them, and heading to the bunkhouse without a word. Several of Jack's men had accompanied him on a previous journey to this mountain and they knew the routine at Jaguar's Call. Within a few minutes, they had unpacked, washed up and were sitting in the shade, exactly as Arthur Borland's men today, talking among themselves as they smoked.

In Spanish Jack spoke to his lead guide. "Open up that nasty stuff your men drink," he said, "and let them have the rest of the day off. They've earned it."

The guide turned to his men, spoke briefly and they scurried off to the bunkhouse to retrieve a bottle of brownish liquid, some locally concocted drink from San Ignacio that looked like brackish pond water and smelled worse. The workers poured drinks into small cups they had brought and leaned against trees while they relaxed and drank.

"Care for something more civilized?" Jack asked Lucky with a devilish grin.

"Thought you'd never ask. What have you brought?"

Jack reached into his pack and pulled out a plastic bottle. "It's Chivas Regal. If it's good enough for the Queen I guess it's good enough for us."

Lucky was thrilled. He hadn't even seen a bottle of Chivas in years. The fine scotch was hard to get outside of major cities in Central America and he didn't get to the city very often. He felt his mouth go dry and he said, "Just a minute. I'll get us some glasses and ice."

"No ice for me, old man," Jack replied. "I'll drink it neat, the British way."

The men sipped their drinks. Lucky savored his, leaning back and closing his eyes after each

ANCIENT

small taste. "Nectar of the Gods," he murmured. That brought a laugh from Jack.

Lucky never asked his visitors any specifics about their journeys. He usually had an idea once he talked to them a bit whether they were looking for treasure, or ruins, or graves and bones. Captain Jack was an exception, of course. His reputation preceded him. But still Lucky avoided the subject, waiting until and unless Jack wanted to broach it himself. And it didn't take long to happen.

"Well, Lucky, here we are once again."

"It's good to see you again, Captain Jack. How long will I enjoy the pleasure of your company?"

"We leave the day after tomorrow. I want to give my men a couple of nights' rest before we move on up. I think I'm really on to something this time, Lucky. I'm going to show you something . . . I don't intend to tell you specifics about it, of course, but I am extremely excited about these things I ran across and I want to show you something."

Jack walked to the bunkhouse and rummaged through one of the packs. He pulled out a wooden case, the kind you might put a large bible in as a keepsake. He brought it back and sat down. Lucky could see that the box appeared to be very old. There were buckles encircling it; they might originally have been capable of being locked to keep the box secure.

Arthur Borland stopped talking for a moment. He looked at Brian, patted the wooden box sitting on the table in front of them and said, "This is the box my father showed to Lucky Buncombe."

The story continued. Jack had sat down and unbuckled the straps. He opened the lid. Lucky could see that the small box was filled but he couldn't tell what was there. There was a folded piece of paper on top. When Jack removed it, Lucky thought there was a glint of metal below. Jack closed the lid and held the paper in his hands.

"I don't want to bore you with arcane facts," he began. "Have you ever heard of Don Pedro de Alvarado?"

"Can't say I have."

"I'm certain you know who Hernan Cortes was."

"Of course. The Aztecs thought he was a god. They accepted him and he obliterated them. He did the same thing with the Maya, as I recall."

"Correct. Alvarado was sent by Cortes to conquer the natives in the very area where we're sitting right now – and he conquered, that's for sure. His cruelty to the Maya people was unbelievable; Spanish scribes who were part of his entourage duly recorded the carnage. Although it's never been proven, I'm certain Hernan Cortes himself was on this very mountain in the 1520s."

Jack unfolded the paper he had taken from the trunk. It was a map, drawn on a piece of what looked like butcher paper. Lucky noticed it was very detailed, with much intricate writing and drawing. He looked at it without getting too close or trying to appear too interested.

Jack told Lucky that he had gone to the archives in Seville, Spain, to learn what he could about Cortes, Alvarado and the journeys both men made in Mexico and Central America in the 1500s. Accounts by the scribes who were present noted that the Mayas were easily able to put their hands on large quantities of gold and silver. The gold often had been pounded into thin sheets and decorated. Cortes told the King of Spain that according to Maya legend the sheets of gold were used to adorn the outsides of buildings in a city in the clouds.

ANCIENT

"So you're looking for Vilcabamba, the lost city of gold?" Lucky smiled. "Haven't the scholars decided it's already been found thousands of miles south of here, somewhere in Peru?"

"Not exactly. I've already found gold. Well not actually 'found' - I bought two hammered gold sheets from a man who said he was from Oklahoma. Met him in a bar in Belize one evening. He was staying in the Emperor Hotel in Belize City, the most expensive hotel in Central America. And he looked like a bum, to tell the truth. He was pretty secretive but when I told him I was both the Governor-General and that I was interested in relics he offered to sell me a couple of sheets."

"'I have plenty,' the man told me. 'I'll never be able to spend the money I already have, so I'm happy to part with a couple."

"I paid him a hundred dollars apiece for the two but first I insisted he tell me where he got them."

The man had told Jack he found them in Oklahoma. He had been treasure hunting his whole life and he had found Spanish gold in a creek bed, he said. But this was different – this wasn't Spanish gold.

Jack was excited. "The man didn't know what he had. Now that I've been to Seville and seen the 1540 accounts of the scribes and the Governor of Guatemala, I think the Maya themselves carried this gold far, far north to hide it from the Spanish. I think they carried it all the way to Oklahoma."

Jack had a flair for the dramatic, especially when he was worked up about a project. "Just wait, my good man. This mountaintop citadel isn't just about gold. I spent days poring over the Spanish documents, the eyewitness accounts by the scribes who accompanied Alvarado. Late one afternoon when

BILL THOMPSON

I had decided my search in the Seville library was done, I was preparing to pack up and head back to London. I turned the last page of a sixteenth century volume and found something tucked into the back binder - these two handwritten pages and a crude drawing." He held them up. "This is a copy of the document and the map I found. If things work out these will lead me to the treasure trove of all time – the legendary ancient library of the Maya."

Lucky didn't respond for several minutes. Instead he sat back and sipped his scotch, thinking that Jack Borland, for all his genteel upbringing and wealth, was exactly like the others – obsessed by the thought that just beyond his grasp there was a gold ring waiting to be grabbed. For Captain Jack the gold ring was this Mayan library. He wanted to be the next Hiram Bingham, the man who had rediscovered Machu Picchu in 1911. He wanted fame but he truly believed fortune would come with it. There would be wealth and notoriety beyond imagination, the explorer firmly believed. They all felt that way, Lucky thought to himself.

It was known that the Maya reached a very high level of development in literature before the Spanish arrived and burned almost every one of their books, or codices. What the Spanish accomplished in the name of the church cost future generations the opportunity to know these remarkable people. And now there existed only a few codices the authenticity of which were beyond reproach.

After carefully choosing his words, Lucky finally responded to Jack.

"I hate to rain on your parade, but isn't it a fact that the Spanish burned every single thing the Mayans ever wrote, except three or four they apparently sent back to Spain as souvenirs? That's

ANCIENT

what I've always heard. So how could an ancient library exist? Why has nobody ever heard about it? And what's so important about a bunch of Mayan codices even if you did happen to locate them?"

"I don't expect you to be enthused about this. Believe me, I've second-guessed myself a hundred times since I found the document in Seville. I found a two-page letter written by Pedro Alvarado, Governor of Guatemala, to the King of Spain. For some reason it appears the letter was never sent. Instead it was tucked into a book. I won't tell you what it says but the circumstances of my finding it lead me to believe its contents are true.

"The books themselves could be the most fascinating hoard ever discovered. I've heard my entire life about the missing library at Alexandria, Egypt, and I've heard story after story about hidden libraries under the Sphinx at Giza. People have devoted lifetimes to searching for these repositories of information. And this would be no different. The mind cannot grasp what secrets these volumes might contain. We've never known how these primitive people with barely any tools mastered the construction of huge pyramids with incredibly heavy stones mounted a hundred feet high. How did they achieve knowledge of time and the heavens, create calendars as accurate as ours, and predict events hundreds of years into the future? Lucky, there literally is no way to say how important these codices could be."

"I can only imagine how famous the discoverer would be. I wish you success. You deserve it. I think you may be the most perseverant of all the men I've seen."

His story about Captain Jack done, Lucky turned to Arthur Borland. "That's all I know about your father's last trip. Two days later Jack and his crew of three men walked out of my camp, and from what you tell me, no one's seen them since."

ANCIENT

CHAPTER SIX

In the Monument Club's bar Arthur Borland picked up the small wooden box lying on the table and excused himself to use the restroom. Brian glanced at his watch - they had been talking for more than three hours. Cell phone usage was prohibited in the bar and dining room so Brian walked to the hallway and quickly called Collette at the gallery, asking her to lock up when she finished for the day since it appeared he likely wouldn't be back. His thoughts turned to Arthur Borland. He seemed very nervous – his hands shook all the time - but that could simply be some kind of health issue.

Arthur returned to the table, set the box down and they ordered a last round of wine. "While I was at the Jaguar's Call, Lucky Buncombe told me my father had left one thing behind when he departed. Jack asked Lucky to store a backpack until he returned. He handed it over to me - as far as I know, that man respected his friendship with Jack Borland enough to resist the urge to look inside the rucksack, so he didn't know what was in there. When I opened the pack I found the small box with straps that my father showed Lucky. This very box." He took it from the table.

Arthur told Brian that the map was missing, presumably because Jack Borland took it up the mountain with him. The box contained the two-page letter intended for the King of Spain, the copy Jack had made from the original in Seville. Underneath that, nestled in the bottom of the box, were two very thin sheets of pure gold, each approximately six inches square. The sheets were marked with various pictographs, similar to hieroglyphs but showing men who appeared to be of Mayan descent, animals, hunting scenes and pictures depicting victories in battle. Opening the box, he handed Brian one of the gold sheets. "Look at the symbols that are at the bottom below the pictographs. I compared this with online images from the Popol Vuh and it appears these are identical to the symbolic writing in it."

Brian was familiar with the Popol Vuh, one of the few books written by the Maya that had not been destroyed by the Spanish. Its pages were filled with Mayan drawings and inscriptions.

Arthur continued. "I've had the gold sheets examined both at Oxford University's archaeological department and the Institute of Maya Studies in Mexico City." He explained that metals cannot be carbon dated but the professors who looked at the sheets were uniformly of the opinion that both the writing and the artwork were Mayan and very similar to others in museums. The Mexican antiquities expert offered his expert opinion that the drawings on the gold sheets were consistent with other such material and therefore were unquestionably created by the Maya, although the Oxford scholars stopped short of issuing a firm opinion as to whether the sheets were genuine.

ANCIENT

Brian stared at the sheet of gold he held in his hand. Could this be genuine? If so, it was unique, priceless. "I have never seen anything like this in my life. And the guy told Captain Jack he found these sheets in Oklahoma?"

"Yes. I'm convinced it's true. The Maya gave the Spaniards everything they wanted to buy freedom for their rulers but the conquistadors executed them anyway. Word had to have gotten around. The people figured out that the Spaniards would kill them for their gold. So they removed the temptation. They moved it far, far away."

BILL THOMPSON

ANCIENT

CHAPTER SEVEN
Ada, Oklahoma
Summer 1955

There are people who spend a lifetime searching for gold. Sometimes it consumes them. They can be as normal as the next person but they are driven – devoured - by the idea that someone, sometime, hid a cache of gold and it's there for the finding.

Vernon Tippington and Charles Edwards were sitting on the expansive front porch of Edwards' Southern colonial home, sipping glasses of sweet tea as they talked. Tippington's homestead abutted the back of Edwards' four-acre pasture and although not close friends, they were neighbors who talked occasionally. In this small town everyone knew everyone, and everyone certainly knew Charles Edwards, who was a successful real estate developer.

"Charles," the man was saying, "I know you've heard this from me before, but this time I'm certain about this map I discovered. I've been looking for this for twenty years, and I'm certain the mother lode is behind your house, right down there in your back pasture."

BILL THOMPSON

Edwards sat back in his chair and looked at Tippington. He'd been hearing stories like this from him since 1939 when Charles had built this house. Everyone in this small southern Oklahoma community had heard them and most people thought Tippington was crazy. He was a social misfit, a man some termed a hermit, who had retired from the Oklahoma City-Ada-Atoka railroad, commonly known as the OCA&A, a short line service which ran some 200 miles between the state capital and several outlying communities. The railroad track ran along the east property lines of both Tippington and Edwards and its construction played a part in the treasure stories that kept Tippington searching.

Behind Edwards' house in a big fenced pasture ran a creek that everyone said had been there forever. When it rained the creek became a small river, carrying water through boulder-lined walls that rose more than eight feet above the creek bed and created what might be considered a small canyon. This creek was part of a system – it ran all the way from one end of Ada to the other. People often found arrowheads along its banks, sure signs that Indians had camped here in the past.

When the railroad was built in the 1920s, massive earthmoving equipment created a large hill nearly twenty feet above the low-lying pasture. The train tracks were laid on top of it to make the tracks straight and avoid unnecessary dips in the landscape. A culvert large enough for hobos to camp in had also been built to carry the creek water eastward from Edwards' pasture under the tracks. As heavy equipment prepared the railroad bed the workers dislodged boulders far too heavy for a man to move. The walls lining the creek bed were altered as machines moved rocks that had stood in one

ANCIENT

place for centuries. Progress was usually accompanied by change. In this case the sides of a creek where Native Americans once camped were realigned as bulldozers shifted giant rocks.

There had been talk of treasure along this small river for well over a hundred years. There was a tale about the Spanish conquistador Coronado; according to legend, he came through Oklahoma and buried a cache of gold here. Others said it was Jesse James' loot from stagecoach robberies. Another mentioned Mayan chieftains who sent parties from Central America far, far north – as far as Oklahoma – to hide gold from Spanish conquerors.

No one had ever found anything and most people considered themselves too normal, too sane, to go treasure hunting. But not Vernon Tippington. He had looked at old railroad records from the time the tracks were laid and he knew the workers had found Spanish coins dating to the 1500s. A strange sheet of gold with writing on it had turned up too. There was no explanation how the things got here and the stories had been forgotten by just about everyone. Except Vernon.

"Vernon, how much time are you going to spend on this frivolity? You're wasting your time and energy on a wild goose chase."

Tippington looked at him wearily and responded, "It's my time to waste. I've got my pension from the railroad and some day just you wait and see – some day this is all going to pay off."

"OK, and I suppose just like last time you won't let me look at your map. Right?"

Vernon Tippington's eyes opened a little wider, and he leaned back in his chair, involuntarily moving away from Edwards. "No . . . no, it's my map," he stammered, like one child keeping a toy away from another.

Charles Edwards smiled. "All right, then. Let's see your contract."

Tippington produced two sheets of typing paper, one a carbon copy. There were two typewritten paragraphs. He handed both to Edwards.

"Vernon, I'm going to do you a big favor this time. I don't want half of what you find. If I had half of what you've found so far, I'd be right where I am now, with absolutely nothing. You can dig on my property. If you find something worth a hundred dollars or more, you owe me a hundred dollars. That's it."

Edwards laughed, took a pen from his pocket and jotted down a few sentences outlining the deal he wanted. He signed both copies and tossed the papers back across the table to Tippington. "I think you're wasting your entire life on this

Vernon signed both pages, kept one for himself, and rose. "You'll be sorry you didn't take a piece of the action, Charles. I'm certain this time that I'm onto the payoff. If I were a betting man I'd say it's Spanish gold. I can feel it in my bones."

Charles Edwards went inside the house as Ella, the family's housekeeper, removed the glasses from the porch table where the men had sat. After she went back inside, the hedge next to the porch rustled loudly. Billy Edwards, Charles' 9-year-old son, emerged from his hiding place and ran over to talk to his best friend and across-the-street neighbor, Tommy Albert. The search for gold on their property was on again. And Mr. Tippington was sure this time!

ANCIENT

CHAPTER EIGHT

An old frame barn sat in the middle of Charles Edwards' pasture. Until a year or so ago they'd kept horses stabled there. Charles had decided they were more trouble than they were worth since neither of his sons was interested in riding much any more.

Tommy and Billy used the barn as a huge playroom. They had their chemistry sets in one room they called their laboratory. Another room housed a lot of junk: lawn mowers that didn't work and things like that. Up a ladder there was a loft where hay used to be kept. It was here where Tommy and Billy sat looking out through a cracked second-floor door.

From here they had a clear shot of Vernon Tippington hard at work in the creek bed about a hundred feet away. He had a pickaxe and a shovel and was working his way rock by rock down one side of the creek. From time to time he would stop, pick up something he'd uncovered, then toss it aside. It was hard work and Tippington was sweating profusely. "He's an old guy," Billy said. "I hope he doesn't keel over down there in our creek."

Tippington worked for an hour without stopping. Finally he sat down and pulled a sandwich and a Coke from a sack. As he ate his lunch, he kept looking at a piece of paper he had pulled from his pocket, then he tried to compare something on the paper with the rocky sides of the creek where he was working.

"I bet that's a treasure map he keeps looking at," Tommy said.

Billy eagerly agreed. "He's looking at it a lot, for sure."

"He sure is. If that map tells where gold is it's probably really old. I bet things have changed a lot down there where they built the railroad. I don't think he's able to figure out from the map exactly what he's looking for."

"Let's go see if he'll let us help look."

The boys scrambled down the ladder from the loft of the barn and ran to the top of the small ravine. They climbed down through the rocks to the creek bed. Tippington had seen them coming – as they got closer the boys noticed the piece of paper was gone.

"Hi, Mr. Tippington," Billy said. "Have you found anything interesting yet?"

Vernon Tippington was a reclusive man at best and his social skills left much to be desired. "What do you boys want?"

Tommy blurted out, "We'd like to help you look for treasure." Billy gave him a stern look. He wished Tommy hadn't said that.

"It's none of your business what I'm looking for and I don't need anybody butting in."

"Can we stay and watch, please?"

"Your father gave me permission to dig here. I'm on your property legally. You boys go on and play. I have work to do." With that Tippington stood, put his lunch trash in the sack and turned away from the boys. He walked a few feet down the creek bed to the area where he had been searching. He turned around. "Go on now, I said."

The boys went back to the barn, climbed into the loft and continued to watch Tippington work until Billy's mother yelled from the house, "Lunch is ready!" They ran home to eat.

The boys were soon tired of watching Vernon Tippington. He was committed, for sure. He worked six or seven hours every day but the boys lasted only a couple. Bored, they soon went back to things more interesting than watching a man move slowly, rock by rock, down both sides of a small ravine. They quit a little early. The morning when Vernon Tippington found what had eluded him for twenty years they were playing across the street.

Charles Edwards found a hundred dollar bill stuck in his mailbox and a note that said two words, "Thanks. Vernon." He called Tippington over and over but no one ever answered. He drove to his house a couple of times but Vernon was gone.

Although tales of a Mayan expedition to Oklahoma actually were true, Vernon Tippington had surreptitiously whisked away the in situ evidence that would have proved it. Except for Vernon, no other person on earth ever knew for sure that the Maya really were capable of making a four thousand mile round trip journey. He had found their gold but he had taken every bit of it away.

Rumors popped up about Vernon and what he'd found. Some people heard he struck it rich and moved to California. Others heard he dug up buried treasure and bought a house in Mexico. But no one knew because no one in Ada, Oklahoma ever saw Vernon Tippington again.

BILL THOMPSON

ANCIENT

CHAPTER NINE

The Monument Club, New York City

Arthur Borland finished his story, telling Brian that Lucky had warned him that the trek up the mountain would be incredibly difficult. "Even if you're a seasoned climber, it's crazy up there," Lucky had said. "The jungle's so thick you can't see your hand in front of your face and sometimes you can't walk a foot without having to hack through undergrowth. There're snakes up there as big around as a human's torso."

He told Arthur that once, long ago, he himself climbed five thousand feet to the top of this mountain. He'd seen what might have been evidence of an ancient civilization – stones set in circular formations and a couple of broken rocks that could have been statues – but he never encountered anything that gave him solid proof that the Maya or any other people ever actually occupied this area. All Lucky could advise was, "If you choose to follow after Captain Jack you have an extremely tough climb ahead of you."

Despite the admonition, Arthur and the two guides headed up the mountain the next morning. They kept to the barely visible existing trail Jack Borland had most likely used until it disappeared among the jungle undergrowth. At that point they began hacking a trail themselves, moving slowly up but going the wrong way. Every difficult slash of the machete blazed a trail in the wrong direction - further and further away from the route Captain Jack had actually taken.

Arthur recalled how difficult things had been. "I spent two weeks in the most inhospitable terrain I have ever encountered. I really began to question my decision to do this, but I felt Father was alive up there somewhere. What drove me further up the mountain was that my father believed in this. He thought the Maya used this formidable jungle to hide their most important secret. That's why Jack Borland tackled this hellish place.

"Every day got more and more difficult. We would find a narrow path and get excited that we were following Jack's route. Suddenly the path would disappear and we were back at square one, facing low-hanging vines, insects of every imaginable type and at one point some kind of jungle cat lounging on a branch ten feet above us. I was afraid to touch a tree or bush to steady myself for fear I would discover another new creature just waiting to crawl on my skin. The guides and I tumbled over massive tree roots dozens of times and were physically exhausted every afternoon by the time the torrential rain started. We just pitched our tents and crashed into them, sopping wet and exhausted, barely able to rise for dinner."

He described the incredible heat and humidity that rose from the floor of the jungle as they ascended step after step, sometimes moving less than two hundred feet in an entire day. Occasionally they felt the prickly sensation that they were being watched. Arthur said he fully expected a Stone Age

ANCIENT

Indian to step out in front of them. But they saw only wildlife – fantastic colorful birds, snakes ten feet long and monkeys that yelled and spit. They knew any people who might inhabit the jungle knew well how to stay hidden.

"I regret to say that after two weeks we made it to the top and found nothing. No ruins in the trees, no evidence of habitation, not a shred of anything to indicate my father had even come this way. Sadly, we returned the same way we had come up. We just didn't have the energy to cut a different path down the mountain. We spent one more night at Jaguar's Call and I told Lucky I was totally unsuccessful. He promised to try and contact me if he heard anything at all about my father. So far, no word."

BILL THOMPSON

ANCIENT

CHAPTER TEN

Brian had really enjoyed hearing Arthur's story. "I'm captivated by the exploits of your father, but I can't figure out why you've come to me. Is there a place you think I can be of help to you?"

"You may be surprised to learn that we members of the so-called aristocracy don't always have the money to accompany those noble titles we hold. Many an estate in England has been broken up into small parcels and sold off to a housing developer because the Earl, or the Duke, or the Viscount of this, that or whatever, couldn't pay the bills to keep the manor house open. The nicest properties usually are deeded to the National Trust and the government keeps them up. Those become tourist sites and although the family doesn't own the land or the buildings any more, at least they can see that the estates remain well preserved instead of going to rack and ruin.

"I say all that to say this – my father always lived well. He inherited a lot of property from my grandparents but Jack was always off searching for one thing or another. Gold here, buried treasure there, the secret of eternal youth somewhere else. He didn't earn money – he just spent it. He always hoped to make everything back someday when he hit that one big jackpot. But so far he hasn't. I live modestly, very much so compared to Captain Jack Borland and the ancestors before him. I paid for the trip to Belize and Guatemala to try to find my father but I frankly can't afford to do a lot more."

Arthur told Brian that he hoped Bijan Rarities would be interested in the project for the possible television rights. After all, Brian had participated in the Egyptian production earlier and was planning an Aztec show soon.

"You know, you've become archaeology's equivalent of the Keno brothers on *Antiques Roadshow*. Yes, you own a famous gallery, but your face is becoming so well known on television that you personally command an audience in that arena. With your notoriety you can pull strings most of us can't – even me, a member of the British aristocracy! I think you're the perfect one to find Captain Jack."

Arthur Borland was right. With Brian's fortuitous ownership of Bijan Rarities happening so soon after the incredibly popular airing of the Inkharaton tomb discovery in Egypt's Valley of the Kings, his boyish good looks and comfortable delivery had made him a go-to person for the networks. When Fox, CNN or the rest needed an authority for a sound bite on an ancient discovery, Brian Sadler frequently turned up on the couch next to the news team. He was becoming the public face of the antiquities business as he talked about new digs, exciting discoveries and theories about lost civilizations. He had weighed in on the Mayan doomsday prophecy of 2012, the theories behind the enigmatic statues of Easter Island, and ideas for how two hundred ton stones ended up hundreds of feet high atop Mayan pyramids when that civilization didn't even have the

ANCIENT

wheel. People frequently stopped Brian on the sidewalks of New York or London to request an autograph. He thought it was interesting.

Brian thought a moment then said, "OK, I could provide funding for another expedition to Guatemala on the basis of those artifacts you've shown me. But my problem now is time. I've committed to get the Aztec Commission wrapped up really soon. Most of the work is out of my hands now but final production begins in a few weeks and I'll be filming segments with the producers. No question I think your father's adventures are interesting and I know you're desperate to find him, but I just don't know if I'm the man for you at this particular time. I just can't be gone right now."

Arthur stood. "I don't want to beg, but I must find my father as quickly as possible. I want to leave the letter and these gold sheets with you. Feel free to authenticate them, study them, ask professionals about them . . . whatever you wish. Just get back to me. I'm blatantly trying to capture your interest so I can find my father. At the same time, if we can find irrefutable evidence that the Maya traveled far, far away from their homeland – over two thousand miles north into the heartland of America – it will be a sensational story the likes of which we have rarely seen. And that's exactly what happened. The Spanish didn't bury this Mayan gold in Oklahoma, Brian. The Maya themselves did."

His hands shaking, Arthur Borland handed the small box to Brian and extended his hand with a business card. He picked up his valise, turned and walked out.

BILL THOMPSON

ANCIENT

CHAPTER ELEVEN

Brian stepped out onto Madison Avenue and glanced upwards. Between the skyscrapers the sky was dark and ominous but the rain had stopped. It was nearly five pm. Pedestrian traffic was intense as thousands of workers poured out of huge buildings, on the way for a drink or a subway ride home. Madison would be less crowded at the moment than Fifth, Brian figured, so he continued south, Arthur Borland's box clutched tightly to his chest and his umbrella ready should the skies open up. In the throng of people Brian never noticed the man who had watched him put Captain Jack Borland's box under his trenchcoat.

At this time of day Brian wouldn't ordinarily have gone back to the gallery but he had to put the box in a safe place. These gold sheets could be unique and it was crazy to be walking around the streets carrying something so valuable.

At 54th Street Brian turned west and walked to Fifth, then turned and reached the gallery just as his assistant Collette Conning was locking the door.

"One second, Collette!" he called as he approached. "Have you set the alarm?"

BILL THOMPSON

"Yes, sir. I'm sorry. I didn't know you planned on returning."

"Actually I hadn't but the man I met left me this box and I need to leave it in the vault for tonight." The alarm on the front door of Bijan Rarities wouldn't be an issue; it could merely be disarmed. The vault however had a twenty-minute time delay once it was locked.

"I'll stay and lock up the box if you want to go on home. I have a few things I could get done in an extra half hour. I really have nothing going on this evening anyway except walking my dog now that the rain's stopped."

Brian thanked her; that was a big help. He had had a long afternoon and really just wanted to unwind. They unlocked the door and went inside. Collette entered a code on the massive vault door that had once graced the lobby of a bank. Then she set an alarm on her watch to remind her when the door would disarm. "Go on home, Brian," she said, shooing him out. She locked the front door behind him and walked to her desk.

The rain had cooled things down considerably and a brisk wind was whipping through the concrete canyons of Manhattan. Brian decided to walk to his apartment house on the Upper West Side instead of hailing a cab. This time of day it was quicker to walk than maneuver the busy streets in a taxi anyway, plus walking gave him time to think.

He went up Fifth Avenue to Central Park South then west alongside the Plaza Hotel. On the spur of the moment he decided to stop in at the Oak Bar for a martini. As always, the place was packed this time of day. Brian saw a couple of heads turn his direction as he snaked through tables on his way

ANCIENT

to the bar. One woman turned and whispered to her husband while pointing surreptitiously at him.

New Yorkers were jaded to celebrity. You could see Ivana Trump on the street, or Jennifer Aniston, or the Mayor. Locals came and went without giving celebrities a second glance. Tourists were different though, and despite a lot of regulars the Oak Bar was also a tourist hot spot. Out-of-towners considered trips to New York extra special if they caught a glimpse of a well-known person. Being both a landmark in itself but also situated in the famous Plaza Hotel, the Oak Bar was a site for people watching that was virtually unparalleled in New York. Brian's face, although not famous, was familiar to many people who watched shows on Discovery Channel, History or National Geographic.

He signaled the bartender.

"Afternoon, Mr. Sadler. Your usual, sir?"

"Please."

As Brian removed his trenchcoat the headwaiter appeared and handed Brian a ticket. "I'll take that for you, Mr. Sadler."

The service at the Oak Bar was always the best. Brian always thought for the price of the drinks it *should* be tops. And it was, even for the tourists. He sat down on a barstool and sipped his XO Vodka martini straight up with a twist, enjoying that perfect drink's first stinging swallow as the smooth liquid went down.

He gazed across the room out the expansive north windows that overlooked Central Park just across the street. He could just see the corner of Fifth Avenue and 59th Street four blocks north of his gallery, and he marveled once again in his mind about where he had been and where he was now. Thanks to Darius Nazir the gallery that had been

Nazir's was now Brian's, and Brian Sadler, the former stockbroker trainee who had been in trouble with the Feds, was now on top of the world.

He thought about John Spedino, the Mafia chieftain who had played such a role in Brian's obtaining the Bethlehem Scroll, and how a veiled threat kept Spedino's name alive in the back of Brian's mind, even though Spedino was going to be in federal prison for many years to come. He had seen first-hand how dangerous John Spedino was. And he hoped he never saw it again.

Brian nodded as the bartender asked if he wanted another. As he savored his second martini his cell phone vibrated. He saw a short text from Nicole Farber. "Evening, sweetie. Hope your day went well. Still hard at work here in Big D. Big stock fraud case. Reminded me of you! LOL!"

Nicole. He'd never thought he would let a woman get this close to him. In fact, despite her beauty and her brains there had been a time when he wanted her out of his life completely. Now he and the blonde lawyer from Dallas were a couple, even if long distances kept them apart. She had a career to pursue in her city as Brian did in his but they met as often as they could, stealing a weekend here, a week there. Occasionally Nicole joined him on one of his frequent overseas trips. She complained playfully that most men took their girlfriends to Paris or Rome, while Brian took her to the deserts of Egypt, the archaeological sites of Jordan or the mountains of Mexico, in search of ruins or ancient documents or yet another mystery Brian had heard about.

Brian's interest in archaeology and ancient history dovetailed perfectly with his ownership of Bijan Rarities, a gallery that was ranked in the top three by the small community of collectors and

ANCIENT

dealers in priceless antiquities. Although Nicole's interests weren't strong in these areas she found his exploits interesting at the least, exciting most of the time, and downright scary on occasion. Brian smiled at the thought – he hadn't expected her to be willing to join him in some of the crazy things he did, but she came along as much as she could, mostly to be with him. And he was glad. He wanted her with him as often as they could arrange it.

Brian had met Nicole when she was a rising star at Carter and Wells, one of the largest law firms in the Dallas metroplex. Her specialty was criminal defense work and it had come in handy once for Brian when he was a stockbroker in Dallas. She had represented some of America's largest corporate and banking executives and had steered them, almost a hundred percent successfully, through fraud, insider trading, stock manipulation and dozens of other charges the federal government had in its arsenal. Brian started out as a client too, then ended up as her romantic partner.

In the past couple of years Nicole had risen quickly in her firm and although she was only in her mid-thirties, she had become one of Carter and Wells' star performers. She earned nearly a million dollars a year and was the youngest full partner ever elected to the firm.

Carter and Wells had a New York office and Nicole was licensed to practice in the state. That had happened several years ago when she began to specialize in white-collar criminal law. New York was where many Federal criminal lawsuits were filed since the major stock exchanges were headquartered here and the Securities and Exchange Commission had a very active branch in Manhattan.

As he finished his drink Brian responded. "Having a martini at the Oak Bar. Wish you were here. Seriously. Can't wait until I see you in two weeks."

He called for his check, paid it and headed for the door, putting on his coat as he stepped outside. The wind had died down since he arrived. He decided to take a brief stroll in Central Park before heading home. He jaywalked across the street and entered the park at 59th and Fifth, chose an empty, mostly-dry bench and sat for a few minutes, watching people pass by and enjoying the beauty and serenity of the park on a cool March evening after a downpour.

He replayed the afternoon with Arthur Borland. Finally he glanced at his watch and saw that over a half hour had passed while he was lost in thought about Captain Jack's exploits. Brian walked back to Central Park South. When he looked toward the broad fountain area in front of the Plaza Hotel he could see that Fifth Avenue was blocked off south of 57th Street. Traffic headed south was backed up for blocks and policemen diverted cars onto 57th in both directions. Brian walked down Fifth until he reached the barricaded area. Pedestrians were still moving on the west side of the street but more barriers blocked the east sidewalk. As he got a block closer Brian saw that there were several police cars and an ambulance parked in the street directly in front of his gallery. He began to run, sprinting the two blocks and heading across the street. At the barricade a policeman told him he could go no further.

"That's my gallery," he shouted. "What's going on?"

ANCIENT

The policeman took Brian's arm and moved him around the barrier. "See that officer standing in the doorway? Go identify yourself to him."

Brian ran the half block and pulled out his business card and driver license. Breathlessly he said, "I'm Brian Sadler. I own this gallery. What's happening?"

The officer motioned him aside as two paramedics pushed a gurney through the showroom. When it emerged on the sidewalk, Brian looked down at Collette Conning. Her face was bloody and he could see a large gash in her forehead.

"Collette! My God. What happened?"

A medic said, "She shouldn't talk. She's in shock."

She looked up at him, her face contorted, terror-stricken. "I . . . why, Brian? Why? The box was already locked up." Then her eyes closed and the men moved her quickly to the waiting ambulance.

He grabbed the medic's sleeve. "Is she going to be OK? Where are you taking her?"

"We're sending her vitals to Lenox Hill so the doctor will be ready when she gets there. She's had a traumatic injury and we need to move her as quickly as possible." The back doors closed, the men rushed to the front and, as police cleared the way, the ambulance moved away from the curb, siren wailing.

Brian returned to the gallery's front door. "Who can I talk to about what's going on?" he asked the uniformed officer blocking the entrance. The officer pointed to to a man in a dark suit that was in the front showroom on a cell phone. Other people were taking pictures and doing measurements, mostly in the back of the showroom where Collette's desk and the vault were located.

BILL THOMPSON

Brian walked to the vault as the man in the suit noticed him and yelled, "Hey! Who are you?" Brian saw the gold shield pinned to his jacket lapel.

"Are you the owner?"

Brian answered affirmatively.

The cop pulled out a card, handed it to Brian and said, "I'm Detective Ron Calvin. What's your name?" Brian told him, and Detective Calvin asked if the gallery was under video surveillance. Brian told him that video monitoring was done by an offsite company so although it would take some time, the service could email the surveillance video file to him in a few hours.

The cop asked if he could get on that quickly. From his desk drawer Brian took a card with the name and contact information for the monitoring company and gave it to the detective, who handed the card to another officer and said, "Find out how soon we can get today's video."

Brian said, "I was on my way home and saw the commotion. I just left here a couple of hours ago. How did you get through the front door? What happened?"

"The front door wasn't locked. We were able to talk to Miss Conning for a few minutes before they took her away. It's pretty sketchy - she had apparently been ready to close the store but then had to put something away in a time-lock vault. Does that make sense?"

"Yes. I stopped by and left her a box I'd gotten at a meeting. I wanted it to be locked up for the night so she agreed to stay to open the vault." Walking to the huge door, he saw it was locked. He entered a six-digit numeric sequence on the keypad.

"It'll take twenty minutes," Brian told the detective.

ANCIENT

"She's in quite a bit of shock and seemed terrified. From what I gather someone apparently came to the front door and either the door wasn't locked or she let him in. We aren't sure and she couldn't remember. She's had a blow to her head and may never recall everything. We can just hope in a few days most of it comes back. Anyway, she had just locked the vault. I didn't find out much after that. She was confused and not making sense."

"Now I understand what happened," Brian said. "The panic alarm. She hit the alarm. That's why the door isn't locked."

"Tell me how that works."

"The front door is never unlocked. Collette can open it with a buzzer on her desk but people on the street can't just walk in. If someone wants in she can communicate through a microphone at her desk linked to a speaker next to the front door buzzer outside. But there's one way the door can be left unlocked. There are buttons all over the store in accessible places that will trigger our silent alarm. My employees also wear wristbands that have a button. When you hit the panic alarm the front door disarms so that a responding officer can get inside."

The detective replied, "We figure the perpetrator left the store just moments before a foot patrolman from 55th Street arrived on the scene. He found no sign of forced entry and Miss Conning lying on the floor bleeding from head wounds. Now let's sit down and let me get some information."

He gave the officer his address, cell phone number and private line at the office. Then he started from the beginning, explaining how his ownership of the gallery happened after Darius Nazir's suspicious death not that long ago. Brian had in fact inherited the gallery, moving from Dallas to

BILL THOMPSON

New York to run it. Collette Conning had been Nazir's assistant - Brian had inherited her knowledge and was thankful every day she was here.

"She's my right hand man," he continued, explaining he'd been at an offsite meeting with a client all afternoon. He said he came back, caught Collette on the way out and she agreed to stay and open the vault.

"OK," the detective said thoughtfully. "Then it was either someone she knew or someone who convinced her he had a reason to be inside. Any ideas about who that might have been?"

"Nothing specific, although it could have been someone she's been working with, or a friend of hers or mine . . . there's almost no telling. There's also Jason, my other assistant. Today's his day off but he might have come by. He wouldn't have done this, though. I can't imagine who would, or why."

"Does she have an appointment calendar that could give me an idea who's been in the store in the past few days? There's one more thing, Mr. Sadler. With all respect, sir, one person she would definitely have let in is you. My job is to rule out everyone. We need to know where you've been all afternoon. I hope you weren't alone. It'll make my life and yours a lot easier." He smiled grimly at Brian, who didn't smile back.

Brian had been in this position before, under suspicion by the authorities, and although he felt secure since the staff at the Oak Bar knew him by name he still got really uncomfortable when this sort of thing happened. He knew it was just the cop's job to tie down every possibility and eliminate everyone, hopefully leaving only the bad guy at the end. He told the detective that he had been at the Monument Club all afternoon, having lunch and meeting with a

ANCIENT

client. That would certainly be easy enough to confirm, Brian knew.

"I went to the Oak Bar about 5:30, sat in the park for a few minutes afterwards and then I saw the commotion so I came down to see what was going on here. Call Frank, the headwaiter who took my coat, or Sandy, the bartender. They'll both tell you I was at the bar. And here's my credit card receipt. It's probably got a time stamp on it."

The detective wrote the information in a little pad he took from his pocket and followed Brian to Collette's desk. He put the receipt from the bar in his pocket. "I'll keep this for now. No offense. Just doing my job."

"I got it," Brian responded curtly. "Let's just concentrate on things that might solve this crime instead of things that won't."

One thing that Brian had kept to himself so far was the comment Collette made before she was put in the ambulance. She had asked *why* twice and then said the box was already locked up. She had looked terrified. What did all that mean? He decided to keep that to himself for now. If Collette could talk to the police tomorrow they would know much more. In the meantime Brian wanted a little time to digest that information.

He shuffled through her papers and came up with Collette's appointment book. In the gallery business, the volume of customers wasn't as important as the value of what they wanted to purchase or consign. Bijan Rarities sometimes had twenty clients in a day. More often it was less than ten. Today was like that – there had been only six, two before Brian left for lunch at noon, then four in the afternoon. The last one had been around four pm, a little over an hour before Brian had come by the gallery and dropped off Arthur Borland's box.

"I know every name on this list," Brian told Detective Calvin. "They're all repeat clients except one, and that one I met with myself this morning to discuss his consigning an Etruscan vase for us to sell."

The policeman assigned to retrieve the surveillance video motioned to the detective. He stepped away and Brian watched the uniformed cop speak quietly. When he came back he said, "Apparently you have to receive the download of the video first unless we have a search warrant. The monitoring company just sent you an email with an authorization for the video to simultaneously be released to me. I presume you're willing to assist us, Mr. Sadler. If so, you need to print this release, sign it and email it back."

Brian went to his office, entered his password and opened email. He found the document, signed, scanned and returned it. The monitoring company said the video would be emailed within two hours.

Brian spent the next half hour giving the detective a summary of each of the six clients' backgrounds and how to contact them. He couldn't think of anything that would remotely tie any of today's visitors to what appeared to be an attempted robbery. He just wondered how someone would have figured out so quickly that Brian had the box, if in fact that was what the intruder had wanted at all. Maybe Collette had just been rambling in shock and maybe she just fixated on the thing that kept her there after hours – Brian's artifact that had to go into the vault. But something nagged at the back of Brian's mind. Maybe it *was* the box they were after. If so, *why?*

ANCIENT

A quiet chime notified Brian that the vault was ready to be opened. He turned the combination lock, entered another numeric sequence and lowered a large handle. The massive door swung open. Like a bank vault, just inside the doorway was a wall completely made out of steel bars. It was like a jail cell with a locked door in the middle. Brian took a key from Collette's desk and opened that secondary door. He and Detective Calvin stepped inside.

The vault had a large open area where a number of items were, some on individual pedestals, others on tables or a wire rack shelf along one wall. Most were ancient relics or examples of art from early cultures. In a back room other shelves had cubbyholes to store smaller things. With every item was an information card.

The box Brian had given Collette sat inconspicuously on a table near the vault's door. It looked as though she'd been under no stress when she set it on the table – it was arranged neatly and very straight just as he would expect from Collette. Then she would simply have closed the barred door, which locks automatically, and finally shut the huge vault door. Although the latter weighed over a ton it moved seamlessly on huge bearings and a simple push closed it. Even a small person like Collette could have easily done it in one minute.

"How does everything look?" Detective Calvin asked.

"Exactly as it should. Here's the artifact I brought back around five and gave to Collette. It's right here, exactly where it should be." He opened the box and verified its contents. "All here."

"Let's talk about that little box, where you got it and whether it might have anything to do with this investigation."

BILL THOMPSON

At his desk Brian told some of the story of Captain Jack Borland. He explained that the box contained the copy of a letter from the archives in Seville, Spain and two gold sheets. Brian said he knew nothing about the sheets. "That's part of what Lord Borland asked me to check out." He omitted the fact that Borland had said the sheets were Mayan and had been found in Oklahoma.

The detective took copious notes and it was nearly eight pm when he said, "I guess we're done for tonight. Here's my card. Please look at the surveillance video the minute you get it – I will too. Call me immediately if you know who the person is that Miss Conning let in. And any other time you think of anything I might need to know." He gathered his coat, walked to the front of the store where a uniformed officer stood, and they left in a squad car parked at the curb.

Brian went through Collette's papers, making sure he knew what was on tap for tomorrow at the gallery, while he waited for the monitoring company's email. By the time it came he was bone-tired. All he wanted to do was finish up here and go home. Reviewing the video could take hours – he could do it easily from home. Forty minutes later he was ready to go. He locked and armed the front door and hailed a taxi, too exhausted to walk.

On Fifth Avenue traffic flowed as if nothing had ever happened. That was New York – even after major problems the city quickly reverted to "normal", whatever that meant. There were always too many pushy pedestrians, too much traffic and loud noise. All those things made this city the exciting place it was twenty-four hours a day.

Brian was worried about Collette. From what he had seen, her injuries might be really serious and

ANCIENT

he hoped it wasn't his fault. He just couldn't figure something out. The vault was locked down tight, exactly as it would have been any other night. She had put the box on the table, shut the inside gate and closed the huge vault door. If she had done all that the intruder must not have arrived until after the door was locked. Did he attack her in furious desperation because he couldn't get in the vault? Or was he after something else?

Brian recalled Collette looking at him in terror, saying the word *why* twice. What was that about? Brian hoped Collette would be able to remember.

BILL THOMPSON

ANCIENT

CHAPTER TWELVE

As the cab snaked through traffic Brian called Nicole and told her about his day. She tried to make Brian feel better, sensing the stress as he recounted first the attack on Collette then the story about Captain Jack Borland. At the end, trying to lighten his spirits, she said, "Well, if you need a good lawyer, baby, I know where you can get one! And she's cheap . . . well, not cheap exactly but for you it won't cost you in cash. I have other ways of making you pay, if you know what I mean." She laughed and so did he. But after the call ended Brian had a new concern. He'd needed a good lawyer once before. Hopefully he wouldn't need one this time.

He placed a call to Lenox Hill Hospital and learned Collette was in ICU and stable. He spoke briefly to the duty nurse who said she'd pass along his concerns to her parents.

When the taxi pulled up at the towering building where Brian lived in the Upper 80's off Amsterdam, he saw a black car parked at the curb with a man at the wheel. Brian saw Detective Calvin talking to the doorman.

"What are you doing here?" Brian asked.

BILL THOMPSON

"Obviously you haven't seen the surveillance video." The detective's demeanor was far more serious than when questioning Brian earlier.

"No. I locked up the gallery, caught a cab and came home. I saw I got it but decided I'd look at it here at home."

"I watched at it in the car after I left your place. Then we swung back by the gallery to see if you were still there but I saw the place was locked up. I guess I made it to your apartment building sooner than you did. One of the perks of having a light bar on your car, I guess. So can we go up to your condo? We have a lot to talk about."

"Sure," Brian said, noticing the obvious change in the cop's attitude toward him. "So we're both on the same page, can I presume from your being here that you know the person who showed up on the video?"

"Yes, I do. Let's go inside." He took Brian's arm lightly, and Brian pulled back.

"What are you doing?"

"It might be better for you, sir, if we talk inside. I don't think you want me to have to read you your rights here in front of your doorman and maybe your neighbors. You're the man in the video, Mr. Sadler. You're the man who assaulted Collette Conning this afternoon."

ANCIENT

CHAPTER THIRTEEN

Brian was stunned. He looked blankly at the detective and said, "This is crazy. You called the Oak Bar and verified I was there – right? You saw my credit card receipt. I was there when she was attacked. What the hell's going on?"

"Mr. Sadler," the detective said quietly, steering Brian by the arm toward the building entrance as the doorman held the door open while averting his eyes. "Let's not talk any more until I've read you your rights. I'm going to play this one strictly by the books."

The uniformed officer joined them at the elevator. No one spoke as the elevator climbed thirty-five floors to Brian's apartment overlooking Central Park. "Nice," the officer murmured as Brian opened the door.

"Can I look at the surveillance video?" Brian asked.

"I think that would be a good idea. Just give me a sec." He pulled a card from his pocket and read the Miranda rights to Brian who listened in silence, acknowledged he understood them and waived his right to an attorney at this time.

Sitting at his desk, Brian refreshed his laptop and clicked on the mail from the monitoring company. "I think we can get this worked out fast," he said. "It wasn't me, so we just have to figure out why you thought it was and who it actually is."

The detective stood behind Brian as he clicked on the video attachment to the email and opened it. The video started at one pm but Brian fast-forwarded it to six at the detective's direction. He watched as foot traffic moved along in front of Bijan Rarities' front door, then he saw a man walk to the entrance. Details of his face were not visible under his black umbrella but he was wearing a trenchcoat.

As the man got to the door it opened, blocking his face from view. Collette had obviously released the lock and allowed the person into the gallery. At that point a second camera mounted on a pedestal ten feet from the door picked up his face. Brian looked at the video streaming on his monitor and saw a man whose mannerisms and walk were similar to his, smiling at Collette and talking to her. He stopped the video, hit a couple of buttons and enlarged the still frame. As the face got larger and larger it was clear there was a resemblance although Brian thought it wasn't possible to form a conclusion from the video itself. He could see why the cop thought it could be him. It wasn't, but it was close. But definitely it wasn't Brian Sadler.

The man suddenly turned his face from the camera and grabbed Collette. Brian watched her face contort in fear. The intruder pulled her into an area out of the camera's view. That was where the assault had occurred, the detective told him.

ANCIENT

Brian leaned back in his chair and looked at Detective Calvin. "That's not me."

"It certainly looks like you."

"If you actually believe that I want to talk to my attorney."

"Then you'd better make that call."

The two cops sat in Brian's living room as he spoke with Nicole on his cell phone. He told her what had happened since their conversation less than an hour ago.

"Has he said he's going to book you?" she asked.

"No."

"OK, I'll be there in the morning. I was looking at flights out of DFW while we were talking and I can get on the six am, arriving LaGuardia at 10:30. Let me talk to the detective and then I'll get back on with you."

Brian handed the phone to Detective Calvin, who listened to Nicole for a few moments then said, "I'm taking him downtown now. He'll be released later this evening, presuming he can make bail." He glanced at Brian with a slight smile. Brian stared back, remaining impassive but frightened inside. The conversation continued with a remark about Bernie Madoff.

What the hell? Brian thought.

There was a long pause as Nicole talked. Finally the detective said, "OK. I'm willing to do it that way. If I get his passport now I'll see you both tomorrow afternoon." Nicole said something and then the cop handed the phone back to Brian.

"Sweetie, try to get some sleep tonight. He has agreed to let you turn yourself in with me tomorrow afternoon but he wants your passport. I told him you're an upstanding Fifth Avenue business owner and not a flight risk, and he said Bernie Madoff was upstanding too before he got a life sentence for fraud. Regardless, he's agreed to let you turn yourself in with me tomorrow.

"Give him your passport and pick me up in a limo at the airport. I'll email you flight info. We can talk in the car on the way back into Manhattan and I'll go with you downtown. He's going to meet us outside One Police Plaza, put you in a police car and take you in for booking. Once that's done, I'll meet you on the other side for your initial appearance before a judge."

He thanked her, hung up and took his passport from a drawer. Detective Calvin took it and said, "Don't fail to be there tomorrow, Mr. Sadler. This thing is serious enough now. If you run out on me after I did your attorney a big favor it's not going to be a pretty sight when I find you. And trust me, I WILL find you."

ANCIENT

CHAPTER FOURTEEN

Brian got less than two hours of sleep. Before bed he'd called Nicole to thank her again and tell her how much he needed her. Then he called his limo service and arranged a pickup for tomorrow. All night he tossed and turned, nightmares plaguing his brain, every sound piercing his senses. He had faced the possibility of spending time in jail once before in his life. Once again, he'd done absolutely nothing wrong but somehow, someone resembling him was in the video. Collette had unhesitatingly buzzed him in. *She thought it was me!* He found himself questioning everything, even his own sanity. What if he was schizophrenic or something? What if he actually *had* done it?

Brian couldn't sleep. At six he got up, put on sweats and jogging shoes. As he left his building he saw an unmarked black police car sitting in the no parking zone across the street, a uniformed officer at the wheel. He ran down his block and turned north on Amsterdam Avenue - the car followed a block or so behind. To see what would happen, he turned up a one-way street going the wrong direction and ran toward Central Park two blocks away. He glanced back; the car was no longer trailing him.

He ran inside the park for nearly an hour, making his body go further and further and thinking only of each next step. The frenetic run kept his mind off lay ahead today. Finally he exited the park and went back to his apartment. The black car and its driver were across the street.

Brian noticed a text from Nicole saying she was boarding the plane and would see him shortly. There was no checked luggage; Nicole came to New York often and everything she needed was at Brian's condo.

He regretted that Nicole had to interrupt her schedule and rush to New York, but he would have been in jail last night if she hadn't convinced a detective to allow her client one more day of freedom. *She's the best criminal lawyer in America. If anyone can figure this out, she can.*

At 9:30 Brian went downstairs, no idea what to expect this afternoon. He was dressed in a sport jacket, slacks and an open collar shirt. He didn't know if he'd be wearing an orange jumpsuit later today but hoped he would be in these clothes when he made his appearance before the judge. The doorman opened the door of the sedan and Brian climbed in.

"LaGuardia, right? American Airlines?" the driver said.

Brian nodded. "Park at the curb and I'll run in and wait for my friend's flight."

He tracked Nicole's flight. It was over West Virginia and would be landing at 10:35 am. He waited at a Starbucks outside security, watching passengers walk up the long hallway from the gates. Soon he spotted Nicole carrying a briefcase. She was dressed in a black St. John suit with a white shirt. He hadn't seen her in a month and she looked absolutely gorgeous. She waved when she saw him.

"Hi, stranger. Can a girl bum a ride?" They kissed deeply.

"I'm really glad you came." He took her case and they walked outside. As the driver headed toward Lower Manhattan Nicole went over what Brian should expect. She explained that once they met up with Detective Calvin he would take Brian from there. It would be up to him if Brian would be put in a cell and forced to wear a jumpsuit. Best case, she said, would be if the officer let Brian wear his street clothes until court.

"I need to tell you what happened yesterday," he told her.

"Not here. Not in front of the driver. We'll talk when we get out. We're going to kill a little time. Arraignments happen between one and four pm so I'm not going to turn you over to Calvin until 12:30. If things worked out perfectly you could be booked and then be brought straight up the elevator from the jail to court. No matter what, I'll be waiting for you outside the courtroom. The most important thing for you is to say nothing about this case to anyone. Especially Detective Calvin. I'll do all the talking from this point on."

The driver took the Brooklyn Bridge and they arrived downtown just before noon. Nicole asked him to drop them off on Broadway and stay in the area. She would notify him after court where to pick them up. They ducked into a coffee shop. They sat and Nicole took his hand. "You manage to need a lawyer pretty often! Are you a bad guy after all?"

Brian wasn't in the mood for frivolity. Ignoring her comment, he told her about the surveillance video and his alibi. "I sat in the park for over half an hour. That's not like me, and I'm having scary thoughts. I'm beginning to wonder if I was really in the park at all. What if I had some kind of mental lapse? Maybe I actually *did* go back to Bijan and hurt Collette."

"We'll go through the entire story tonight. For now just stay calm. You won't have to say anything except maybe to enter a plea of not guilty if the judge chooses to ask you instead of me."

"Are you certain I'll be able to get out on bail?"

"Absolutely. Don't worry about it. You're accused of assault. Although your situation may be more high profile because it's a Fifth Avenue case, it's the same charge as hundreds of people a day get in New York. There aren't enough cells to hold all these alleged assailants."

It was time to go. Nicole asked Brian for everything in his pockets, plus his watch, saying, "It'll be easier not to have anything to pick up later." They walked to Pearl Street and Brian saw the detective standing next to a black and white NYPD sedan.

The cop introduced himself to Nicole and turned to Brian. "I'm taking you over to central processing. You'll meet back up with your attorney in the courtroom."

Nicole kissed Brian and said, "See you shortly, baby."

Brian got in the back seat of the squad car. There was a wire cage between the front and back seats. "Thanks for turning yourself in, Mr. Sadler. You saved yourself a lot of grief. Same for your attorney, or whatever she is to you." The car drove less than five hundred feet, around the corner and into a garage area. When it stopped Brian could see a

ANCIENT

doorway with a sign that read "PRISONERS ONLY." Instinctively he tried to open the rear door but it was locked. The detective hopped out and opened it from the outside, ushering Brian through the door and into a busy area. The place looked like an ancient hospital waiting room – tile floors, folding chairs along one wall and a series of bulletproof windows that resembled bank teller cages. Behind him was a wall made of bars. There were four large holding cells and people stood at the doors yelling as he came in.

"Hey, pretty boy," one large man said with a wolf-whistle. "Hey cop, put that one in here with me!" The noise level was deafening and it smelled like floor cleaner, urine and sweat. One cell held only women, mostly prostitutes, Brian figured. Some were dressed garishly and all looked tired and bored.

"Just stay with me for now, Mr. Sadler," the detective said, and Brian was glad for that. Using an access card they walked through a set of doors and a metal detector into a large room.

"Sit here." He gestured to a chair at a folding table. He sat across from Brian and got some paperwork out of a folio he carried. He walked over to a fat sergeant who lounged in a chair by a camera on a tripod. "Time to get to work," the detective said laughingly as he handed papers to the cop.

"Come over here, Mr. Sadler," the detective said. "You'll go through a process now where you're photographed, searched and fingerprinted. Do you have any personal belongings on you? If so this man will take them, give you a receipt and return them when you're released on bail."

"I gave Nicole my personal effects. Will I be able to keep wearing these clothes?"

"Possibly. I'll be back in about twenty minutes and let you know. If's court's delayed for any reason you'll have to stay in a holding cell down here until we go upstairs. If that happens you'll be required to wear a jumpsuit and be brought over by a uniformed policeman. Hopefully we're going straight to the Criminal Courts Building. If that's the case I'll take you myself and you can wear your street clothes."

He turned Brian over to the fat sergeant who instructed Brian to raise his arms above his head. He frisked him thoroughly then told Brian to stand against a wall that had a ruler on it to mark Brian's height. When he was positioned, the cop put a sign in front of Brian with an intake number on it.

This is bizarre.

He was passed to another officer for fingerprinting, then to a third who said, "OK. Strip down."

Brian removed his shirt, t-shirt and pants, laying them on a chair. He turned to the officer who said, "Everything, buddy. Get your panties off and your socks too." The officer was putting on a rubber glove.

In what had to be one of life's ignominious moments, Brian stood naked as the man looked him over, felt under his testicles, then said, "OK. Fun time. Turn around and bend over that table."

When the humiliation was complete, the cop said, "Detective Calvin said for you to put your street clothes back on for now. Just sit right over there in that chair and wait."

After he dressed he asked, "May I have some water?"

The cop looked at him and laughed. "This ain't the Ritz, buddy, and I ain't your waiter. You can tough it out. You're in the Jailhouse Hilton now!"

Brian sat for what seemed like an hour but was probably ten minutes. Detective Calvin came

ANCIENT

back and said, "Good news and bad news, Mr. Sadler. Court is on schedule this afternoon and we're going right on over. The bad news is I have to handcuff you."

The Criminal Courts Building of the City of New York was next door to One Police Plaza. Once Brian's hands were cuffed behind him, the police detective walked him over. They took an elevator to the eighth floor. As the doors opened into a broad hallway, Brian saw over a dozen men and women in orange jumpsuits with the word "PRISONER" on the shirt and down the left pant leg. All were handcuffed like Brian and all were accompanied by police officers. He was thankful for the small favor of wearing his own clothes.

He looked around and spotted Nicole coming toward him. "Hey, how'd it go?"

The detective moved away slightly so they could talk. "As well as could be expected, I guess. At least I'm still in my clothes."

Nicole said, "This may take awhile. I've looked at the docket and you're twelfth on the list. If they're all here everyone has to enter pleas and be arraigned. It could take an hour, maybe a lot longer."

Brian looked anxiously at her. "There's no reason why they wouldn't get to my case today, is there? I damn sure don't want to spend the night here."

"It should be fine. I've been here before and it usually goes pretty smoothly. It's in their interest to move cases as fast as possible. Tomorrow will be busy just like today, and anything the judges hold over just backs up the system."

She looked at her watch and motioned to the detective. "You OK for us to go on in now?"

BILL THOMPSON

He nodded and the three of them went into the courtroom. He led Nicole and Brian to a cordoned off area below a sign that said, "DEFENDANTS." They sat and Detective Calvin stood at the end of the aisle. In a few minutes all the other people whom Brian had seen outside in jumpsuits were similarly seated.

Exactly at 1:30 pm a man stood and said, "All rise for the Honorable Judge Marvin Andiamo." The Judge, who appeared to be in his 50s with graying hair, entered and took his seat. The Court Clerk called off the first case.

Some cases went quickly, some more slowly and some were postponed immediately because one of the parties wasn't present. It was 3:15 when the Clerk announced, "Case F175948, State of New York vs. Brian Thomas Sadler."

Nicole and Brian moved to a table in front of the Judge and Detective Calvin walked to a matching table across the aisle, next to a man whom Nicole told Brian was an Assistant District Attorney. The detective whispered briefly to the ADA as Nicole said loudly, "Represented by Counsel, Your Honor."

"Approach the bench please, Counselors," the Judge said. Nicole and the ADA walked to the bench. They conversed quietly for a few minutes and returned to their seats.

"What was that all about?" Brian whispered.

She shushed him as the Judge said, "Mr. Sadler, please rise." Brian and Nicole stood. She pressed a button on her cell phone then set it on the table. "You're charged with felony assault. Do you understand the charges against you?" the Judge asked.

"Yes, Your Honor."

"And what plea do you wish to enter?"

"Not guilty, Your Honor."

ANCIENT

Since you are a business owner in Manhattan, and since you have no prior criminal record, your attorney has asked that you be released on your own recognizance. I find that unsatisfactory considering the gravity of the crime with which you are charged. Mr. District Attorney, do you have any objection to bail of one hundred thousand dollars?"

The opposing counsel stood. "That's satisfactory to the State, Your Honor."

The Judge then said, "Bail is therefore set at one hundred thousand dollars. If you post bail you are ordered to reappear on May 20th for a preliminary hearing. You must also surrender your passport until then."

"Thank you, Your Honor." Nicole stood with Brian as the detective rejoined him.

"Where do you stand on bail?" Detective Calvin asked Nicole.

"We'll meet the bondsman in the hall. I paged him while the Judge was talking to Brian."

Brian whispered to Nicole, "I can put up a hundred thousand dollars myself if you give me a couple of hours."

"You don't have a couple of hours. You're charged with felony assault. You have to stay in jail until bond is posted. I know you can do it yourself but it's just easier right now to use a bondsman. It's going to cost you ten grand but I think you'd spend that right now to walk free and not spend a single second in a cell." She didn't wait for his response. Pushing through the doors into the hall, she looked around and found the man she was searching for. She raised her hand in a wave and a man in a gray suit walked toward her.

"Stay here for a sec, Brian," she said. Detective Calvin moved closer to Brian as they stood out of the way of the human traffic moving through the hallway. She spoke to the bondsman who finally nodded and walked away.

Nicole looked at the detective. "He's posting Brian's bail now. If you don't mind, can we walk into the Court Clerk's office and get this finished?"

"Sounds good to me. I have other people to catch, you know." He smiled but neither of them returned it.

It took only a short time before bail had been posted. The detective read the paperwork the Court Clerk's office submitted then asked Brian to turn around. He unlocked the handcuffs and said, "OK, you're free to go. I'll see you in court, as they say." He walked toward the elevators and entered the first open car.

They waited for a different elevator car. "How in the hell did you get bail so fast?" he said to Nicole as they rode down.

"I would hope by now you'd think I know how to do my job. Every white-collar client I bring here wants to be out fast. My firm has these bail bondsmen on retainer and they jump through hoops when we call them. I texted this one last night before I went to bed and told him to be on alert and ready to go if I paged him this afternoon.

"The biggest fear to a bail bondsman is whether his prisoner might disappear and leave him having to pay the bail. When bondsmen deal with Carter and Wells they know they can't lose. The firm guarantees the bail bond. Now we turn right around and collect the entire amount from you and put it in an escrow account. Once everything is settled and bail's no longer required, we give your money back. Simple, huh? We get great service because Carter and Wells guarantees payment if you skip town. The

ANCIENT

bondsman is happy because he's making a fee with no risk. You're happy because you're out of jail. I'm happy because you're happy."

BILL THOMPSON

ANCIENT

CHAPTER FIFTEEN

The sedan dropped Brian and Nicole at the gallery. Jason Hardesty, the newer of Brian's assistants, was with a client as they walked through the showroom to Brian's office. In a few minutes they heard the soft ding of the front door and then Jason stuck his head around the corner.

"Have you gotten an update on Collette?" he asked.

"I called early this morning and they said they couldn't give me any information."

"Her father called here for you. I told him you hadn't arrived yet. He said she's out of danger but still asleep. They say she's not in a coma but she had a hard blow to her head. I . . . I guess you know about that, though," Jason stammered for a moment as if he'd said something wrong. "Mr. Sadler, I want you to know . . . I, uh, both Collette's father and I don't believe you were involved. That would just be crazy. So if there is anything I can do to help you, and Collette too of course, just ask." He looked embarrassed and was saved by the bell, literally, as the front chime softly rang. "I'll be up front," he said, making a quick exit to see who had rung the bell.

"That was awkward," Nicole commented.

"It sure was. I wonder if Collette's father really believes I have no involvement. It's pretty hard to refute at the moment."

"Show me the video, Brian."

Nicole asked him to rerun it several times and she paused frequently to look closely at one frame, then another. She watched the man come into the gallery, then rewound and watched it again, over and over.

"That's not you."

"Well thanks for your vote of confidence. But you have to admit it looks like me."

"It does, but he doesn't have the same gait as you do. That's probably not enough to convince a judge, but it does allow us to begin picking at the rest of this to see if there are other things that corroborate my thinking. Let's think for a minute of every way possible for someone to look exactly like someone else. Give me some ideas – way out of the box is fine – anything you can come up with." She took a yellow legal pad from Brian's desk and pulled a Mont Blanc pen from her inside jacket pocket.

Brian thought for a moment and said, "OK, it could be my twin brother."

"Which you don't have, but some people believe that somewhere in the world every person has a twin." She wrote it down.

"The guy has a passing resemblance to me at a distance but up close he's completely different."

"That might fly. He'd have to look pretty similar though. Collette let him in and didn't appear afraid of him even when he was fairly close to her."

"The guy is wearing a latex mask."

"Now that's a possibility. The market for that kind of stuff is pretty specialized, mostly in the spy world, but there are people who for a price can make a latex mask from a photo. It might not stand up to inspection a foot away from a close friend but I hear they're pretty good even a short distance away." She jotted a note.

"Any other ideas?"

"Not at the moment."

"OK, next topic. What did he want so badly, how did he know you had it, and what'll happen next, since it appears he didn't get it?"

There was no progress as they considered how and why this all happened. They reviewed the video another time. The man's clothes were similar to Brian's but that would have been easy to duplicate. Brian wore dark pinstripes or solids every single day, with a muted tie and a white shirt. When it was cool he wore a trenchcoat like a million other New Yorkers. That's what Brian had had on yesterday and what the man in the video had on too, except it looked as though he wasn't wearing a tie. The resemblance to Brian was close but not perfect. But as Nicole said, it had been good enough for Collette to buzz him in.

Brian suggested they run up to the hospital to see if they could find out anything about Collette. They caught a cab to Lenox Hill Hospital and got her room number at the front desk. There was a "No Visitors" sign taped to her door, so they stood in the hall. In a few minutes a lady who appeared to be in her fifties or sixties came out. She looked tired but her facial features showed she was unmistakably related to Collette.

"Excuse me. Are you Mrs. Conning?"

"You're Brian Sadler, aren't you?" She seemed friendly enough, especially for a person who's daughter's attacker might be standing in front of her.

BILL THOMPSON

"Yes. I hope you don't mind my coming here. Mrs. Conning, I had nothing to do with Collette's injuries. This is my friend and my attorney, Nicole Farber. We're doing everything we can to figure out what happened."

Nicole shook the lady's hand. "I'm so sorry about your daughter. How are things going?"

"She's been awake off and on but her short term memory seems to be gone. The doctor says shock can do that to a person. Her father and I can only hope and pray she'll recover and be the person she was. The doctor says the blow to her head was severe and that she likely suffered a concussion."

Mrs. Conning looked at Brian intently. "She has enjoyed working with you more than anything else she's ever done. She considers you a fair, honest and exemplary employer and above that, a friend. She goes on about you every time we're together. She absolutely loves everything about you and her job at Bijan. For now I'm choosing to believe you had nothing to do with this attack. Once Collette regains her memory hopefully she can cast some light on this whole thing."

"Please let us know if there's anything we can do," Nicole said.

"Sounds like you both have plenty of things to work on at the moment. I hear the video shows that you were there. I don't understand that."

Brian started to respond – Nicole held up her hand to him. "Unfortunately Brian can't really say anything at this point; I hope you understand. All I can tell you is that he was *not* there. Whoever it was, he did a good job of convincing Collette to let him in. We need to figure out what he was after. Concentrate on taking care of your daughter; I know she'll be in good hands with you and her father here. Please

ANCIENT

contact Brian if she wakes up and feels that it would be OK for us to see her. God bless your family, Mrs. Conning."

BILL THOMPSON

ANCIENT

BOOK TWO

BILL THOMPSON

ANCIENT

CHAPTER ONE

Three months later

Within a month after the attack Collette Conning had made almost a complete recovery. She returned to the gallery, eager to participate in the Aztec Commission sale. She and her parents conferred with the District Attorney and expressed their deep feelings that Brian Sadler could never have been a part of the attack. In fact it made no sense – he had full access to the gallery, its vault and the items inside – so motive was impossible to establish as far as Brian's charges were concerned. The Connings refused to support the State's action against Brian. Without the victim to testify, the District Attorney's office dropped the charges in a procedure known as nolle prosequi, which gave the state the option to re-file in the future if evidence warranted. The case remained open and unsolved and Brian hoped there would be an answer someday to explain what happened.

The Aztec Commission broadcast on *History* was a resounding success. Brian went to Mexico City for a total of sixteen days over several trips. He and

BILL THOMPSON

Dr. Nunez, the archaeologist from the Museum of Antiquities in Mexico City, narrated the show, with voiceovers when the producers inserted video and stills of Tenochtitlan, the ancient Aztec capital where the artifacts were found. Brian thought adding the well-known professor to the broadcast was a valuable decision. He also praised the network's producer for his editing and presentation of the broadcast.

As *Antiques Roadshow* appraisers do, Dr. Nunez and Brian had stood next to each artifact in turn. The archaeologist gave a brief narrative as to what was known – the item's history, provenance, rarity and other interesting details. Brian then added the estimate of the price each of the ancient items would bring at auction. As the show progressed each value was added to a large ticker and the total recalculated. In a dramatic climax, Brian disclosed the final auction estimate at more than eight million dollars.

The show aired on a Sunday night at nine pm and ranked among the most watched documentaries ever. Two weeks later Bijan Rarities held the auction itself, simulcast from three sites so the attendees in each venue could see all bidders and each item up for bid. Brian was on site in New York, his assistants Collette and Jason were at the new Bijan gallery in London, and Dr. Nunez was in Mexico City at Tenochtitlan, where the artifacts were found. There were far more bidders than they'd anticipated, due in no small part to the publicity Bijan Rarities had generated through the *History* documentary.

The sale was a huge success, exceeding Brian's estimate and grossing slightly over ten million dollars. The gallery's percentage was almost a million dollars, but even better was the

ANCIENT

immeasurable publicity from the television broadcast. The New York Post interviewed the couple that had consigned the Tenochtitlan artifacts for sale. They had high praise for the gallery and its illustrious owner, Brian Sadler.

As Brian spent countless hours on pre-production work for the show and auction, he often thought of Captain Jack Borland. Shortly after they met, Brian had told Arthur although he was committed for these three months, they should talk afterwards. If Jack were still missing Brian promised to help.

Brian had split up the items Arthur left with him. He delivered the box itself to one expert and a gold sheet to each of two others. He guarded their background and provenance carefully. If the gold sheets were truly Mayan they were priceless. Further, the idea that they somehow turned up in Oklahoma added an element of mystery to the story. Brian had to be cautious not to betray Arthur Borland's confidence or even to potentially endanger Jack Borland, if he were still alive.

The box went to the director of Mesoamerican studies at Columbia University. The educator had spent his adult life studying the Maya society. He told Brian it was likely the item was Mayan. He consulted several reference books and finally showed Brian a picture. It showed a similar box found in Palenque, Mexico at the Temple of the Inscriptions.

The scholar said, "It's impossible to say with certainty if your box is Mayan, but we could certainly carbon date it and at least confirm the period from which it comes."

A couple of days later he took one of the gold sheets to the prestigious Bryant Park Museum of Ancient History, having called his friend Anthony

Fuselman, who had recently become Assistant Curator for Pre-Columbian Civilizations. Fuselman held a doctorate in archaeology and specialized in ancient artifacts. Brian had read his thesis on the writings of the Aztec and Maya civilizations with an emphasis on whether they came from similar root languages. He was a recognized expert in the symbology used by both.

Fuselman took one look at the sheet and said, "This is incredible. Where did you get this?"

"I'm sorry but at the moment I'm under strict confidentiality with a client and I can't tell you anything. Hopefully you can still help me. Is it possible that the writing shown here is sixteenth century Mayan?"

"And my payment for this project is . . . what?" he smiled at Brian. "When are you going to have *me* be an expert on one of those television shows you produce? I could have been famous by now if I'd been your Aztec go-to guy!"

Brian smiled, knowing the man was half-kidding. He explained that Dr. Nunez' presence on the show was a capitulation to the Mexican government to allow Brian to remove the artifacts from their country.

"OK, I get it. I'm mostly kidding. Dr. Nunez did a great job and he was the right guy for that production. Just don't forget your old friend Anthony and the Bryant Park Museum over here, ready to help in exchange for a little positive press now and then!"

They got down to business. Fuselman told Brian the gold sheet might or might not be authentic – provenance would be critical for that determination. Since the sheet had been removed

ANCIENT

from where it was found, provenance could never be firmly established.

He added optimistically, "That said, the writing and symbols are perfectly correct for Mayan civilization in the 1500s. Do you want to know what it says?"

Although a translation wasn't critical, Brian listened as Dr. Fuselman explained that the sheet was one of a series. It was the continuation of a story of conquest of one Mayan city by another. "I see no names either of cities or people, but I feel very comfortable telling you this all fits. Unless someone went to a hell of a lot of trouble to create a fake, even going so far as to use a real gold sheet, I'd say this is authentic."

That was good news. Now Brian scanned a portion of the letter from the Governor of Guatemala, Pedro de Alvarado, to King Charles V of Spain. According to Arthur the letter itself had apparently never been sent. Captain Jack had copied the original during his visit to the archives in Seville, Spain. Brian's scan omitted enough of the verbiage to mask its meaning but it was still sufficiently long to give a flavor of the writing itself.

He emailed the scan to the Institute for Mesoamerican Studies at the University of Mexico. Since Brian didn't have a personal relationship with anyone who could authenticate Spanish letters, he had called a couple of colleagues in London who had dealt in similar items. He got the same name from both, a professor named Moreno. Brian asked him if the words appeared consistent with how the letter would have been crafted and written in 1540.

Soon Brian received his response – the letter's sentence structure, words and other nuances were identical to thousands sent from the colonies to

BILL THOMPSON

Spain in the sixteenth century. The archives in Seville and Mexico were full of examples that perfectly matched Alvarado's letter.

Now Brian was convinced he was dealing with real Mayan artifacts and a letter from the 1500s.

Brian called Arthur, told him the items had passed authentication and arranged to meet him the next week when Brian planned to be in London. Over lunch at The Savoy Grill, Brian handed the box and its contents back.

From prior conversations Brian knew Arthur had heard nothing more about Captain Jack. He said, "I've gotten things arranged so I can take a couple of weeks off very soon. I'm sorry it's taken so long but now I'm happy to help if I can."

"I'm absolutely convinced you can help me figure out this enigma. There's only one hitch. I wanted to go with you but my mother has fallen ill. She's getting old and is very frail. As you can imagine, my father's disappearance has only exacerbated her failing health. Now she's constantly nervous and jittery. There are no children but me and I can't leave her at this point." He explained that in-home care was too expensive so he and his wife were looking after his mother and staying at the family's manor house outside of London.

Brian expressed concern over Arthur's mother's situation and he was disappointed that they wouldn't both be in Guatemala. He changed the subject, telling Arthur that one of his oldest friends had left the United States many years ago, giving up the corporate boardroom for a more serene life as a charter boat captain on the Belizean island of Ambergris Caye. More recently he and his new wife Odette had decided to buy a hotel in San Ignacio, ironically the same jungle town from which Captain

ANCIENT Jack Borland's expeditions had always begun. Not surprisingly, Brian's friend Sam Adams knew Captain Jack, just like almost everyone else in the area.

Brian laid out his plans. "I'm going to San Ignacio before the end of the month. I'll look around and see what I can learn. I can't promise results but I'll go into the jungle and give it a shot. I've taken my friend Sam into my confidence about this whole thing and he's happy to help. He's met your dad and he's nosing around San Ignacio right now to see what rumors are out there. I'm planning a brief trip to the mountain in Guatemala and he's trying to work out things so he can come along. His knowledge and background could be a big help."

Arthur agreed and then mentioned payment. Since he had no funds to contribute to the cost of the expedition or to reimburse Brian for his time, they quickly reached an agreement. It was possible Brian might discover something valuable during his quest to find Captain Jack. If he did, and a sale subsequently occurred, Arthur and Bijan would split the proceeds. Bijan would handle any future sales of items by the Borland family and receive a standard commission for its work. Brian promised within a couple of days to prepare and forward a contract for execution by Arthur and his mother.

Arthur was pleased that at long last something was going to happen. He said, "I wish I had his map, but at least I'll hire the same two guides who accompanied me, if that's acceptable. They know which paths *not* to take and they know how to cut a swath through a forbidding jungle."

BILL THOMPSON

ANCIENT

CHAPTER TWO

During the next two weeks the contract was executed and Arthur lined up the Belizeans who would accompany Brian into the Guatemalan highlands and up the mountain.

Over the past weeks Brian had told Nicole everything he knew about Captain Jack and that he was going to Belize and Guatemala very soon.

"Come on this trip with me. We haven't been anywhere interesting in months and this will be exciting to say the least. Our accommodations will be good – we'll stay in San Ignacio at my old friend Sam's hotel – we'll have a proper martini and a great meal every night we're in town."

Nicole had recently finished the trial of her high-profile client in the stock fraud case. The jury couldn't agree if he was simply naïve or deceptively conniving, so he went free. The government dismissed the case and Nicole's near-perfect record of acquittals continued. She always enjoyed the frenzy of trial preparation much more than routine client problems and now that trial was over she was feeling a little down. A trip to Central America could be the elixir she needed both for her professional life and her personal involvement with Brian. She agreed to go with the caveat that she could only stay a week.

"I'll come back when you leave San Ignacio to go into Guatemala," she told him.

Brian called the San Ignacio Inn and spoke with Sam's wife Odette. She expressed how much they both looked forward to seeing him and meeting Nicole. He bought two round trip first class tickets on American including a night in Dallas before the early morning flight to Belize City.

Everything he needed fit in a carry-on rolling bag and a backpack. Everything was on time and by 1:30 he was having a glass of wine at Seaview, the hottest new restaurant in Uptown Dallas. Nicole would be arriving soon.

Uptown is a compact area of shops, apartments and office buildings just north of downtown Dallas – this chic restaurant was only three blocks from Nicole's office and just slightly further away from Brian's old building that had housed the investment banking operation of Warren Taylor and Currant where Brian had been a broker. Not long after Brian left for Bijan Rarities the firm had shut down after a Securities and Exchange Commission investigation. He occasionally was reminded of those exciting crazy days selling penny stocks and winning huge prizes like convertibles for stupid things like spelling someone's name correctly. Those were heady, exciting, greedy days – a time when Brian learned the hard way that everything comes with a price. Then his thoughts drifted to the amazing turn of events that allowed him to meet Darius Nazir, move to New York and assume the ownership of Bijan Rarities after Nazir's untimely death just a couple of years ago.

ANCIENT

Brian glanced up and saw a flash of blonde hair heading his way. Nicole could turn heads just by walking into a place and today was no exception. Everyone knew when Nicole Farber arrived. Men and women alike paused to watch this beautiful woman. She made a statement with no effort whatsoever. She carried herself as though she were a woman on top of the world – a girl in her thirties who was already a success. And it was true. She was all those things and far, far more to Brian Sadler.

Nicole was dressed more casually than usual, wrapping things up before her trip, working with her office door closed and no client appointments scheduled. She was wearing designer jeans and black spike heels. A black blazer topped her white button-down shirt - she looked absolutely incredible, just the way she always did to Brian.

She paused and spoke casually to two men at a table nearby. She waved to Brian and walked to his booth. As he kissed her cheek she said, "Hi, baby. Long time no see."

The waiter appeared. "Good afternoon, Ms. Farber. A cocktail perhaps? Or do you prefer to enjoy the wine the gentleman has ordered?" She chose the wine.

Brian asked the waiter to give them a few minutes, promising to signal when they were ready.

"I'm finished at the office. Let's catch up, enjoy our lunch and skip dinner. I have ideas for you tonight, Brian Sadler. And they don't involve sitting in a restaurant. In fact, they don't involve sitting at all!"

She winked at him and patted his leg. "Glad you got a booth instead of a table. I always want to be as close to you as I can. Especially when I haven't seen you in a couple of months." She moved closer and snuggled up. "Man, I've missed you."

As they chatted they finished half the bottle before they ordered lunch. They had plenty of time – it was a leisurely meal followed by coffee. Around four pm Brian gathered his suitcase and backpack and they walked the five blocks to Nicole's condo at the Ritz-Carlton on Pearl Street. Her assistant had delivered her stuffed briefcase there so she wouldn't have to carry it to the restaurant. As usual, it was full of work she could handle while she was out of town. The concierge handed the case to her as he held the elevator door and welcomed Brian back to town.

Nicole had bought her two thousand square foot condo on the twentieth floor at the perfect time and from the perfect person. A dip in the real estate market and a motivated seller who was facing foreclosure meant that she paid half what the six-room condominium was worth only a few months later. She had windows on the north and south and a small terrace opening from her living room on the east.

"Care for another glass of wine, Mr. Sadler?" She smiled at him and tossed her jacket on the back of the couch.

"I think I'd rather have you." He took her in his arms and kissed her deeply. They held each other close, enjoying the moment. She moaned as his hand moved inside her blouse, caressing her breasts. "Good thing you forgot your bra," he whispered.

"Oh, I didn't forget. In fact it was very deliberate. Wait'll you see what else I forgot."

While they kissed, she deftly removed her shoes and belt and unzipped her jeans. She backed away from Brian for a moment as she wiggled out of

ANCIENT

her pants. She had nothing on from the waist down. Her shirt came off quickly – now Nicole was totally naked and Brian was incredibly aroused.

"Look what you've done. You've made me feel like I have way too many clothes on."

"Then let's get them off." As he cupped her breasts, Nicole began unbuttoning his shirt. She removed it and unbuttoned his slacks, zipped them down and off. "Uh oh," she said, smiling. "You forgot something too."

"Seems like boxers just get in the way around you."

Bending down, she took off his socks and now they were both naked. "Brian Junior's really happy to see me, I think," she said, running her fingertips up his shaft.

By now Brian could only moan in agreement.

"Follow me," Nicole said, leading him out to her terrace. "I love this condo because no other owner can see my patio. I've told you it makes a great place to sunbathe au naturel. Tonight it's a great place to get together for something I really want, with someone I really want." She told Brian to lie on her chaise lounge and she sat on the floor beside him.

"How about a little fingertip massage?" she said as he lay with his eyes closed. She began at his forehead, lightly grazing his skin with her fingers as she moved in circles, first along his cheeks, then his ears, his neck and his chest, moving to his nipples and caressing them until they were hard, then sliding slowly around and around down his chest. He moaned as she moved further.

Brian softly said, "I'm getting all the attention here. What about you?"

BILL THOMPSON

"I'm fine, Brian. I'm so glad you're here with me and I'm so glad we're going on a trip tomorrow. Tonight's your treat. I'll get my turn tomorrow night. I promise. You owe me!"

She climbed on top of him, facing him so he could see every inch of her tanned body. As she slowly settled down on him she groaned with anticipation as she felt his shaft go higher and higher inside her. She moved up and down very deliberately as he joined her rhythm, meeting her and moving together until in one huge rush they both climaxed. In the afterglow, she laid her body on his and he held her tightly.

"I love you. I've never told you exactly how I feel, but I love you, Nicole."

"I know you do, Brian. And I love you too." She began to cry. "I want to be with you all the time but I don't see any way we can do it. We're fifteen hundred miles apart and it might as well be a million. Our lives are a million miles apart too. I can't live where you live, Brian. And you can't live where I live. We have to figure this out somehow."

ANCIENT

CHAPTER THREE

The flight from DFW to Belize City's Philip S.W. Goldson Airport is an easy two-hour trip. Brian and Nicole ate a light lunch in first class and were first down a set of stairs to the tarmac. The humidity and temperature were high but not unlike that of Dallas. They walked to the small terminal building and were guided toward immigration. Soon they cleared customs and walked outside where a jumble of taxis and greeters waited.

"Brian!" Nicole saw a nice-looking guy Brian's age in a linen shirt and khaki shorts walking toward them. He smiled broadly and hugged Brian. "This must be Nicole," Sam Adams said, hugging her too. "Welcome to Belize!"

Sam guided them through the parking lot to his pickup, loaded their bags and pulled two brown bottles from a cooler. "Have a Belikin. You're now officially in my country!"

As Nicole took the cold bottle Brian told her that Belikin beer was an institution in Belize, brewed locally and served everywhere in the country. They sipped on the brews as Sam drove through the busy streets of Belize City then onto the Western Highway, heading toward San Ignacio and the Guatemalan border two hours away.

Nicole checked emails on her iPhone while the men talked about Captain Jack. Sam said that he hadn't heard anything new about the missing explorer but that Arthur had done his job. The two guides who had accompanied Arthur a few months ago had already contacted Sam and were awaiting further instructions. Brian was also glad to hear Sam was coming along too.

"Everything worked out and I'm in for your expedition up the mountain. I hope my extra set of eyes and ears, and hands for that matter, might help you out. Plus it gets a tiny bit boring playing Bob Newhart the innkeeper. I need a little spice in my life!"

"I'm really glad you're coming. How soon do you think we can leave?"

"We have to get the provisions. I've already begun a list of supplies we'll need. This kind of expedition isn't as rare as you'd think so there's a pretty basic checklist of essentials, and everything's available in the stores in town. One good thing about the particular mountain we're climbing is a midpoint rest stop called the Jaguar's Call. It's a good place to regroup before the hard climb and we can replenish water and other stuff we need. Back to the original question, I'd say we leave in four days."

Brian mentioned he'd been told about Jaguar's Call and its proprietor from Arthur. It was an essential stop, he said, because Jack Borland had been there too. They needed to interview Lucky Buncombe. He might have been one of the last to see Jack before his disappearance.

ANCIENT

Nicole tuned in as they talked. "OK guys. When you explorers leave for the boondocks this gal is winging her way back to Big D."

"Let's plan to leave on Tuesday," Brian said. "That gives us four days to get everything ready and enough time for me to show Nicole the sights."

Sam thought that was fine. "Done deal. On a different subject, I've lined up something interesting. There's a great guide I use whose name is Alfredo. He's discovered a cave that has ancient pottery and even a Mayan skeleton. He's been back to it a couple of times since but it's virtually pristine from the standpoint that no tourists have been there so far. Since we have a little time to kill and I've really wanted to see this cave, are you guys up for a mini-adventure on Sunday before our real jungle adventure even starts?"

Brian replied immediately, "Sure!" Suddenly he glanced into the back seat where Nicole was frowning.

"Sweetie, you can stay at the hotel if you don't want to do this. I know you didn't plan on visiting an unexplored cave, so make it easy on yourself."

"I'll think about it. Sounds a little scary but hell Brian, half of the things you do sound scary to me."

Finally they turned off the main highway onto Burns Avenue, the main street in San Ignacio. Within five minutes they arrived at the San Ignacio Inn where Sam introduced them to Odette. She greeted them warmly.

"Sam has told me so much about you, Brian. He's really been anticipating your arrival so I'm glad you're finally here!" She showed them to their second floor room, one with a balcony overlooking the street. "Usually there's not much noise from down below but Saturday nights in town can be drunk and late so if you decide you want to switch to a room on the back it's no problem." They decided to stay with this one – the balcony gave them a great view of the town and the open French doors provided a cool breeze.

Brian had left Jack Borland's box and its contents securely locked in his vault in New York City. He brought pictures of the things that were in the box - the gold sheets and the letter to the King of Spain along with a translation into English. Everything was in a manila envelope that he stuck behind a mirror on the wall of their room.

They walked downstairs to the bar just off the lobby. "You must be Mr. Brian and Miss Nicole," the Belizean bartender said with a broad smile. "I'm Leo!"

Before the evening was over Brian was convinced Leo was the best bartender in Belize if not the entire world. It was hard to get XO Vodka in Dallas or New York and impossible here. But somehow Sam Adams had arranged it and Leo had made an extra dry martini up with a twist, exactly as Brian preferred it. Life was good, Brian decided, ordering a second one and later a third just for good measure.

On Saturday Sam took Nicole and Brian a few miles on the Western Highway to the site of a hand-cranked ferry that took cars and pedestrians across the Mopan River. Nicole took over the crank and moved the ferry slowly across the narrow canal. Soon they were at the ancient ruin of Xunantunich. It was a beautiful morning and Nicole was fascinated to see her first Mayan temples rising over a hundred feet high around a central plaza. Although she professed to have a fear of heights she gamely accompanied Brian, Sam and a guide from the plaza to the top of the highest structure. From there it was easier to

ANCIENT

imagine the size and former grandeur of this ruined city.

They sat outside for lunch at Rosita's, a little Mexican place nearby. Nicole went to the restroom after lunch and when she returned Brian and Sam were deep in whispered conversation. "What's up, guys?"

Brian smirked and winked. "Just planning our afternoon. You'll have to wait and see."

Sam drove a few miles down the Cristo Rey Road out of San Ignacio, turned off onto a deeply rutted dirt road and stopped when they reached the Macal River. "End of the line," he said to Nicole as Brian jumped out and held the door for her. Sam opened the tailgate of the truck and got out two lawn chairs and two towels, handing them to Brian. "See you in an hour and a half." Nicole watched as the truck headed back on the road they had just taken.

"What are we doing?"

"We're going to have some sun and some fun in the water."

"OK. Did you bring our swimsuits?"

"Please, Nicole. Swimsuits? Do you really think we need those out here in the jungle?" Grinning at her, he walked to the edge of the river and looked out. "The bottom is flat and sandy right here, only about a foot deep. Let's take our chairs out and sit in the river." He pulled his t-shirt off, unbuttoned his shorts and dropped them on the shore. He was naked except for his tennis shoes. "Come on. Nothing like sunbathing in the nude."

"You don't have to ask me twice." She pulled her tank top over her head, unhooked her bra and pulled off her shorts. She took off her shoes and socks. "I want to feel the sand between my toes."

BILL THOMPSON

They sat in lawn chairs in the Macal River for nearly an hour, talking and enjoying the time together au naturel. At one point they heard the sound of people talking and they looked at each other, wondering where it was coming from. In a moment a canoe came around the bend, manned by a twenty-something couple. It was absolutely too late for modesty, so Nicole and Brian just sat in their chairs and waved as the canoe went by.

"Looks like fun," the guy yelled.

"Oh yeah," Brian called back. "You should try it."

"Thank God there weren't a bunch of little kids in that canoe," Nicole laughed as the boat drifted away. "We might have brought new meaning to sex education in Belize. Speaking of that, do you think Sam will be back on time or will he be early? We've just finished one exhibition – I don't really want to give Sam a show!"

"He knows exactly what I had planned for this afternoon. He'll be on time just like he said."

"OK then. We have less than a half hour left." Nicole got up, turned and knelt in front of Brian's lawn chair. In almost no time his body convulsed as he finished what she had started. "Wow, that was a fast one. You must be into this outdoor stuff!"

"Well yes, I'd say so. When I'm sitting in the jungle in a river stark naked with a nude goddess in front of me doing something like that, I think any red-blooded man would get things done pretty fast."

"Glad I could be of help." She smiled and sat back in her chair for ten minutes. They finally got up, took the chairs to shore and were drying off as they heard the truck approaching. Nicole quickly pulled on her shorts, fastening her sports bra just as

ANCIENT

Sam pulled up. She glanced at Brian – he had gotten his shorts up and was zipping them.

Nicole pulled her tank top on as Brian donned his shirt. "Looks like you had a great afternoon for sunbathing," Sam said. "Did you see any canoe traffic?"

Nicole laughed. "Yes, actually we did. And they got a great show because they came around the bend faster than we could react."

"Oh well. Hopefully you weren't in too compromising a situation!"

Brian replied, "It was fine. We had a blast. Thanks for suggesting this."

They drove back to the inn, walked to the town square for a quiet dinner on the street and turned in early, hoping the Saturday night revelry in town wouldn't keep them from sleeping. They had a big day ahead of them tomorrow – after climbing a ruin and sitting in a river all afternoon, they fell asleep quickly and never woke until Brian's iPhone alarm went off at six am.

Around seven the guide Alfredo met Sam, Nicole and Brian in the hotel lobby, ushered them out to his ATV and they began the two-hour ride to the cave site. The first twenty minutes of the trip was on a paved road. When they reached the tiny village of San Antonio, Alfredo turned off the main road onto a fairly well defined dirt pathway that snaked through a couple of farms before entering a forest.

A hundred feet in the woods the pathway narrowed dramatically. "Watch your arms," Alfredo said as the ATV brushed saplings on both sides of the road. They rounded a corner and Alfredo cursed quietly as he saw a large tree lying across the road in front of them. "OK, end of the line, amigos. We walk from here."

"How far are we from the cave?" Sam asked.

"Two miles, more or less. If this tree hadn't been here we could have gotten about a half-mile closer, but that would have been it anyway. So we haven't lost much."

Each person was assigned a backpack. One contained their lunch, another had rapelling gear and there was other equipment for their descent into the cave. Alfredo had extra ropes and equipment that he decided to leave in the ATV. He told them, "This is just emergency gear. No need to carry the extra weight."

They loaded up and began the hike, stopping occasionally as the guide or Sam pointed out flora and fauna, interesting tidbits of information or to note the tracks of various animals that inhabited the jungle.

"Watch out!" Alfredo suddenly stopped Nicole as she headed down the trail. "Look at the leaf-cutters." He pointed to a long line of ants marching single-file across the pathway, each carrying a leaf twice its size. "If you interrupt them they can inflict a painful bite." They stopped to look at a huge bulge on one of the trees. "Termite nest," Sam said. "They're very tasty."

"You've got to be kidding," Nicole laughed.

Sam tore a piece of the nest away and reached inside, pulling out several termites that he picked out of the nesting material and stuck in his mouth. "This is one of the most-eaten insects on earth," he said, swallowing. "They're full of protein and taste like nuts."

"I hope I don't ever get that hungry," she commented, astonished at what she'd seen Sam do.

Nearly two hours later they arrived at a small opening. Alfredo stopped and took off his pack.

ANCIENT

"We've arrived. Let's put our packs down here and rest for a minute, then we'll begin our descent." He handed each person a headlamp. "Please put these on. You'll need them very soon after we start down."

After drinking a little water the foursome entered the cave, Alfredo in front and Brian bringing up the rear.

BILL THOMPSON

ANCIENT

CHAPTER FOUR
Four hours later

Brian was resourceful. Sitting at the bottom of the cave in the dark, he thought of ways he could save himself. He had no idea where Nicole, Sam and the guide were, but he knew something must have happened to keep Alfredo from returning on time to rescue him. He was concerned for himself but even more for Nicole and his good friend Sam, who both were only along for the ride. It was Brian who had really wanted to see this cave and now maybe they all were in trouble, trapped down here somewhere. Brian thought about Alfredo's admonition to stay put. If he left this room it would be easy to get lost. Maybe forever. Finally he decided if he was going to get out he'd better think of a way himself. Alfredo wasn't coming back.

He figured the toughest part of the trip up would be climbing a ten-foot slick rock they had slid down shortly after entering the cave. Alfredo had installed a rope there already but climbing with a bum shoulder would be a challenge. Brian decided he had no choice but to go. The risk of remaining here with no rescue was worse than trying to get out.

BILL THOMPSON

He turned on his iPhone and the light from the screen gave him a little visibility. As fast as he could he unpacked the backpack completely to see what resources he had available. There was a small pickaxe, a five-foot length of rope and two carabiners stuck in a side pocket. Most importantly Brian found a second headlamp and two extra batteries in the bottom. Apparently Alfredo had ensured each pack contained minimal necessities for survival or climbing. *He's a good guide,* Brian thought. *Thank goodness he included this stuff. It may just help me get out.*

Turning on the failing headlamp, Brian shut off his phone and put it in his pocket. He coiled the rope and hooked it to his belt, using one of the carabiners. He stuck the second headlamp and the batteries in his pants pocket, had a sandwich and a bottle of water, then he prepared to ascend.

I can always come back down if I have to, and I won't starve for days. Knowing he couldn't manage the backpack with his damaged shoulder, he stuck a bottle of water in his pocket and left the pack with the rest of the food and water on the cave floor. He stood at the base of the rock he had fallen down earlier.

Carefully he raised his right arm as high as he could to find out what range of motion he had. He winced and cried out loud as he forced it to shoulder height. He discovered when his arm was raised he couldn't tighten the fingers on his right hand enough to grip. He probed his right shoulder with his other hand, poking and prodding to see if something was broken or out of place. Hopefully it was just a torn muscle. Optimistically deciding it was the latter, he had to endure whatever pain there was, in order to climb up. Instead of thinking of the seven hundred

ANCIENT

foot ascent he concentrated on just one rock - the next one. The first ascent, the one directly in front of him, would be one of the hardest. He'd have to to climb up on small stones, face the rock down which he had fallen and raise his arm above his head. If he could do that, he'd face his next challenge. He had to grip the top of the rock and pull himself up.

Brian wasn't sure if he could lift himself one-handed. If he couldn't, he'd have to use his injured right arm and work through the pain. He hoped he wouldn't make things worse and end up losing the use of his arm completely.

What choice do I have? If I don't try to use both hands I may end up dead down here at the bottom of this cave. So let's get started.

He climbed up and raised his left hand to the top of the slick rock. He tried several times to lift himself using only that arm. Since he was right-handed and weighed 170 pounds, he got nowhere. He gritted his teeth, raised his right arm to shoulder height, seized it with his good arm and pushed it even higher. He screamed in pain but he forced the arm higher and higher. Suddenly something happened. He heard a click and the pain lessened immediately. He felt his shoulder and decided there must have been a separation that he'd just repaired. The right shoulder area was tender but nothing like it had been a few seconds before. He flexed his right hand and found that although it was still painful, he could at least form a fist.

Brian raised both hands, took hold of the top of the rock and raised himself up. His right arm wasn't functioning well but with effort he was able to scale the rock. Once in the cavern above it he could walk up. Occasionally he used his sore arm for balance or to help steady himself as he walked back up the pathway he had previously come down.

Soon his headlamp died. He stuck it in his pocket and put the other one on his head. It had taken less than an hour for his group to descend seven hundred feet. Brian knew it would have taken longer to ascend even without injury, just because it was more strenuous work to go up rather than down. After nearly an hour he thought about where he was and calculated that maybe he was about one third of the way to the top. He turned off the headlamp and looked up. He could see no outside light whatsoever; everything was absolutely black. There were many more twists and turns ahead, Brian knew, and no light filtered down this far.

He continued up another fifty feet or so and came to a large room he remembered from the descent. It contained several Mayan pots and Alfredo had stopped to comment on them. Brian's heart fell at what he saw ahead. Directly in front of him were two broad openings. He had no idea which one they had come down. If he chose incorrectly he had no idea where the other passageway would take him.

Brian looked closely at both openings for footprints, slide marks or any other indication that his group had come one way rather than the other. Both passages were rocky and slick with seeping moisture. Both headed upwards with a steep incline and there was no clue which was the right one.

Here's where Alfredo would say, I told you so. If his friends and the guide were somehow trapped too then he'd become the rescuer himself once he reached the surface. But if he was lost in a labyrinth hundreds of feet below the surface of the jungle it could mean death for the entire group.

ANCIENT

There was always a little pad of paper and a pencil in Brian's shirt pocket, an old habit of his. He made his choice and wrote a note saying, "Brian Sadler took the left passage." He left it under a small rock on the floor of the cavern. If the guide returned and Brian was lost at least he'd know which tunnel Brian had taken.

As he entered the narrow passage, he sketched a crude map to help find his way back if it was a dead end. He had noted the time when he started up this aperture. After an hour he was still climbing, sometimes with little effort, sometimes not. Parts of the passage were narrow, so tight his arms rubbed on the sides as he inched his way up.

Soon the passage began to constrict even more tightly. It felt like he was in a chimney – he was certain he hadn't come down this way but decided he would keep moving up until he couldn't go further. He could always go back down. At least he hoped he could.

The passageway got narrower and narrower as he climbed. Now he couldn't raise his hands above his head because there was no room to move them. He was slithering like a snake, arms at his sides, twisting his way up as he found footholds on the rocky sides. Suddenly a wave of nausea overtook him. What if he couldn't go on? What if this passage came to a dead end? He'd be done when he couldn't slither any more or when a rock marked the tiny chimney's end. There would be no further progress. He looked up. There was nothing but darkness above him, lit for a couple of feet by his tiny headlamp. His mind raced - what if he couldn't get back down? What if he got stuck? What if the headlamp died now? If it did Brian had no way to move his hands to the batteries or the lamp to fix it. He would be trapped in absolute darkness. Suddenly he began to hyperventilate, using up precious oxygen and finding himself breathing his own stale air in the tiny passage only inches wider than his own body. He forced himself to calm down. He took slow breaths and thought about Nicole and the others. *I have to find them. I have to be strong. I may be the one who saves us all.* Again he prayed and again he slithered upwards.

After a couple of minutes that seemed like hours the narrow passageway began to widen. Finally he popped into a round room about ten feet in diameter and with a high ceiling. This room had a sand floor and there were dozens of shoe and boot prints. Brian breathed a sigh of relief. He clearly remembered how difficult it had been for all of them to stand here together with their packs, because of the tight space. Five feet in front of him were two dark openings in the wall. He felt a momentary jolt of fear – what if one was another claustrophobic flue like he'd just traversed? He didn't know if he could do it.

Just then something encouraging happened. A bat flew by his head and went into one of the openings. Brian turned off his headlamp and saw a faint glow of light far up the hole where the creature had flown. This was the way out!

Brian sat down and drank his bottle of water. He was excited that he was getting close to the surface but he'd been climbing for well over two hours and the last half hour inching his way up a narrow chimney had taken a toll on both his mind and his body. His muscles ached and his throbbing shoulder was hot to the touch.

He had no idea where Nicole, Sam and Alfredo were but he had to assume they hadn't made it back

ANCIENT

to the surface. If they had Alfredo would already have retrieved ropes and rappelling gear and come down for him. Standing at the opening he yelled each name loudly, then listened for a response. Nothing.

Putting the empty water bottle in his backpack, Brian walked over to the hole that led upward. He moved with a renewed enthusiasm both from having had water and from being pumped up about getting out.

It's not that far now. You've come this far – you can do it.

Facing this last part of the climb was the scariest of all. It wouldn't be narrow and confined but there was the steep rock ahead of him. He had to navigate the rope with an inflamed shoulder.

If I can't make it, I'm stuck ten feet from freedom. I could yell but if no one's there I'm no less trapped than if I were still at the bottom of the cave. My food and water are seven hundred feet below me. I could die of starvation ten feet from the surface.

He forced those thoughts out, concentrating instead on each step that took him closer.

Finally Brian reached the sheer rock that rose over ten feet in front of him, his last obstacle. Shafts of daylight glimmered far above. He shouted again but got no response. He gazed at the rock, trying to decide how to scale it. He stretched his right arm upwards to see how mobile he was. It still hurt like hell but if he pushed himself he could use it to climb. Better a sore arm than a dead man, he figured.

There were outcroppings along the left wall next to where the rope hung down. Brian took out the pickaxe and hacked at one that was about two feet off the ground. He made an indentation in the wall that would be large enough for him to stand on. Putting both hands against the rock face he raised his left leg and put his foot on the rock. He grasped the rope, took his pick, raised it high above him and hacked until he had lodged it into a small hole. He put his weight on the pick, praying it wouldn't come loose, and lifted himself until he could stand on the small outcropping he'd cut.

The pick came loose as Brian lifted himself on it and he let go of the rope. He fell backwards, landing on his back on the ground. He got up, flexed arms and legs and except for his arm problem everything was working.

Unable to think of a better plan, he tried the same one again. Holding the rope he raised himself high enough to dig a small hole with the pick and gave it a major last thrust that lodged the axe into the wall. He took hold of the handle and again raised himself onto the small ledge. This time the axe held and he was only four feet below the top of the rock if he stretched his arms out. But what could he do next? He couldn't remove the pickaxe to make another handhold because the axe itself was the only thing to hold onto. He couldn't scale the rope because he only had one arm that worked. He was six feet off the ground, four feet from freedom, but it might as well have been a mile. Once again he was stymied.

He looked at the rocky outcropping where he was perched, his good left hand holding the axe handle and his right lightly gripping the rope. Not far above the handle a rock protruded three inches from the wall, enough for Brian to grab hold of. If he held that rock he could use his other hand to remove the pickaxe and make another step higher than the one he stood on now. He could stair-step his way to the top. There was another outcropping above the first

ANCIENT

one - another place to create another step. This might work.

That was the good news. The bad news was that Brian would have to use his good left arm to hold on to the rock while he fully extended his damaged right arm and shoulder, removed the axe and then hammered it higher into the wall.

He had to try. He extended his left arm and took hold of the rock face next to the sheer cliff. It was firm and gave him a good handhold. This next move was the hardest. He had to steady himself by holding onto a rock, and use his other hand to remove the axe. That meant letting go of the rope. If he did, it would swing away from him where he could no longer reach it. So if this plan didn't work Brian would have to somehow get back down eight feet without the aid of the rope and without falling. There was no other way. He let it go.

He slowly raised his right arm and gripped the axe handle. Pain shot through his arm as he jiggled it back and forth, finally releasing it from the hole where it was tightly jammed. Now he extended his right arm fully. Tears streamed down his face from the pain as he concentrated on holding on with his good hand. He was eight feet above the ground, his left hand holding a rock above him, his face against the cave wall and his right hand holding a pick. He began to strike the rock.

Every blow sent excruciating waves of pain through his shoulder. He screamed at the first one but he continued hitting the wall. He began to feel resistance after about five minutes and knew he was making progress.

God, help me do this. I know I have no right to ask you for anything, but please don't leave me this close to the top. Please help me get out.

BILL THOMPSON

He closed his eyes, gritted his teeth, drew back his arm and struck the hardest blow he could muster. This time it stuck. The tool was once again lodged in the wall.

Brian tested his weight on the handle of the small axe. At the moment it held. He pulled hard, knowing he couldn't put his full weight on the handle for fear of breaking it. He had to raise his other foot two feet to the second rock while he held the handle. It was tricky. If he broke the axe handle his plans for rescuing himself were history.

He gingerly moved his right foot above his left, placing it on the next outcropping of rock. This protrusion was a little wider and he got his foot planted solidly. He used the axe handle to raise himself once more. If he fell from this height he would surely break something; in the back of his mind he prepared so he wouldn't land on his back or his head.

The pickaxe held. Brian lifted himself, using his right arm and shoulder. He worked through waves of pain. At the top, he took both hands and placed them on the overhang of the sheer rock. It was chest height, but he didn't think he could lift himself with only one good arm. He shined his headlamp around until he found what he needed – a small boulder about four feet away sitting on the top of the cliff face. Holding on with his left hand he removed the rope from his belt, knotted it four times about a foot apart then made a lasso. He tried a couple of times to rope the rock. *Third time's the charm.* He tossed the rope and it fell behind the rock. He pulled slowly then tugged hard. It held firmly.

Thank you, God.

Brian held the rope tightly with his left hand. It would have been so much easier with his right, he

ANCIENT

thought briefly. He pulled himself up, arm over arm, using the knots he'd made. It seemed like an eternity and it hurt like hell but in a couple of minutes he was over the top, lying on his stomach.

From here it was merely an uphill walk. He moved with renewed vigor. Light from the surface was pouring in overhead. One last time he yelled the names of all three of his companions. Again there was silence.

He rounded the final bend and saw the trees that lined the cave opening. He looked at his watch. It had taken him nearly four hours to climb out but he'd made it!

He scrambled up twenty feet to get out of the hole and yelled, "Nicole! Can you hear me?" He heard a groan on his left. Sam lay on the ground, bound and gagged, bleeding from his nose and a long cut on his forehead. Brian untied him and removed a dirty rag that had been stuffed into his mouth.

"Sam! What happened? Where's Nicole?"

Sam said that two men came to the cave entrance. He had never seen either of them before. One appeared to be in charge. He asked Nicole where Brian was and when Sam told her not to answer he kicked Sam in the face.

"I passed out, I guess. When I woke up the men and Nicole were gone. I don't know where Alfredo is either. He went down to the ATV to get more ropes to rescue you but he never came back. I hope they didn't kill him. The guy in charge was on a mission – he wants you."

"Dammit, Sam! What's going on? We have to find her!" He grabbed his phone but there was no service. "Does your phone work?"

Sam stood unsteadily. He grabbed the trunk of a tree next to him for support, pulled his phone out of his pants pocket and gave it to Brian. "I don't know. But when you're ready I think I'm good enough to start down the hill."

"Oh God. What am I doing? I'm sorry, Sam. You're hurt and I'm thinking only of Nicole. Come on. Let's get you back to town where a doctor can look at you."

"No. I agree we need to find the others. I'll be OK. Just check my phone then let's get moving. Let's see if the ATV's there and if we can find Alfredo."

Sam's phone also had no signal so they started walking. They had to leave Sam's backpack; in his condition he couldn't both carry it and maneuver down the steep hill.

Brian picked up two long sturdy sticks to use for balance. He gave one to Sam and took the other for himself. With his shoulder throbbing he couldn't grip with his right hand so the stick stayed in his left. He walked close to Sam, grabbing him once when Sam stepped on a root and lost his footing. Later they both fell on a patch of slippery moss but kept on going. Even with their injuries the trip down was easier than the ascent.

As they walked Brian asked Sam to tell everything he remembered. "We have to figure out where they could have taken her. I have to find her. This is all my fault!"

Sam struggled to recall details. "There were two guys – the one with a thin mustache was the boss. The mustache guy did all the talking. When he kicked me the party was over. I'm sorry. I'm sorry I don't know any more than that."

"No worries. I just need to get to a phone and call the police. How are you feeling?"

Sam said he was doing better and asked Brian how he escaped from the cavern. An hour later they

ANCIENT

heard rustling in the underbrush next to them. Brian used his stick to move aside the thick growth and they saw a pair of legs bound at the ankles. They pulled Alfredo from the bushes, tied up and gagged as Sam had been. He was stiff and sore and had a lot of insect bites but he wasn't hurt.

"I was heading down the trail when I came upon two guys going up. They asked where you were, Brian. I told them I was alone but they knew exactly what they were doing. I think they followed us out here. I'm so sorry. They pulled a gun and threatened to kill me. Where's Nicole? Is she OK?"

"We don't know. Are you OK to head to the ATV?"

Alfredo was fine. As they walked he described his attackers and Sam confirmed they were the same men who'd taken Nicole. Finally they came to the rough path they'd walked earlier.

"The ATV's a half mile away," Alfredo said. "Let's move it."

They stepped up the pace and covered the remaining distance quickly. They spotted the fallen tree and could see the ATV on the other side.

When they reached it they found all four tires slashed. Brian said, "Shit. What the hell do we do now? We're a million miles from civilization."

Alfredo and Sam looked things over. The only damage was to the four tires. The ATV started fine and the fuel gauge showed half a tank.

Brian tried his phone again but he was still out of range. "Can we take the tires off and drive on the wheels?" he asked. "Would it work?"

Alfredo shook his head. "We wouldn't get far."

"All we have to do is get back to one of the farms we came through after we left San Antonio. Someone has a landline phone. We could even walk it in two or three hours. I have to do something." Brian's voice broke as he struggled to get the words out. "I have no idea what's happened to Nicole but the more time that passes the more danger she could be in. I have to help her."

Night would come quickly; the trees around them cast deep shadows as the sun fell ever lower in the sky. The time of day was the primary danger to Sam's suggestion. An unarmed man walking in the jungle is no match for the creatures that come out after dark. It would be pitch black by the time they got to a farmhouse.

Alfredo said, "I'm willing to try to drive on the ruined tires as long as we are on dirt roads. If we can make it to a farmhouse or close enough to San Antonio that our phones work we can call for help. There's no way I can drive on pavement but this might work. At least it will get us closer to a house. We can't walk in the jungle at night. There are dangers out here you can't imagine. Brian, you don't know what we might find but Sam certainly does."

They piled into the ATV and Alfredo started it. He backed up and turned around as the tires slapped the dirt path noisily. The ride was so rough they could go less than ten miles an hour. While he could see, Alfredo frequently checked the wheels but suddenly darkness descended like a curtain. Within seconds, they could see nothing except the rutted path in their headlights and trees brushing both sides of the ATV.

Their trip into the jungle had taken almost two hours on the rough back road. Now they were simply bumping along. They could probably have walked faster, but even though it offered no protection from predators the ATV was safer than going on foot.

ANCIENT

Brian was lost in thought, running every possibility over in his mind. *Where is Nicole now? If they're using her to get to me surely they'll keep her safe. But what if they've already killed her?* He had to find out if Odette had heard from Nicole. His hands shook as he desperately tried to keep calm. *I can't lose her. I just can't.*

Suddenly a large cat darted across the path directly in front of them. His green eyes shone as he looked directly into the headlights for a second before disappearing into the dense jungle. "Tiger cat," Alfredo said quietly. "Hope he's not hungry. Or curious."

Sam added, "That's what we know in the States as an ocelot. They're nocturnal, on the endangered list in Belize and usually they steer away from humans. Out here at night in his territory I wouldn't hazard a guess as to whether he'd be afraid of us. My initial thought, I doubt it."

They drove for half an hour, making slow progress. Finally the right front tire had enough. In one large piece it tore away from the wheel and flew into the bushes. The ATV lurched sideways and Alfredo stopped immediately. The forest was totally black. Only the gleam of the vehicle's headlights provided any light.

Alfredo said, "Unless we took off all four tires I don't think we could continue in the ATV. And I don't think we could get them off. There's not enough room on the sides of the path to get to the tires. I wish I'd brought my rifle, guys. I didn't think it was necessary on a short day trip. I hate to say it but we have to walk. It's not safe but neither is staying here."

Brian asked how long it would take to get to the farmhouses. They figured maybe a half hour if everything went fine. He tried to remain calm. Dread filled his mind as he imagined Nicole out here somewhere, the captive of men who wanted God knew what from her. Would she be the same person after they were through with her? Would he ever even see her again?

ANCIENT

CHAPTER FIVE

In 1953 the Alta Vista Consortium moved men and equipment into the eastern Guatemalan jungle in the area known as Montanas Mayas, the Maya Mountains. The company constructed a very basic camp two thousand feet up a mountain. Local workers built six buildings and dug a mine to extract tungsten. A hundred natives at a time lived in a communal structure, ate in a common dining hall and slept in barracks constructed of lumber and thatched roofs. It was a lonely outpost and they were the only humans for hundreds of miles.

The consortium closed the Montanas facility in 1990, having taken as much tungsten as was commercially feasible to extract from the mine. The site was abandoned and soon was reclaimed by the jungle. After several years only a handful of people remembered that the place had ever existed. The site was so remote that no one ever came to see if anything was left of the old mining camp.

Today the place was being used again. With machetes a clearing had been made and three of the old buildings repaired. Inside the former dining hall, a round hut fifty feet in diameter, a single metal table stood in the middle of the building's only room. They'd welded an iron pipe to each corner of the five-foot square table. It was heavy and the pipes made it easier to move around.

Nicole was tied on the table, face up and totally naked. Her arms were lashed to the iron pipes in the upper corners, her legs to the lower ones. Netting stretched across the room a few feet above her and thirty feet above that was a small hole in the center of the peak of the domed, thatched roof. She could see daylight through it and also through open window holes high in the walls.

Nicole remembered very little of her kidnapping. The three of them had made it out of the cave without incident. They stayed at the cave's entrance while Alfredo went back to the ATV for equipment. He'd retrieve his pack of ropes and come back in half an hour.

She and Sam had yelled down the cavern's entrance every few minutes, hoping Brian could hear them. They knew it was fruitless since he was seven hundred feet below but it made them feel better to try.

After awhile they heard someone coming up the trail. Sam looked at his watch. "Wow, that was fast. Alfredo made better time than he figured. I guess he's in a hurry to get the rescue over with and eat lunch!"

In a few minutes they saw two strangers come around a bend. They were dressed in fatigues and had packs on their backs.

"Hola," a man with a pencil mustache said, raising his hand and smiling at them.

"Hello," Sam responded. "Did you happen to see our guide when you were on your way up?"

ANCIENT

"Of course we did." The man smiled again, and pulled a handgun from his pocket. Sam started to get up and the man said, "Perhaps you had better keep your seat, Mr. Adams. There's no need for you to get hurt and it's not you we're after." He turned to Nicole. "Where is Brian Sadler, Miss Farber?"

"Don't tell him, Nicole," Sam yelled. The second man took a few steps to where Sam was sitting and kicked him hard in the face. Sam fell backward and lay motionless on the ground.

Nicole felt her heart racing. "What . . . what's going on?"

The man with the gun smiled again. "There will be plenty of time for talk, my dear. One last time, where is your boyfriend?"

"Until you tell me what you're doing I'm not saying anything."

The mustached man nodded at his companion, who was standing behind Nicole. Suddenly she felt him reach around her and clamp a dirty cloth over her nose and mouth. She remembered nothing else until she awoke in this room, tied to the table. She had an overpowering thirst and a violent headache.

"H . . . help." Her tongue felt thick and her lips were parched. "Help!" she said loudly. Making the word was difficult. She must have been drugged.

Nothing happened and no one came to see about her. There were no sounds except buzzing insects and the loud cries of birds. She had no idea where she was.

She pushed waves of fear out of her mind. *I have to be calm. I have to think. I can survive and I will.*

BILL THOMPSON

Still in a fog, she attempted to reconstruct what had happened. She had a misty recollection of being carried on a gurney and dumped in the back of some kind of truck but that might have been a dream. She raised her head, looking for her clothes, but the part of the room she could see was empty. She laid back on the table and closed her eyes.

Maybe she'd slept. Maybe not. When she opened her eyes there was a man standing next to the table. The man with the mustache.

Ah, I see you are finally awake," he said in accented English. "I hope you aren't too uncomfortable."

Nicole studied him. He was the man who'd taken her – tall and lanky, dressed in khaki trousers, a jungle shirt and a Panama hat. He didn't look like a kidnapper. He looked like a businessman.

"What do you think you're doing? Why have you brought me here? Brian won't stand for this, you know. He's already getting the authorities and they will find you."

The man laughed. "Enough questions, little lady. You need to lie still and not worry so much about things. You need to know only this. Mr. Sadler is looking for something that my associates want very much. I've been asked to ensure he finds it and gives it to me. Now that you are my guest I believe he will be very willing to cooperate. I expect he will hand over what he finds with no qualms whatsoever. Don't you?"

"I . . . I don't understand. What do you mean, something he's looking for? He's looking for a man, not a 'thing'. And why do you have me spread eagled on this table? Give me my clothes!" Her voice became frantic as she twisted and tugged at her restraints.

ANCIENT

"My dear, don't fight. You'll just use up your energy for no reason. Your boyfriend is actually looking for a 'thing' - something I myself have spent a lifetime seeking. And now another man wants it even more than I. He is very wealthy and is willing to pay a fortune for the chance to own something so dear. He's hired me to get it for him. And I've retained you, so to speak, to help Brian. I will let your boyfriend know that not only am I interested in his finding it but you are as well.

"Now to your second question. Why are you naked? You have me to thank for that, actually. I made that decision myself. There are several reasons. The primary one is so you understand who is in control. It is I, not you, who will determine everything about your life for the next days or weeks. Second, if you should ever try to escape you will not get far, naked in the jungle. Third, it is a special treat for my guards to get to see a perfect American woman in her natural beauty. Just so you know, I have told them they are forbidden to touch you as long as you behave. But they may look all they want. So if you get far more than idle glances you may blame me for that. You are extraordinarily attractive all over your body," he said, looking from head to toe. "But surely you know that already."

He laughed heartily. "Enough for now. Here is what you need to know. Listen to me closely."

The man explained that Nicole would be released from her constraints twice a day to eat and use the bathroom. Her toilet was simply a corner of the room, and the guards would watch her at all times to ensure she didn't escape. When she was not eating or using the toilet she would be tethered to the table's four corners.

BILL THOMPSON

"You are deep in the jungle, Miss Farber. You may scream as much as you wish. It makes me no difference. No one will ever hear you. Two things I must warn you about, however. If you scream and thrash about after dark it is possible a jungle animal such as a jaguar might be curious about you. Besides the open doorway there are high window openings behind you and also there is a hole in the roof. Things might come in. If a jaguar were to enter this room you have no defense whatsoever except to call the guard, who might or might not be able to save you from a jungle cat. So I caution you to remain quiet at night.

"The other danger comes if your table were to fall over somehow. If you make the table move by swaying or rocking, for instance, and it falls sideways to the floor, the ants and scorpions would eat you alive beginning with every orifice they could find. I assure you it would be the most violent and painful death imaginable . . . far worse than anything I might dream up myself." He smiled again. "My men will put oil on the legs of your table every day. That will keep the bad things from climbing up to reach you."

He pointed up. "See the net over the table between you and the ceiling? It is there to keep insects or perhaps a snake from falling onto the table. If something does happen to reach you please call out to the guard. He should always be nearby."

The man turned and started across the room. "Wait," Nicole shouted. "Wait! You can't leave me like this! I'm going to die here!"

"Most likely you won't. It is in our interest to keep you alive. The guards will enjoy having you here as a diversion and although they do not speak English, they will respond to your call. Oh yes, one

ANCIENT

more thing I need to do." He pulled a phone from his pocket, walked closer to her and held it up. "A little insurance to get your boyfriend to cooperate."

He smiled appreciatively at her body and snapped a picture of her, naked and bound to the tabletop.

"You bastard! What's this all about? Why are you doing this? Who the hell are you?" All her fear had gone - she felt nothing but unbridled fury.

"Ah, Miss Farber. Everything in its time. I really don't care one bit about you. You're nothing more than my insurance policy. But Mr. Sadler - he's the important one. I truly *am* interested in him. Now I suggest you lie back and relax. It is . . ." he looked at his watch. " . . . three o'clock in the afternoon. In about two hours you will be released to eat and do your business. Shortly thereafter it will be dark. It is your first night in the jungle. I hope you sleep well. It is better to sleep than to stay awake. Trust me on that one."

He left the room.

Panic rose in her body as Nicole thought of Brian trapped at the bottom of a cave. The man with the mustache had said he was very interested in Brian. If that were true, surely he would rescue him. Did he even know Brian was there? Had Sam told him where Brian was? Would the man ultimately kill Brian once he got whatever he wanted? She had nothing but questions. No answers. Regardless, she felt she must keep Brian's whereabouts a secret.

She drifted in and out of a state of slumber. It was hot and she was sweating, although she could do nothing about it with her arms and legs tied to the table. She did notice that the iron pipe holding her right hand was slightly loose. The entire time she was awake she gripped the pipe with her palm, trying to move it. It had a slight give but was still solidly welded to the metal table.

A different man walked into the hut. He walked to her and smiled, showing gaping spaces where teeth had once been. He leered at her body and put his hands above her breasts. She twisted and he laughed but he didn't touch her. He began removing the ropes around her legs. Once they were free she bent her knees, feeling the blood begin to flow again through her calves and thighs.

The guard untied her arms and motioned to the corner. She sat on the table as he stood a few feet from her, his hand on a pistol in a holster. Sliding her feet to the floor, she stood and walked where he had pointed. There was nothing – not even a pot. She turned her back to him and urinated on the dirt floor. He applauded and she turned around and raised her middle finger to him defiantly. He laughed and motioned her back to the table. She sat, crossing her legs in a fruitless attempt to cover herself.

He handed her a dirty pan with bread slices and a sloppy lukewarm concoction that looked like thick soup. He gave her a plastic bottle with no lid.

"Agua fria." Cold water.

The sight of food made her stomach growl. She was starving. She sat naked in front of the guard and used her fingers to devour the meager meal. She took a drink of water and nearly gagged; it tasted awful and she thought she'd die from a dread disease if she weren't killed first. But she had to have it.

One thing had to happen, she thought to herself. *I have to get out of here while I still have my strength.*

"What are you looking at, you jerk?" she snapped at the guard.

ANCIENT

He merely smiled and watched her small, pert breasts move up and down as she drank the disgusting water. When she was finished he motioned her to lie down and he retied her restraints. He took his time with her legs, using the time to gaze at her body. He smiled broadly as he checked her thoroughly. She decided not to waste effort on this so she merely closed her eyes and let him finish his work. He took the pan and bottle and left.

It was almost dark and Nicole felt totally alone. She shivered from fear as she thought about the animals that could be lurking everywhere. If the man with the mustache was telling the truth - if she really was in the middle of a jungle - she could be in serious danger whether she cried out or not.

Sometime during the night she awoke. Disoriented, she remembered a dream that jolted her senses. Suddenly she remembered she'd been scared – she'd heard a terrifying scream. Now she heard it again. It wasn't a dream! It was real! There was an animal out there somewhere close by, probably a large cat. The dim glow of moonlight filtered through the openings and she looked around. There was a flicker from the doorway – the glow of a fire.

Once again she worked her right hand around the metal post to which it was tied. She spent what felt like hours moving the pole back and forth ever so slightly, hoping to loosen it. She yearned to move her arms and legs more to get the circulation going and she debated calling the guard to see if he'd let her loose for a few minutes. But she remembered her captor's warning about crying out during the night. So she remained silent and eventually dozed off.

When she awoke it was morning. A new guard was standing next to the table. Once he saw her eyelids flutter he set to work removing the ropes from her feet, then her hands. He offered her his hand to sit up and she accepted, since her limbs were stiff and sore. She sat on the table for a moment then walked unsteadily to the corner and turned to the wall. When she was finished she looked around. Instead of ogling her as the other guard had done, her captor was applying a greasy substance to the legs of the table. Nicole found herself surprised at the gratitude she felt that insects or small animals would not be able to make their ways up to where she was tethered.

She raised her arms above her head to stretch her muscles then quickly dropped them again when the guard began staring at her. She saw the plate and water bottle sitting on the table and she ate standing up this time with her back to the man.

She ate at the end of the table and ran her hand lightly along the metal post she'd worked on earlier. The guard didn't notice - he was checking the netting above the table. She saw that one of the weld spots had begun to pull apart. If she could break the weld, the pipe would break away from the table and one arm would be free.

Finally her guard said, "Senorita, sientate!" and slapped the tabletop. She sat, and then lay down with her arms raised. As he began to tie her wrists, she moaned.

"Too tight!" she said, wincing. He responded by loosening the ropes significantly.

"Muy bien," she smiled at him, using some of the few words of Spanish she knew. "Gracias, senor."

He loosely tied her ankles then he ran his rough hand up her left leg far above the knee, letting it rest there for a moment. This was the first time any of the men had touched her and she shivered

ANCIENT

involuntarily. He smiled at her and she managed a feeble smile in response. She knew the price for getting her ropes loosened might be more than she wanted to pay, but she had to keep her limbs working if she was going to make it out alive. There might be worse things than death but she was determined to maintain her inner strength – to do anything she had to do to free herself and escape.

Alone again, Nicole began working at the metal post by her right hand. Now that she knew where the weld was failing she concentrated on that area. It was a slow process and she eventually drifted into a restless slumber.

BILL THOMPSON

ANCIENT

CHAPTER SIX

Throughout the day Nicole catnapped. When she was awake she was working on the pipe, and by late afternoon she had made some progress. She worried that when the guard came to untie her he would notice the loose pipe so she decided to stop working on it until after she was fed. Once she was tied again she would give it her hardest effort and see if she could achieve success.

As she lay on the table she again thought about Brian. Was he still lost at the bottom of the cave or did Alfredo return to rescue him? She hoped he had but worried that he had run into the kidnappers as they came up the same trail to the cave while Alfredo was coming down. Tears ran down her cheeks as her thoughts turned to what-ifs. *What if Brian were dead? What if this was the end of the wonderful relationship they had experienced so far? What if the man who kidnapped her now had Brian also? Please God, save him. Please.*

Time passed slowly and Nicole's arms and legs throbbed painfully. The slightly loosened ropes allowed her to move her limbs a little. That helped but the only relief came when she concentrated on something else and tried to forget her sore body. The insect noises were constant; she undoubtedly really was deep in the jungle. She set her mind to thoughts of escape. How would she free herself from her guard? If she were loose would she find others outside? She doubted it, because she never heard conversation. She sometimes heard noise that sounded like music on a Spanish radio station. She figured they posted only one guard who listened to the radio while he killed time.

How would she get clothes - especially shoes? Were hers still here somewhere? And how would she get out of this place? Was her only route of escape to flee through the jungle? There had to be a road. She hadn't heard the sounds of a vehicle but also she didn't know how big this place was. If there were a road, maybe she could flag down a passing vehicle.

She was awake when the guard entered. He was the same man from this morning – the guard who had left her ropes looser.

"Hola, senorita." His eyes spent plenty of time on the merchandise as he untied her tethers. He released her legs first then her left hand, and was getting ready to untie the rope from the loose pipe. She had to be sure he didn't discover it so she moved her free hand to her breast, feeling it and pinching her nipple slightly as she smiled up at him. He watched her, transfixed. His mind was a million miles away from a loose pipe with a rope tied to it. *That was easy,* Nicole said to herself, thinking this might be a means to overpower him when the time came.

She paid a price for enticing him. After he fed her and she had gone to the bathroom he motioned for her to sit on the table and put his nasty hands on her breasts. He felt them roughly, squeezing and

ANCIENT

pinching her nipples in his fingers. She sat and took it, smiling, putting the scene out of her mind and thinking instead of freedom. *I can endure anything. I can endure anything to get away.*

After what seemed like forever he motioned her to lie down and he retied the ropes. Once again he watched her naked body instead of noticing that she was holding on to the pipe to keep it from moving. He tied the tethers even looser than before - she was grateful that she could move her arms and legs around somewhat and that her effort to break the pipe would be easier with the rope loose. The guard stood over her, moved his eyes down her body approvingly from head to toe.

"Buenas noches, senorita."

Now we're telling each other good night. If I'm lucky, maybe this is the last time we do that.

At some point during the night the shift changed. It was dark when she heard the sound of voices. Two men were talking softly in Spanish some distance away. Soon the conversation stopped; one of the two men had ended his shift and gone home.

For a couple of hours she worked hard to loosen the welded pipe holding her right hand. Finally she gave it a valiant effort and heard a loud snap as it came free. *Oh God, please don't let the guard have heard that.* She lay still and quiet for a long time but nothing happened. She figured either he was asleep or too far away from her door to have heard. That was lucky.

She was careful not to bang the metal table with the pipe when she moved her right hand. It was still roped to the pipe as she swung it over her body to her left side. She used her left hand to separate the pipe from the rope, which fell silently to the ground. Holding the pipe with her left hand, she used her right to loosen the other tether. Both hands now undone, she carefully set the pipe on the table next to her. It was about two feet long and over an inch in diameter. It would be a decent weapon for someone who had nothing else.

Nicole untied her feet and she was free. She stood and flexed her arms and legs until they were in perfect working order. It was very dark both inside the building and out. She cautiously looked through the open doorway – there were two other buildings in the moonlight, each of them thirty or forty feet from her. Outside one of the buildings there was a small campfire that had dwindled to dying embers. The guard was probably asleep in that building since she could hear nothing except the jungle sounds to which she was becoming accustomed. It was time to put her plan into action and she prayed that she was right about there only being one man here during the night.

The guard with almost no teeth who had leered at her the first night was asleep in the building nearest the campfire. He lay on a small cot and there was a powerful rifle sitting by the door in case a predator came into the camp. He was supposed to check on Nicole every couple of hours but she was quiet and other than looking at her naked body, there wasn't much to check on. It was hot so he took off his shirt and trousers and slept on the cot in a dirty undershirt and shorts.

He woke suddenly to sounds of shouting. "Help me! Help me!" Although he spoke no English, he sensed the panic in the words the woman was yelling. He grabbed the rifle and ran the short distance from his building to her makeshift prison.

He stopped short of the doorless frame to her building and yelled, "Senorita! Esta el gato?" *Is it a*

ANCIENT

cat? Although he feared retribution if Nicole died on his watch the man standing in his underwear in the middle of the jungle was far more afraid that a jaguar might pounce from the doorway and eat him alive before he had a chance to shoot it.

The woman didn't answer. He listened closely. He didn't hear any sounds from her nor did he hear any rustling or movement from an animal. He carefully entered the building, the rifle ready to fire if necessary.

He literally never knew what hit him. Nicole was standing just to the left side of the entrance in the darkest part of the building. She held the iron pipe with both hands above her head - as soon as the guard was inside she brought it down with all her might. There was a pulpy, sickening sound as his skull fractured and he fell to the ground without a sound. She knew he was dead and was surprised that she felt nothing but relief.

Nicole grabbed his rifle and ran outside. Naked, she walked to the building she had watched him leave and carefully looked in. There was a cot near the door and the man's clothes and shoes were sitting on the floor in a heap beside it. There were other cots, some lockers and furniture but there were no other people. She ran to the third building. It contained a stove and an old-fashioned icebox and a rickety table with some chairs around it

She was alone. Thank God for that. She went back to the building with the cot and rummaged through the lockers. She found her clothes and her totally dead iPhone. Nicole put on her clothes and the guard's combat boots, thinking they might be more functional than her own shoes if she had to run through the jungle. She glanced again at her phone, bitterly disappointed, but she doubted she would have had a signal anyway. She stuck it in her pocket. Once she got away she could work on finding Brian. She hoped that he wasn't still lost in the cave after all this time. If he was it could be too late.

Nicole went back to the dead guard's body and gingerly removed his wristwatch, averting her eyes from his ruined head. It was almost midnight. If the shift change had happened after dark it was possible no one would come back for twelve hours. On the other hand, after daylight all bets were off. Anyone could show up and anything could happen. She only had a few hours to decide what to do next.

She rummaged through the guard's pockets and found a little money. It was Guatemalan, a good indicator that she was no longer in the country where she had started out. She stuck the money in her pocket along with the watch.

Keeping the rifle ready, Nicole walked the perimeter of the camp. Since the moon was almost full she could see clearly. The place was very high – on top of a hill or a mountain. There were no lights in the distance so she figured it was really remote. On the first day her captor had told her she could yell all she wanted – that alone was a sign there was no one around.

A road led away from the site down a steep hill. She followed it for a hundred feet and saw a clearing. There was a tired old Toyota 4Runner parked there! The car was parked so far from the camp that she knew why she had never heard an engine.

She looked inside. The key was in the ignition. Nicole jumped in and turned the key. The vehicle started immediately and she saw that the gas tank was over half full.

ANCIENT

She turned the car off, hopped out, ran back up the hill and looked in the icebox. There were sandwiches that looked old and stale and bags of chips lying on the table. She guessed those were the guards' food. She left that stuff but took three large bottles of water and a backpack that had a few basic tools in it. *You never know what you'll need.* She tossed everything plus the rifle and her shoes in the back seat and turned the Toyota around and drove away, hoping she wouldn't run into one of the bad guys coming up.

The rough road had only recently been dozed out of the jungle. The SUV brushed branches on either side as she bounced down the hill. After what must have been two or three miles she came to an intersection with a two-lane asphalt road. She looked at the moon; morning was only a few hours away so it had to be in the west. She turned left on the road going what she figured was east. In a few miles she saw a sign that indicated Tikal was one direction, Melchor de Mencos the other. She now knew she was in Guatemala. She also knew how to head back toward Belize; Sam had said that Melchor was the first Guatemalan town just beyond Belize's western border, and San Ignacio was only a few miles from it. All that was great except that Nicole was on the wrong side of the border. She turned east on the road and headed for the little town of Melchor de Mencos, the town on the Guatemala side of the western border station into Belize.

She had no passport, no money except for what she had taken from the guard and no entry documents for Guatemala. There was no way they would let her cross into Belize without papers so she needed help. She had no idea where Brian, Sam and Alfredo were. She would have called the San Ignacio

Inn to talk to Odette but she didn't know the number. Escape was her primary goal – she couldn't help the others unless she got away from her kidnappers and back to Belize. She decided to call her office.

Worried that someone might recognize the old Toyota she had appropriated, she parked it in an alley off the main street in Melchor, noted its tag number and locked it up. The sun was rising; nearby she heard roosters crowing as she walked a block to the main road. She went from shop to shop until she found what she needed – an Internet café. The sign said the shop opened at 7 am. She had an hour to kill.

She needed coffee but had no idea what the bills she'd taken would buy. Her craving for caffeine finally overcame her concern. A teenage girl had just unlocked the front door. She spoke to Nicole in Spanish.

Nicole replied, "Do you have coffee?"

The girl looked at her blankly for a moment, not understanding a word she said, but finally it clicked.

"Un café?" she said, smiling.

Nicole nodded and watched the girl take boiling water off a stove, use an old one-cup coffee press and brew her drink. It smelled wonderful and she held out a bill.

"No es suficiente," the girl said.

Nicole shook her head, not following the Spanish, and the girl said in broken English, "One more, senorita. Por favor."

"Oh, OK," Nicole smiled weakly and pulled another bill out. The girl took the money and handed her change.

ANCIENT

She took her coffee and sat down on a curb half a block from the alley where the SUV was parked. Now that she knew two of the brown bills were about enough for a cup of coffee she could determine the value of the other bills she had. She had plenty of money for an hour on a computer and a recharge for her iPhone.

She watched as a couple of people walked past the alley, looked down and gave the Toyota a stare. One even walked up to it and glanced inside. She was glad she had left the rifle covered with a tattered blanket - she figured the man was casing the vehicle to see if he could steal something. She couldn't afford to stop him and make a scene but when she stood up he saw her, turned and walked away down the quiet street.

At seven Nicole walked to the Internet café, entered and said, "Do you speak English?"

"Yes, a little," a kid behind the counter replied.

"I need to charge my phone." She held it up and pointed to the place where the charger plugged in. "And I want an hour on the computer. How much?"

He replied in Spanish – she didn't understand so she handed him the largest bill she had. It was enough - he made change, pulled a phone charger from under the counter and handed it to her. He took her to a computer and pointed to the power strip behind the monitor and at the phone. She nodded, sat down and plugged it in. Nothing happened for a moment but then the phone began charging.

Nicole opened her mail account on the computer and used Skype to call Ryan Coleman, her assistant at Carter and Wells. It was a little early for him but she hoped he was there. She left a voicemail saying she'd call back every fifteen minutes until she reached him.

Finally Ryan answered. "Good morning, Miss Farber. I think I just missed your last call so I waited by the phone for this one. What's up?"

"Ryan, what day is it?"

He laughed. "I beg your pardon? Have you had too many margaritas?"

"Dammit, this is no joke, Ryan. What day is it?"

He got serious quickly. "Uh, it's Wednesday."

She had been kidnapped on Sunday. Three days ago.

She briefly said what had happened. She said she was in Melchor de Mencos on the eastern border of Guatemala and needed to get back into Belize fast despite having no passport, no exit papers showing she had ever left and almost no money.

He was astonished. "Are you OK?"

"I'm good but have to go. Talk to Mr. Carter as soon as you can. He'll think of something. And try Brian's cell phone. If you can't reach him call Bijan in New York as soon it opens. Ask Collette if she's heard anything from him."

Randall Carter was the founder and name partner of the law firm where she worked. He was also one of the most politically well-connected people in Dallas. He had forsaken the family oil business for a law degree. Thanks to generations of family connections the firm he started had prospered from its first day. The Carter name was everywhere in Dallas, the latest being the city's new symphony hall and a wing in the Science and Nature Museum, just two in a long line of places bearing witness to millions of dollars the family spent on charitable causes in the Metroplex every year.

ANCIENT

"I rode up the elevator with Mr. Carter when I came in this morning. I'll go see him right now. What else should I do? Should I ask him to try to find out who captured you and where you were being held?"

"First get me out of here. I'll give you as much as I can about where I've been." She told him as much as she could remember about the camp where she'd been held captive. She didn't mention the dead guard.

"Brian, you have to hurry. I need to get away before they find me. Just concentrate on getting me out of Guatemala. Call my phone in exactly one hour. If for any reason I don't answer, presume something's gone wrong."

She told him she was at an Internet cafe, gave him the location and tag number of the Toyota SUV she'd stolen and said she would be laying low in town until his call.

She leaned back in the chair. Three days. She'd been in the jungle for three days. Again she wondered where Brian could be. The last thing she knew was that he was waiting for rescue at the bottom of a cave. What if her kidnapper had killed all of them? Since he was stranded deep in the cavern, what if Brian died of starvation? She began to feel a rise of panic and forced herself to calm down.

Nicole. Get a grip. You can't help Brian unless you think clearly and you get yourself out of this jam. So keep your head on straight.

She looked at her phone – it was charging fast. She called Brian's phone but again got nothing – it went straight to voicemail. She left a message telling him she was all right and asking him to call her. She ended by saying, "I love you. Don't leave me, baby."

She checked mail – maybe Brian had emailed her somehow. If he were alive and had been rescued, then he also had no idea where she was.

There was no mail. She sent one to him explaining what had happened and where she was. She said she hoped to be back in Belize shortly.

Nicole prayed she would see him soon. She couldn't consider any alternative. She wouldn't let herself think he might be gone forever.

She accessed the website of Sam's hotel and got Odette's email address. She sent Odette a copy of the mail she'd sent Brian, so she'd know where Nicole was.

Once her phone was fully charged and her hour on the computer was up she logged out, dropped the phone charger off at the desk and left.

It was hot in this dusty border town. Now that it was mid-morning there was activity everywhere. People walked down the dirt streets leading donkeys and carts loaded with straw, fruits and vegetables. She looked in both directions, keeping her eyes peeled for anyone who might appear interested in her. She didn't see a man with a pencil mustache standing inside a store across the street watching her intently through a store window.

Nicole strolled nonchalantly down the opposite sidewalk toward the alley where the Toyota was parked. She glanced at it and saw everything looked just as it had when she left it. Then she turned right at the next corner, aimlessly killing time until Ryan's call.

ANCIENT

CHAPTER SEVEN

Ryan Coleman was a highly intelligent paralegal with a master's degree from SMU. He knew how dangerous Nicole's situation was and he rushed to Randall Carter's office three floors up. He told Carter's assistant there was an emergency involving Nicole Farber and he must speak with him immediately.

The assistant sent a message, stood and ushered Ryan through massive double doors into her boss's office. Ryan was surprised at its opulence. The office was easily fifteen hundred square feet and wrapped around two sides of the building, its floor to ceiling windows giving incredible views of downtown Dallas.

Carter was on the phone. His assistant motioned for Ryan to sit.

"Governor, I'm sorry to interrupt but it seems we have some sort of crisis here. May I call you back shortly?"

He turned to Ryan. "What's going on with Nicole? Isn't she on vacation in Belize?"

BILL THOMPSON

Ryan told him everything he knew. Carter was concerned.

"This is serious news and I'm afraid we don't have much time. I'm worried about the men who are after her. Stay outside in the waiting area while I make a couple of calls. If I haven't gotten back to you by the time you're supposed to call Nicole, come back in here and we'll get her on the line."

Once Ryan stepped out, Randall Carter hit a speed dial number on his phone and spoke to a United States Senator on his private office line. He made it brief – he needed help getting one of his partners rescued from an emergency situation at the Guatemala border with Belize. He told the Senator she had escaped from a kidnapper and her papers and passport were stolen. She needed safe passage back into Belize. He emphasized that time was critical and his partner believed herself to be in grave danger.

Less than ten minutes later Carter's assistant forwarded a call from the United States Ambassador in Belmopan, the capital of Belize. The Ambassador advised that he would contact his counterpart in Guatemala City and that he would send his first deputy to Melchor de Mencos to personally escort Ms. Farber back into Belize under diplomatic immunity. Once back, he would arrange a new passport for her within 24 hours. His deputy would leave now and he would likely be in Melchor on the Guatemala side in less than an hour, barring traffic problems on the Western Highway, the only road leading from the capital to the border forty-five miles away.

Randall Carter brought Ryan back into his office. He tasked the assistant with gathering things the Ambassador needed – Nicole's passport number,

ANCIENT

her flight information for her trip to Belize and where she was staying in San Ignacio.

"How much time until we call Nicole back?" Carter said.

"About ten minutes, sir."

"Stay here so we can make the call on time. Then get the information I need for the Ambassador and email it to me immediately. I'll call him back and he can advise his deputy who's going to find Nicole."

Randall Carter dialed Nicole's phone exactly when she had instructed. It rang six times and went to voicemail. He tried again, then a third time. Nicole didn't answer.

BILL THOMPSON

ANCIENT

CHAPTER EIGHT

Five minutes before Ryan was supposed to call, Nicole again walked to the alley where the SUV was parked. As she peeked into the alleyway she saw an obese policeman in a dirty uniform, shirttail hanging out over his belt. He stood on the driver's side of the Toyota and peered inside. Nicole stopped but not before he noticed her.

"Senorita," he called, motioning to her to come to the car. "Senorita, necesito hablar con usted." *I need to speak with you.*

Summoning almost all the Spanish she knew she replied, "No hablo espanol."

"No hay problema." She approached and in heavily accented English he said, "This is your car, yes?"

"Uh, yes. It's actually a friend's car. I borrowed it."

"Your passport, please."

"I . . . uh, actually I left my passport in the hotel," Nicole stammered. "Everything is bueno. No problema."

BILL THOMPSON

She managed a feeble smile as her phone began to ring. Turning away from the man she said, "I need to take this."

Before she could answer he grabbed her wrist and said, "No es bueno, senorita. It is not good for you. You will come with me."

Running was smarter than being detained, she quickly decided. She turned and ran directly into a man standing behind her whom she hadn't realized was there. She was startled to see the man who had originally kidnapped her, dressed in a linen suit and wearing the same straw hat.

"Muchas gracias, Senor," the man with the mustache said to the slovenly officer. He smiled as he gave the policeman a wad of bills. "Muchas gracias."

"Help! Help! I'm an American! Help me!" Terrified, Nicole yelled as loudly as she could. People walking in the street turned and looked her way but with the policeman standing right there no one chose to become involved.

The man in the suit gripped Nicole's upper arm tightly. As he pulled her toward the Toyota she heard a loud voice say in Spanish and English, "La policia Federal! Federal Police! Release that woman!"

Three men ran down the narrow alleyway. Two of them were dressed in crisp brown uniforms and had rifles slung over their backs. The third, the one who had yelled, wore a coat and tie and had a badge on a lanyard around his neck. They ran to Nicole.

"Stop those people!" she shouted as her kidnapper and the policeman disappeared around a corner a half block away. But the three men ran to her.

Displaying an identification card, the man wearing the suit said, "Ms. Farber, I'm Ronald

ANCIENT

Singleton, Deputy Ambassador for Foreign Affairs at the US Embassy in Belize. You have some very important friends in the States who are interested in only one thing – your safety. We're in a strange situation here. I have authority only inside Belize - I have no jurisdiction to order these Guatemalan Federales to do anything so let's just get you out of here and back to San Ignacio. We'll let the local officers here in Melchor worry about finding your abductors."

She relaxed once she was safely inside the embassy's black Nissan sedan. She asked if the deputy could get her back without a passport.

"Absolutely. Fortunately there's no need for documents when you're in the hands of the American government. We're traveling under diplomatic immunity. May I ask you about the others? Once you were reported missing . . ."

"I was reported missing? When?"

"Two days ago, by Odette Adams, the owner of the San Ignacio Inn. She named four missing persons - two Belizean nationals, one of whom is her husband Sam, and two Americans - you and a man named Brian Sadler."

Nicole figured the other Belizean national would be the guide.

"Have they found the others?" she asked hopefully.

"I don't know. Missing Americans aren't in my direct area of responsibility, so I wouldn't have heard. Surprisingly, people disappear more often than you'd think, and it usually involves getting lost in the jungle or staying out overnight at some local person's house after getting drunk in a bar. Violent crime in Belize is extremely rare and usually drug related. I wouldn't worry too much. Your friends may be back at the hotel when you get there. We should arrive in less than a half hour. There'll be some paperwork to deal with but we can save that for later. I'll leave you to unwind and get back with you in a day or so."

Nicole thanked him then picked up her phone. First she called the Dallas number that she had missed several times earlier. It was Randall Carter's private line and he picked it up on the first ring.

"My God, Nicole. Are you all right?" he said loudly.

"I'm OK, I'm OK, Mr. Carter. I'm safely in the hands of the American Embassy. I can't tell you how much I appreciate your facilitating my rescue." Nicole explained to him what had happened, and said she didn't know where Brian was.

The deputy motioned to her as they approached the border. "You'll need to hang up for a moment," he whispered.

She told Randall Carter she'd keep in touch and disconnected as their car stopped at the Guatemalan border station. The driver lowered his window and presented diplomatic papers to a guard with a semi-automatic rifle slung on his back. A few words were exchanged and without a single glance into the back seat where Nicole and the Deputy Ambassador sat, the car was waved through. Three minutes later a similar scenario played out on the Belize side and the car sped down the Western Highway in Belize heading toward San Ignacio.

While they were clearing the border Nicole asked the Deputy Ambassador if he had the phone number for the San Ignacio Inn. He gave it to her.

The desk clerk answered and immediately transferred the call to Odette. Nicole could hear the fear in her anxious voice.

ANCIENT

"I'm so glad to hear from you! I've been worried sick. I got your email. Can I talk to Sam?"

"He's not with me, Odette. I'm back in Belize on the way to the hotel. You're saying Brian and Sam are still missing?"

Her voice became shrill, tense. "You're not with them?"

"I'm not. I'm scared to death Brian is trapped in the cave. And Sam. God, Odette. Where is he?"

"No one has heard from any of you since you left here Sunday to go to that new cave. Searchers are looking everywhere. They found Alfredo's ATV in the jungle but no sign of you. I filed a missing persons report with the Federal Police and the Embassy. I need to go - I have to tell the police I've heard from you. I'll talk to you when you get here." She hung up abruptly.

When they arrived at the San Ignacio Inn, Deputy Ambassador Singleton went inside with her. As Odette rushed up to hug her Nicole glanced at a uniformed police officer sitting in the lobby.

Singleton handed her a business card. "I'll call you tomorrow to finish up the paperwork and deliver your replacement passport. Meanwhile if there's anything further we can do please don't hesitate to contact me."

"Thanks for all you've done. I can't imagine where I'd be right now if it weren't for your showing up at just the right time."

Once he left Odette gestured toward the policeman and said, "Nicole, this officer wants to talk to you about the others."

The officer took notes as Nicole told him about Brian's injury at the bottom of the cave and about her abduction. Once she finished he commented that there was considerable difficulty with this particular case because of where the abduction happened.

"The border is not well defined in the area where the cave is. We are dealing with two different countries, Belize and Guatemala. We know where the cave is, so it is clear you were kidnapped in Guatemala. There is also Alfredo's ATV. It was a couple of miles away from the cave, probably in Belize although that's not certain. As I said, the border is not easy to determine when one is in the jungle.

"We have a major problem, Senorita Farber. Although we are concerned about Mr. Sadler and our two Belizean citizens, we have no legal right to search for them in another country. Until I heard your story today, no one was certain if a crime had occurred at all. The officials in Guatemala have so far chosen to ignore our inquiry. But you were kidnapped at the entrance to a cave that is definitely in Guatemala. Now I can contact the police in Melchor and ask them to start searching for your friends and to look in the cave for Senor Sadler.

"I want to be frank with you, Senorita. We can hope the Guatemalan authorities will be interested in helping us. Sometimes such requests are honored, other times they resent what they see as our intrusion into their business and we are ignored." He looked at Odette. "Senora Adams, I will get to work on this and be back in touch with you if we have anything to report." The policeman turned and walked out.

ANCIENT

CHAPTER NINE

Last Sunday night while Nicole was tied to a metal table in the jungle, the rest of her party had decided to abandon the damaged ATV and walk out of the jungle. Brian, Sam and Alfredo donned headlamps. There were two more in the glove box of the ATV plus a small LED flashlight. They walked down the path. The darkness was intense – tall trees reached toward the sky on both sides of the road and the only light was the dim glow from three headlamps as they walked.

"Remember when we came in?" Sam asked. "There was an open field before we came to the jungle. It probably won't be too long until we get back to it and things should be easier. At least we'll have moonlight once we get there."

"It is easier to see once we get out of the forest, that's true," Alfredo replied quietly. "Easier both for us and for anything that wants to find us. How do you say it in English? A sword with two edges?"

Noise was everywhere – Brian was surprised how loud it was after dark. Insects buzzed mightily and the men frequently heard the rustle of things moving about in the thick growth of trees and bushes only a few feet from them. As he walked Brian kept thinking about Nicole. *I have to be strong so I can get out of here and find her.*

His mind was turning over possibilities, ways he might locate Nicole, how to learn what might have happened, when he suddenly snapped back into reality. Alfredo was walking in front. He stopped in his tracks and whispered, "Shit. Baalum."

Sam put his arm out in front of Brian. "Stop now," he hissed. "Don't move."

Brian was in the back. It was so dark he couldn't tell what Alfredo had seen. He whispered, "What is it? What's Baalum?"

Sam shook his head and whispered, "Shh. It means "king" in Mayan. It's what the locals call a jaguar."

Brian peered ahead and saw two gleaming eyes. He could barely make out the sleek form of the cat standing fifty feet ahead of them in the road.

Alfredo took a few steps backwards until he was with the others. "Stay together," he said. "It's very rare to see a jaguar and he's probably curious. Aim your headlamps into his eyes. If he were interested in killing us we wouldn't have seen him until it was too late. He was probably crossing the path and we're simply an inconvenient distraction."

They stood in a line elbow to elbow across the path and watched as the beautiful animal slowly turned his head away from them. Suddenly he uttered a terrifying, ferocious roar and walked slowly into the forest.

"Holy crap," Brian said. "What the hell was that roar about?"

ANCIENT

"Just establishing that he's the king. This is his jungle, not ours. He didn't know for sure about us but decided to let us know who was boss."

"Is it safe to keep walking?"

Sam and Alfredo talked for a minute, deciding that there was nothing to lose by moving on down the road. Since they had no weapons, if the cat wanted them they were as good as dead no matter what.

Soon they reached the open field. They could see lights from a house across the expanse.

"Let's pick up the pace," Alfredo said, "but still walk, don't run. We don't want to attract a predator."

Staying close together, they walked through waist-high grass. On the other side was a crude farmhouse with an old Land Rover sitting in the yard. They knocked on the door and heard someone turn a lock. A local woman stood in the open doorway, a frantic look on her face.

Alfredo conversed quietly with her in a mixture of Spanish and Mopan, the local dialect that many people in the area spoke. She said something then closed and locked the door, leaving them standing outside.

Alfredo said, "She will let us use the telephone but she is very afraid of something, I think. Maybe us. She says to wait here."

Suddenly the door opened. A man holding a pistol said, "Come in, gentlemen."

Sam yelled, "You! Brian, this is the guy who assaulted us!"

"Calm down, amigo. My issue is not with you. It's Mr. Sadler here that I want."

"What do you want with me?"

"I've been looking everywhere for you." He gave a low whistle and a second man with a pistol thrust the old woman into the living room.

"Why hurt this woman? What's going on?"

"The woman has no part in this," the man with the mustache replied. "This is the first house you three would come to if you were walking from the cave. I knew you would come here to call for help. And here you are!"

To demonstrate my good intentions, my friend here and I will put away our weapons. He spoke a few rapid words in Spanish and they holstered the guns. "Now I will explain myself."

Suddenly Alfredo rushed to the man with the mustache, grabbed his pistol and held it on him. Brian was surprised the man didn't appear to be concerned in the least. In fact he said something that astonished all of them.

"Ruiz, hand over your weapon," he told his man. He looked at the boss quizzically but did as he was told.

Brian took the gun and said, "OK, what the hell's going on? Alfredo, tell the woman to call the police!"

"The one thing I know you will not be doing is calling the authorities. In fact it's time to put down the guns."

"Fat chance," Sam smirked. "I don't know why you let us take your pistols but that was a dumb-ass move."

"I no longer need weapons to control you. Why, do you ask? Because, gentlemen, I am holding Nicole Farber as my prisoner."

Brian grabbed the man's shirt and hit him squarely in the jaw. "Where is she? Talk, you bastard, or I'll kill you."

ANCIENT

The man rubbed his jaw. "Back off, Mr. Sadler. I am going to show you something. This is something you may not want your friends to see. It is a very personal picture of your girlfriend."

He reached into his shirt pocket and pulled out a cell phone. He clicked a few times and handed it to Brian. Brian looked at Nicole's picture. She was naked, each of her limbs tied to a corner of a metal table. She didn't look afraid – her face was contorted in anger. Even as he feared for her safety Brian thought about how much fight Nicole had in her, how she would try with every ounce of energy she had to free herself from captivity. If she could. If she were even still alive.

Brian started hyperventilating but took a deep breath. "You'll never escape me if she gets hurt. I will track you down anywhere you go. I will find you and kill you myself." His voice shook with emotion as he passed the phone to Sam, then Alfredo. Naked or not, they had to see what she was facing.

Sam spat, "You bastard. You'll regret this."

The man laughed. "We're taking back the guns now and you're coming with me. If you follow my instructions you will see her again. And this lady . . ." He gestured at the woman, ". . . will live as long as she keeps her mouth shut."

He spoke to her quietly in Spanish. She fell back into a chair. Terrified, she held her hands to her face.

"No Senor. Por favor, no." She was frantic.

Alfredo said, "He promises to return, hunt down her children and kill them all if she ever speaks about tonight." The pathetic woman sobbed as the two captors ushered them out to the vehicle.

By daybreak the five men had been in the car for hours, much of it on back roads but now on a paved two-lane highway. They were in an old Land Rover, its roof piled high with gear. The man with the mustache was in the right front seat as the other man drove. Sam, Alfredo and Brian were in the back. The man had taken their phones and thrown them out the window as they traveled and he had made two very brief phone calls, speaking quietly and rapidly in Spanish.

"He's checking in with someone," Alfredo translated, talking under his breath to Brian and Sam.

Their captor had said almost nothing to them since the trip began. Finally he turned to the back seat. "I will tell you a few things now. You may call me Tomas. Tomas Rodriguez. That name is as good as any, I think. It is my usual nom de plume." He laughed heartily. "Mr. Sadler, I hope you don't mind if I call you Brian now. We are going to be associates, even if we are not friends.

"I am going to help you. And in return you are going to help me. Of course it will be important for you to know that your girlfriend is always safe. To make that happen I will be in contact every few hours with someone who wants to hear from me very much. In fact if I fail to make a call for any reason, Miss Farber will no longer be safe. Quite the contrary, in fact. She is deep in the jungle in a place where there are many predators, including the human ones." He smiled again. "She must be protected. My regular telephone calls are her lifeline. Do you understand?"

"I got it, you son of a bitch. I don't know what you think you're doing but you'll never get away with it. I can get you money if that's what this is about. A lot of money. Is that what you want from us?"

ANCIENT

"Where are we going?" Sam Adams asked. "Don't you know people will be looking for us everywhere?"

"So many questions, my friends. Brian, this is not about money although eventually I believe what my friends and I want from you will bring untold riches. And Mr. Adams, of course people are going to look for you. Each of you has friends and family whom I am sure care about you very much. And the police - they will certainly be looking too although I'm afraid they are not as diligent as your police in America. They may look for a time then maybe they will hear a rumor. Maybe a story about how you three men just wanted to disappear for a while. Maybe a fling on the beach on a remote caye. A macho man thing, you know?" He smiled.

"Where we are going there are no people who will come looking for you. We are going to find something my friends and I want very much. And Brian, if we are very lucky perhaps we will also find something you want very much. Captain Jack Borland."

BILL THOMPSON

ANCIENT

CHAPTER TEN

Tomas would tell them nothing more. After an hour or so Brian saw a sign that read "Tikal" and had an arrow pointing left. Brian knew that Tikal, one of the finest Mayan archaeological sites, was in Guatemala and they were heading west toward the mountains. He now knew almost certainly where they were going and after about an hour Tomas spoke quietly in Spanish to the driver, who soon pulled off the road in front of a small café.

They sat outside on a shady patio and ate. "I'll pay for lunch, men," Tomas said with a smile. "It's the least I can do after inconveniencing you three so much."

Sam spoke up. "I'd like to wipe that shit-eating grin off your face, 'Tomas'. You'd better hope things go the way you think they will. Once Nicole's safe, you're a dead man."

Tomas merely smiled and gestured toward the Land Rover. They continued westward. Brian said, "So all this is about searching for the ancient Mayan library?"

"You are a very intelligent man. Of course it is. In less than a half hour we will be at the spot where the famous Captain Jack Borland started up the mountain. We will follow in his footsteps just as his son Arthur did. But you already know the things Jack and his son did, don't you?"

Brian ignored the question. "We have to climb. We'll need gear to do that. Is that what you have on top of the truck?"

"No worries. We have everything we need for a trip to the top. We're missing just one thing - Jack Borland's map. I presume you don't have it either. At least it wasn't in your hotel room."

"You searched my hotel room? You son of a bitch! What the hell do you think you're doing?"

Sam was dumbfounded. How had this man had gotten into his hotel, past a desk clerk and Odette herself, then upstairs to Brian's room? His mind racing, he listened quietly.

Tomas continued. "Don't get excited, Brian. You will need your stamina and strength to climb this formidable mountain. To briefly answer your question, I was looking for something Jack Borland had. Lucky Buncombe, the proprietor of the Jaguar's Call up the mountainside, told me that Jack had a box that contained a map and perhaps some gold. He gave that box to Jack's son Arthur. You have that box. I doubt you brought it to Belize but I know you have it. But I don't need Jack Borland's box any more. I know what you know."

He tossed a manila envelope into the back seat – the one Brian hid, the one with pictures of the gold sheets and the letter from the Governor of Guatemala to the king of Spain. Brian showed it to Sam, who stared at the sheets in amazement, then handed it back to Brian.

Tomas continued. "I know exactly what you are here for. You're looking for Captain Jack himself

ANCIENT

but you and Jack's son also want the ancient library of the Maya. The man for whom I work will be happy to leave you with that if you also find the gold sheets. My employer and I think they actually are there. After all his fruitless searches, that crazy Jack Borland finally figured out what he was doing."

BILL THOMPSON

ANCIENT

CHAPTER ELEVEN

The Jaguar's Call in the Guatemalan rain forest
Four months ago

Not long after Arthur Borland left, Lucky Buncombe was clearing brush around the perimeter of his rustic retreat when he heard someone approaching. Looking up he was startled to see an attractive female probably in her early forties standing before him. She was dressed in fatigues and combat boots and had a backpack that she threw on the ground.

"Got any water?" she said to Lucky. "And could you try to look a little less astounded?"

Lucky stopped staring, closed his mouth and stammered, "Sure . . . sure I have water. What the hell are you doing here?"

"How about the water first, then we talk," she responded, smiling slightly. "I'm exhausted from the climb and I ran out of water about an hour ago."

Lucky walked to his old refrigerator, opened the door and retrieved a thermos. He unscrewed the top, wiped the bottle with a rag in his belt and handed it to the girl in front of him. She took it and turned it up, swigging the water and letting it run down her neck. Lucky watched as rivulets went into her partially unbuttoned shirt. He hadn't seen a woman since the last time he went to San Ignacio; he made a quick calculation in his head and figured it had been months. And this was no ordinary woman. The more he observed her the better looking he realized she was.

They sat in chairs under a tree, a breeze making things tolerable.

"I'm Lynne Parker. I'm an anthropologist from UCLA. And what am I doing here? I'm hoping all these people who believe the Maya were on this mountain are correct. I'm looking for evidence of their civilization and chasing rumors of an ancient library of Mayan codices. If it exists I want to be its discoverer."

Lucky glanced at her. She had bright eyes that sparkled when she talked about her goals. Even though she was dressed in fatigues he could see she had a great figure. Lucky thought this was one sexy package of woman.

"Are you finished with the once-over?" Lynne said with a smile.

Nice smile, Lucky thought. "Oh, sorry," he said. He found himself stammering again. He usually was in complete control with the ladies but he couldn't figure out what it was about this one. He guessed he was older than she was by fifteen years although he couldn't be sure. And she was really, really cute. Long dark blond hair pulled into a ponytail, olive skin, that cleavage . . .

"Um, I . . . I was just wondering how a girl like you got up here by yourself." Lucky had trouble putting words together. He found his mind wandering like it always did when it had been awhile since he had been to town. "I . . . uh, are you going to be here for a day or two?"

She laughed and it sounded like music to Lucky. "I'd like a bunk for the night, and some provisions to get me on up the mountain. Do you have separate lodging for females?"

Now it was Lucky's turn to laugh. "We haven't had a female at Jaguar's Call in years. But unless someone else shows up today, which isn't likely, you'll be the only person in the bunkhouse tonight."

Lynne spent that one night, began her trek up the mountain the next day and returned a week later, empty-handed. No indigenous population, no evidence of a secret Mayan library, no nothing except an exhausting five thousand foot hike, six nights in a tiny tent and a ravenous appetite for something besides granola bars and water.

She told Lucky she was still convinced that the Maya had once inhabited the mountaintop because of the area's similarity to other sites she had explored. It made sense that the Maya rulers would have picked this place to build a city. It was on a mountaintop that could have been the site for a temple complex even grander than the majestic ruined cities of Tikal or Chichen Itza. And the stories about an ancient library had been around for hundreds of years. This was the right mountain. Everything was right for it to be the one. Lynne was certain of it.

The night she returned from the top she and Lucky had the last of his beans and rice for dinner. He explained to her that he had to go back to town for provisions soon and didn't look forward to the journey. The camp was unattended when he was away and it always bothered him that a jaguar or other creature would vandalize the place looking for food.

They sat by the fire pit, logs blazing before them and a canopy of stars in the dark sky overhead. Insects trilled loudly all around and occasionally a grunt or growl or caw reminded them there were plenty of other things besides bugs in the jungle just outside their field of vision.

"Tell you what, Lucky. I have a proposition for you. A quid pro quo if you will. You go to town – what does it take? A week or so all said and done? I'll stay here and mind the camp. Then when you get back I'll be your bartender and right hand man. I'll do whatever you want me to and every few weeks I'll go up on the mountain and look around. Someday I'm going to find my Mayan library up there. I feel it. So whatta you say, Lucky?"

That was two months ago and since then Lucky felt his life had indeed lived up to his nickname. He brought her back some t-shirts and shorts from Melchor and she appreciated the gesture. They talked every night. He found out she was forty-five years old although she could easily have been ten years younger. She had been married and divorced long ago, had no kids and now considered herself wed to her career. She was an adjunct professor of anthropology at UCLA, on leave for a year and armed with enough grant money to get her to the jungle and home again.

She cooked the meals every day – she could make even the most basic food taste wonderful. When she served the occasional guest Lucky figured the men liked the food mostly because of the scenery. She wore tight-fitting t-shirts that hid none of the curves of her gorgeous body, since a bra was something that wasnt part of Lynne's wardrobe.

ANCIENT

She went up the mountain again a month later and returned empty-handed like before. She said, "I guess at least I'm narrowing down my choices. I've reached two dead ends. Something has to work sometime."

One night she and Lucky were washing dishes from dinner. He had killed a peccary. The meat of the hog-like mammal wasn't unlike ham and they had feasted on it, along with potatoes grown in a garden Lucky had planted. They even had a bottle of wine – Lucky picked up two or three every time he went into town.

Standing next to each other at the washtub, she washing and he drying, he suddenly felt her move closer to him. "So," she said in a sultry voice, "what does Lucky want?"

He turned to her. They had not shared so much as a goodnight kiss up to this point. He was intensely attracted to her but had kept his feelings in check. *She's so much younger that even in the jungle – even with nothing else available – she's not going to be interested in me.*

"What does Lucky want?" he repeated back to her. "We agreed to always be honest with each other. So honestly, what the hell do you mean by that?"

"I want to know what Lucky wants. From me. Right now."

"OK, Lynne. You asked. More than anything else . . . I want to sleep with you."

"Wow," she replied, turning her body into his and lifting her face. Her lips were inches from his. "Wow. That's what I was thinking you were going to say." She stood on tiptoe and kissed him deeply.

For Lucky Buncombe that night was unlike any other. The attraction was both completely mutual and absolutely instant. "First, we shower," Lynne laughed. "We can do it together or separately."

"If you're looking for my vote, I say together."

"Then it's unanimous." They walked outside to the crude shower Lucky had built. Clothes came off quickly. Completely naked, she deftly unzipped his jeans and pulled them off. In one swoop his boxers hit the ground within seconds.

The shower was lukewarm because the blister bag that held the water was warmed by sunlight during the day. She took biodegradable soap and washed herself all over, then him. "Looks like you're ready for some fun," she laughed as she soaped his body.

"Kind of hard not to be, with you right here!"

They dried and walked through the office to Ralph's bedroom. She knelt in front of him as he stood by the bed, pale moonlight filtering through the window. Her body was absolutely incredible, he thought. And on her knees when she moved to take him a shudder of excitement shook his body.

Lynne was an experienced lover. She taught Lucky how correct his nickname was that night and sleep came for them both only as the first rays of sunlight were visible. After a short couple of hours of slumber she rolled over, smiled at him and said, "Hey, Lucky. Did you get what you wanted?"

He smiled and moved his body next to hers. "Oh, wow," she said, grinning. "Feels like you didn't quite finish getting what you wanted, after all!" And it all began again.

Lynne and Lucky had a talk not long after that night. She told him she was a flop with men in general and had had far more success with short stints than long-term relationships. "I realize we're both out here in the jungle, but I want to be honest with you. I'm here to find the Maya civilization that I'm looking for. I want to find that Mayan library, Lucky. If someone shows up at your camp with information that can help me get it I'll do anything, and I mean anything, to find out what he has. Until that man comes along," she said, smiling and rubbing her hand on his thigh, "I'm all yours, baby."

Lucky knew exactly where he stood although he hated to admit it. After only a short time he had found out what amazing things Lynne could offer a man and he knew she would use every trick in the book to get what she wanted.

She was insatiable, Lucky learned, willing to try absolutely anything that sounded interesting. She was loving and intimate beyond imagination. The nights in bed totally surrounded by her were passionate, incredible experiences. Her sexual knowledge and willingness to please him made him feel lucky indeed. Her body was flawless – from her small, perfect breasts to the wonderful rest of her, he had explored it all in every way imaginable and Lucky was totally hooked. She was like a drug – once you tried it, you could only hope for more and more forever. And when she inevitably pulled back someday he knew he would be like an addict without a fix. But he was willing to stay - to have her in the here and now - until some man showed up who could give her the one thing she really desired. A key to the Mayan civilization. A clue to the ancient library. The gold ring she reached for to seal her successful future.

Lucky could only hope it would be a long time before someone like that came along.

BILL THOMPSON

ANCIENT

CHAPTER TWELVE

The terrain became more and more mountainous as the Land Rover continued on the highway. Beyond a narrow shoulder on each side of the road the jungle was dense and dark. Tomas consulted a map then spoke to the driver. Within five minutes they pulled off onto the shoulder and stopped the Land Rover.

"Ready for some exercise?" Tomas said, opening the car door. "All of you, unload the vehicle."

"Where?" Sam asked. "There's hardly room on the side of the road for all that gear."

"Mr. Adams, you have no faith in my mapping skills." He pointed to the tree line. "Take a look - there is the beginning of our adventure. Right there in front of you. We will unload our equipment there."

They walked ten feet to where Tomas had pointed and saw an opening in the trees. The jungle growth let little light filter to the highway below and with reduced visibility none of them had noticed the cut until Tomas showed it to them. A small hand-painted wooden sign was stuck in the ground. It said, *Jaguar's Call. Food and lodging. 1000 meters straight up.* And it had an arrow pointing right into the air. Exactly as Arthur Borland had described it.

The men unloaded equipment and carried it into the jungle a hundred feet to a clearing. Tomas issued instructions. "We will hike along this trail for an hour and then stop for the night. All of us are tired after last night with no sleep. We must be rested in the morning for the ascent." He spoke quickly to the driver of the Land Rover, who soon drove away.

Two hours later they were eating dinner that Alfredo had prepared over a campfire. Using a satellite phone from his pack, Tomas checked in with someone regularly. Brian calculated the calls at approximately every four hours, although the times varied, indicating there was no exact schedule.

Three pup tents were erected. Tomas took one and said, "You can choose among yourselves who gets the other two. It makes me no difference. I want to tell you that I will not be guarding you. Should one or all of you choose to leave our campsite I only have to utter one word to put Nicole Farber into a very big problem. Or fail to make one phone call on time. You must be very careful, gentlemen. You must protect me as closely as you protect yourselves. I am Nicole's lifeline. Her *only* lifeline. And her life is in your hands."

They sat around the fire before turning in. "So who's your employer?" Brian asked Tomas.

"There is no need for you to know that."

"Sounds like he must be someone pretty important. And I guess he has money. Rich drug lord?"

He laughed. "That is of no concern to you. My employer knows your reputation for success in the field of ancient artifacts. He has faith that you can find the treasure that eluded Captain Jack Borland. That's all you need to know."

ANCIENT

Alone in his tent, Brian lay awake for some time. Who *was* Tomas' employer, a man who knew Brian at least by reputation? Why was Brian so critical to all this? Why couldn't Tomas just go himself and look for Jack Borland's treasure? Brian mulled other thoughts in his mind. He had to get a phone. The logical choice was to take Tomas' but if they overpowered their captor, a simple task with three against one, his required calls to protect Nicole would end. If Tomas was telling the truth Nicole's life could end as well. Brian struggled to stay awake and think of a solution but suddenly awoke with a start, rays of sunlight hitting the tent above him. It was morning and he could hear activity outside.

Tomas rummaged through a pack and brought out food, water and coffee. Sam took over the coffee detail while Tomas told Alfredo where plates and cups were. They drank coffee and ate powdered scrambled eggs. Tomas walked away and made a very short call. Brian noted the time on the pad of paper in his shirt pocket.

"Tell me Nicole's all right," Brian angrily said. "Tell me."

"My calls are not progress reports, Brian. My calls are merely to ensure things are well on both her side and mine. If something were wrong I would be told about it. If the calls are short you may rest assured everything is going well. It may not be a five star hotel, but Nicole is relatively safe. If she behaves, that is. And if you behave."

They cleaned their campsite, loaded up and began to walk on a trail that led upward on a slight incline. Brian knew this was only the start of the serious climb that lay ahead. Tomas took a handgun and holster from his pack and hooked it to his belt. In an odd way it comforted Brian. The jungle could be a forbidding place. A gun might be no match for a huge cat but it could help protect them.

They continued to walk as the incline got steeper. The trail was fairly easy to see but still they stopped occasionally to ensure they were heading in the right direction. Insects buzzed everywhere and it seemed to Brian as though the jungle was like a living thing – moving, undulating, swaying in light breezes. They saw hundreds of birds flying about and dozens of howler monkeys in the trees, each screaming in a screeching yell, trying to fend off these intruders who were moving through *their* jungle – a place which belonged to the animals, not the humans. In this forbidding place brains didn't triumph over brawn. Logical thinking took a back seat to stealth, cunning and raw animal ingenuity. Eat or be eaten. Survive or die. The creatures of the forest were in charge, not these puny humans walking along a path.

Brian asked Tomas about the two workers Brian had lined up to help him, the same two who had accompanied Arthur Borland on his trip several months ago. Tomas replied that the two men were in fact still retained and they would be at Jaguar's Call when Brian arrived. "That is one reason why this trail is fairly easy for us to navigate," he explained. "Your guides were on this same pathway only a few days ago. They cleared it for us."

They stopped for a brief lunch. Tomas made another call – Brian wondered if the phone's signal would work all the way to the top of the mountain. If it didn't he wondered if Tomas would have some alternative means of checking in.

The humidity increased dramatically as they began a much steeper climb. They passed another Jaguar's Call sign so they knew they were still on the correct trail. It would have been hard to go anywhere else; the brush was incredibly thick all around them and occasionally Alfredo used a machete that Tomas had provided to clear the pathway ahead of them.

At five pm Tomas said, "We stop here for the night. Tomorrow we will reach the Jaguar's Call by noon if things go well for us."

They set up camp, cooked dinner and Tomas assigned a two-hour watch period for each of them. "We don't want to let our fire die down and be eaten by a hungry jaguar," he said, handing the pistol to Brian, whose watch was first. "If something comes near, what is your saying in America? Shoot first and ask questions later!" He laughed but no one else did.

The night was uneventful. There was considerable activity in the bushes around the campsite but each man in turn tended the roaring fire and nothing came close enough to generate interest.

Wednesday morning was the third day of their captivity. Tomas stepped away and made his call. This one took longer than usual and Alfredo put a finger to his lips as he listened to Tomas' side of the conversation. "Something is wrong," he whispered. "Tomas says his employer will not be happy."

The call took nearly ten minutes. When it ended Tomas returned to the group and began to break down his tent. "What's going on?" Brian said loudly. "What took so long? Is something wrong? Is Nicole OK?"

"Nicole is fine. She is a strong-willed woman, as I am certain you know. Apparently she managed to free herself and she killed one of my guards. However everything is under control now and she will be watched far more closely in the future. I fear she will regret the action she chose but we are many miles away so I have no direct control over her. Her decision was dangerous but I trust my men will not harm her. At least those are their orders!"

Brian noticed a significant change in Tomas' demeanor from then on. No longer did he appear happy, smiling or cocky. His face was grim and he seemed deep in thought.

Something's up, Brian thought. *I guarantee Nicole has done something that really pissed this guy off. Maybe it's because she killed a guard. Whatever's going on, he's definitely not telling me everything.*

By midday they reached their destination. Brian had watched Tomas on the climb – he had been uncharacteristically uncommunicative during the ascent and seemed worried. Brian tried not to think what could happen if as her punishment the men were given free rein to use her as they wished.

They were hot and tired as they walked into a broad shaded area surrounded by the crude buildings that made up Lucky Buncombe's 'resort.' A beautiful woman dressed in a tight t-shirt, shorts and a camouflage jungle hat walked toward them. "Welcome to Jaguar's Call. I'm Lynne Parker."

Tomas stepped in front of the group. "Good afternoon, Ms. Parker. My name is Tomas Rodriguez. Are there two men here awaiting the arrival of Brian Sadler?"

She pointed to a couple of Belizeans sitting in the shade by a building smoking cigarettes. They waved and Tomas walked over to them, speaking rapidly in Spanish.

A man came out of a building and introduced himself as Lucky Buncombe, the proprietor. "Lynne here is my right hand man," he said proudly, putting his arm loosely around her shoulders.

ANCIENT

Making sure we all know who belongs to whom, Brian thought to himself. He also considered how beautiful this young girl was and what a lucky man the proprietor was if she was indeed his girlfriend.

Tomas returned and shook hands with Lucky. "These five men are going up the mountain the day after tomorrow," he said. "We will need accommodations for two nights."

Lynne smiled. "Senor Rodriguez, just let me know what you need from us. Bunkhouse is over there – your two guides have already claimed a couple of beds and you guys are welcome to pick any one you want. In case you're hungry I was just fixing some stew for lunch and there's plenty for you guys too. Dinner's at seven, drinks before, presuming you brought something to drink, that is." She laughed. "We don't have much of a stock of beverages here but we sure would join you in a drink if you happened to have anything with you."

Tomas smiled back. "I do in fact have some rum and you and Mr. Buncombe are welcome to join us. I look forward to getting to know you better, Miss Parker, and to find out what a beautiful woman such as yourself is doing so high up a mountain in the Guatemalan rain forest."

"Likewise, Senor Rodriguez. I can't wait to learn what you fellows are looking for up on the mountain."

"Call me Tomas, I insist."

"You got it, Tomas. And I'm Lynne." She turned to the others and got their names, pausing afterwards to point to each and say "Brian, Sam, Alfredo, Tomas," to ensure she had the right name with the right man. "Wow, we haven't had this many people at one time since I've been here!"

BILL THOMPSON

While Brian, Sam and Alfredo unpacked their packs and chose bunks Tomas stood at the edge of the clearing far away from them, talking on his phone. His worry was evident – his face was serious and his jaw set. He looked angry and spoke at length in a voice too quiet for Alfredo to hear.

"It's obvious something's gone seriously wrong," Sam said. "I just hope that Nicole's . . ." He stopped. "Sorry, Brian. I don't want to put negative thoughts in your space. I know she'll be fine. You've told me what a fighter she is in the courtroom and I bet she can handle herself just fine against a bunch of illiterate thugs."

Brian couldn't reply. He held back tears as he thought of the ordeal Nicole might be going through this very moment. They could be raping her or they could have killed her for what she did to one of their own. He turned away from Sam and put his gear on the bunk.

Sam patted him on the arm. "She'll be OK. Let's be positive about this. It does us no good to think negatively. We have to work on one major thing – we have to get that sat phone away from Tomas long enough to see if we can find out anything about Nicole."

Through the open holes that served as windows they could see that Tomas had finished his call. Brian left the bunkhouse and walked over to where he stood.

"You said the five of us are going up the mountain. What about you?"

"I'm going back. I never intended to make the trip with you. I have Nicole, therefore I have no fear that you will continue the quest for Jack Borland. When you find what you are seeking I will be happy to assist you in claiming it. You and your two friends need to concentrate on getting your goal accomplished as quickly as possible so your pretty little girlfriend won't be simply a plaything for my men."

"Something's gone wrong, Tomas. Want to tell me what it is or should I just guess? Has Nicole escaped? It's obvious you're really worried about something. Has my 'pretty little girlfriend' outsmarted your men? Are you in trouble with your boss?"

Tomas snarled, "Everything is under control, *Mister Sadler*. Don't let your mind fantasize too much about how you would like things to be. Concentrate instead on finding the treasure Jack was seeking. That way everyone will be happy. Including you and Nicole Farber." He strode across the clearing to the office and went inside.

For most of the afternoon the two Belizean guides went through all the gear they had brought up plus what Tomas had provided. They laid everything out to determine how best to carry it. A plastic bladder of rum and a liter of Coke were chilling in Lucky's old icebox in anticipation of happy hour later on. Brian watched Tomas closely – after his long conversation earlier the regular check-ins had stopped. He was no longer calling at periodic intervals. Brian didn't know what to make of that.

Sam sat in a chair outside the bunkhouse, lost in thought. Brian pulled up another chair and sat next to him.

"Lynne Parker has a cell phone," Brian said quietly. "After lunch I asked her and she said she did and why didn't I have one too. I told her we'd lost our phones. It was a pretty lame story, all three of us losing our phones while Tomas still has one, but it was the best I could do on short notice. I don't think she believed me - she said she wanted to know what we were doing at Jaguar's Call before she did us any favors. Point is, we have to get her to let us use that phone."

"You actually think a cell phone will work up here?"

"Lynne says the phone company installed a cell tower twenty miles south of here to boost signals from town to town through the mountains. It's not perfect and it doesn't always work but she says it does the job at least half the time."

"Who're you going to call?"

"I want you to call Odette. If Nicole can communicate at all she'll talk to Odette once she realizes she can't talk to me. I'm going to tell Lynne what's going on so I can persuade her to let me use the phone. But I have to make sure she doesn't tell Tomas what I'm doing."

They discussed how little information they'd have to reveal in order to get her to hand over her phone. The biggest problem would be explaining why they didn't just use Tomas' phone.

Suddenly they heard a familiar sound – the ring of his satellite phone.

Tomas walked out of the office with his phone to his ear. He walked away from them but as he passed they heard him say, "No hay problema, el jefe."

Brian pulled out his pad of paper and wrote something down. "I'm going to ask Alfredo what this means," he said as he jumped up.

"I know a little Spanish," Sam said. "What did you hear him say?"

"He said something like 'No eye problems, el Heffe.' Does that make any sense?"

ANCIENT

"He said, 'No hay problema, el jefe.' Is that what you heard?"

"Yes, that's it. What does that mean?"

Sam looked concerned. "It means, 'there's no problem, boss.' He's not talking to someone named Jeff. He's talking to his employer – his jefe, his boss. And obviously there *is* a problem."

BILL THOMPSON

ANCIENT

CHAPTER THIRTEEN

Brian walked into the office. Lynne and Lucky sat at a table they both used for a desk. "I need to tell you both something," he began quietly. "We're prisoners of that man out there who calls himself Tomas. I know it doesn't look like we're his captives but he's holding my girlfriend hostage until I find a treasure he thinks is on the mountain. You have to help me - I have to use a phone. He took ours . . ."

Suddenly Tomas walked in. The talk abruptly stopped and they all looked up in surprise like burglars caught in the act.

"My, my, what is going on?" Tomas shouted. "It appears I have walked in on a very private conversation. I apologize. Do go on and don't worry about me."

"No problema," Brian said emphatically, using the words he had heard Tomas say on the phone call. "No hay problema, el jefe."

Tomas' face was red as he spat his response. "Mr. Sadler, you know very well it *is* a problem if you and I don't see eye to eye on absolutely everything. There's no need to involve these people in our affairs. Actually it's better for you two," he looked at Lynne and Lucky steadily, "if you don't know much. A little knowledge is a dangerous thing, they say. I will tell you that Mr. Sadler here is in a bit of trouble with the authorities, something about an assault on his girlfriend whom he brought to Belize with him. So although he is on a legitimate quest up this mountain he also is trying to stay out of sight of the local police. I'm sorry to have to tell these nice people your secrets, Brian, but apparently you were saying something to them – undoubtedly not the truth. Our friends must recognize the good people from the bad."

Tomas smiled at Lynne and continued. "Mr. Sadler will not be a danger to either of you. If I had thought he would be I would never have brought him here. He is on a mission for me; I have incentivized him greatly to be both prompt and diligent in his quest. And I am confident that he will."

Lynne glanced at Brian, concerned about the conflicting stories she'd been told. She turned to Lucky.

"I . . . Lucky, are you OK with this crew staying here a couple of nights now that we know all this?"

Lucky leaned back in his chair confidently. "I think we can pretty well take care of ourselves here, Mr. Rodriguez and Mr. Sadler. I get a lot of people here who are searching *for* something, or running *from* something, or both. It's really none of my business so long as nobody gets me involved in his affairs. You boys play nice and keep things between yourselves and I don't give a rat's ass what secrets you have. You mess with me and maybe you'll wish you hadn't. Know what I mean?"

Tomas smiled and said, "Of course, Lucky. We don't intend to get you involved with us, do we

ANCIENT

Brian? Come on, we have work to do." He ushered Brian out of the building before him.

Outside, Tomas grabbed Brian's arm roughly and swung him around. "What the hell do you think you're doing? Do you care so little about Nicole that you will jeopardize her life? You have one mission and one mission only. Find the treasure and I will be out of your life forever. Fail and it will be fatal. For both of you."

He turned and walked away.

Happy hour was anything but happy. Tomas seemed troubled, deep in thought, saying very little. Lucky made small talk with Sam about how things were in San Ignacio. Lynne sat next to Brian sipping a beer and making small talk.

Everyone's afraid to ask anything about anything, Brian thought. *Tomas has everyone spooked.*

Tomas' phone rang again. As he walked away Lynne put her hand lightly on Brian's arm, moved closer and said, "So what are you after up there on the mountain?"

She was so close Brian could smell her hair. It was nice but it made him feel as if he were betraying Nicole somehow.

He moved his arm and replied, "Do you remember Arthur Borland, a man who came through here several months ago looking for his father, Captain Jack?"

Lynne looked at Lucky. "I haven't been here that long but I'll bet Lucky remembers."

Lucky nodded. "Everyone knows Captain Jack. And I spent a long time with Arthur when he came through here, both on his way up and his way back down."

BILL THOMPSON

"I'm here at Arthur's request. I'm looking for Captain Jack but also for the ancient library of the Mayas. Have you heard anything from Jack since Arthur last saw you?"

"Sadly, no. So he's still missing? That's a damned shame. I told Arthur he might have gone back down the mountain another way but I haven't laid eyes on him since he left my camp on his way up. That was months ago. I also told Arthur if anyone could survive it would be Jack. But if there's been no word, he may not be alive. That would be a tragic loss. Jack Borland is, or was, a remarkable man. That's for sure."

Brian glanced at Tomas, who was deep in conversation. He whispered to Lynne, "I have to use your phone tonight. Get with me after everyone goes to sleep."

"Why sir!" she whispered back, smiling. "Are you inviting me to your boudoir?"

He snapped, "This is no joke. I'm the good guy here and Tomas is a kidnapper. I have to do what he says because he's holding my girlfriend. I have to see if anyone's heard from her."

"OK. You have to tell me what's going on first. I want to know what you're looking for. You give me what I want, maybe you get what you want. And in the deal maybe we both get a little extra we both might want. From each other."

Lucky heard her. What she said both angered and saddened him but his face remained impassive. She wasn't his property, although losing her would be tough after all this time.

Brian started to respond but saw Tomas striding back and watching the interaction between Brian and Lynne closely.

ANCIENT

Brian changed the subject, saying to Lucky, "Arthur has high hopes we can find his father alive."

Lucky picked right up. "How do you think you can find anything up there? Arthur tried and got nowhere. Jack had to have taken the map with him. Without it, how do you even know where to start?"

Tomas leaned forward, waiting for Brian's response. "I know which way Arthur went, and I know it was the wrong way. Our two guides also accompanied Arthur. I think they can help figure out where he went wrong. My goal is simply to see what I can learn. Any clue that will ultimately help find Captain Jack will be a success in my books."

Lucky stared into space for a minute, then spoke. "You know Jack Borland thought there was an ancient city up there. He talked like he was the next Hiram Bingham, walking up the mountain and finding another Machu Picchu lying there undisturbed and waiting. As dense as this jungle is, that's always possible. Unlikely, but possible. Jack wanted to find that Mayan trove of information – the Ancient Library, he called it – the codices that would unlock the secrets of the Mayan civilization. If he found that he knew he'd be famous. Rich too, I guess, although it might take more than a bunch of old books to make all that happen. Jack figured it would take finding Mayan gold too. He believed that was of the realm of possibility."

"Enough speculation," Tomas said, abruptly closing the subject. "When do we eat?"

After dinner Sam, Brian and Tomas sat around the campfire drinking coffee. Alfredo and the Belizean workers talked quietly among themselves as Lucky and Lynne washed dishes in the dining hall.

As they stood at the sink Lynne quietly said, "Lucky, tell me more about Jack Borland. I want the whole story so I can figure out what these guys are doing."

Lucky told her everything he knew, all the things he had heard both from Captain Jack himself and later from Arthur.

Brian confronted Nicole's kidnapper. "What's going on, Tomas? You obviously have a problem. You haven't been your usual cheery self all day and suddenly you're receiving phone calls instead of making them. Now you're talking a long time in private instead of having your one word 'check-ins', as you described those little quickie calls. I want to know what's going on. I'm beginning to think maybe you don't have Nicole at all. I want proof."

Tomas snapped back, "You are in no position to make demands. Concentrate on your job and I'll do mine. Nicole needs you. In fact she can't survive without you. The day after tomorrow you will continue Jack Borland's quest and if you're lucky you will find out what happened to the old man himself. I could personally care less about him but my employer and I want the fruits of your labor – the Mayan gold. Just think of Nicole lying naked out there in the jungle somewhere, tied to a table and watched by some men whose carnal instincts are just beneath the surface. You must be successful in your quest so your girlfriend's beautiful, totally nude body can get back home to you safe, sound and unblemished." He smiled maliciously. "And maybe you had better think more of Nicole's welfare than the charms of this anthropologist you just met. Don't get too chummy with her. You have enough problems as it is."

Brian didn't reply. Lynne was a source to get a phone – nothing more. It would be fruitless to argue with Tomas, even to dignify his comment with an

ANCIENT

answer, and Brian had other ideas anyway. The rest of the evening was spent double-checking the equipment the men would be taking up the mountain. Alfredo told Sam and Brian that tomorrow he and the workers would go over everything one last time and then load the backpacks. Since Tomas was leaving there would be five men going up.

Everyone turned in at ten o'clock. Brian lay in his bunk watching shadows on the ceiling as the campfire flickered outside. He had to get Lynne's phone, no matter what. At some point he fell asleep then awoke suddenly, aware that someone was kneeling next to his bed.

"Shh. Don't say a word." It was Lynne and her fingers were lightly pressed to his lips. "Come with me." She tiptoed out of the bunkhouse.

Brian was careful to make as little noise as possible. He was wearing just boxers and he thought how strange he must look as he put on his shoes to go outdoors. Lynne stood near the office twenty yards away. In the moonlight he could see that her tiny t-shirt was frayed – it was so torn it barely covered her breasts. Her bare midriff was taut and solid all the way down to the tiny bikini panties she was wearing. She looked incredible and he found his mind wandering. He focused back on Nicole and his situation.

Once they were in the office she whispered, "I'm taking a huge risk here. I don't know who to trust but I think Tomas is creepy so I'm going to take a chance. We have to be careful, Brian. If your girlfriend is really his hostage he won't be happy with either of us if he finds out you've used my phone. Before that I want to know everything you're doing. Lucky told me about Captain Jack's last adventure and his hope to find the ancient library of the Maya.

He also said Jack had information he located in Spain, including a map he took with him. Lucky said he thinks Jack had gold in a box. Mayan gold. What do you know about that?"

"I've seen everything but the map. And I authenticated it all. As far as my experts can tell the gold is real. But you're an anthropologist. Why are you so interested in the gold when your search should be centered on the civilization?"

"I'm way more interested in the ancient library and the possibility of finding Mayan codices than I am the gold. Plus your buddy Tomas may end up taking the gold anyway. Although if there were a little left over it wouldn't hurt the career and the bank account of a starving anthropologist from UCLA. My job doesn't pay much. I could stand a little boost of fame and fortune. Now tell me more about the gold. Was it Spanish coins you saw?"

Brian explained that the gold was in small square sheets. He presumed it had been removed from the outside of a building where it had been used for decoration.

"There's no direct evidence that the Maya had buildings covered in gold," Lynne remarked. "That sounds more like the Inca. The pictographs on the sheets – they were definitely Mayan, right?"

"Absolutely. They matched some of the pictorials in the Popol Vuh."

"OK. Just because no one ever heard of the Maya covering buildings in gold doesn't mean it didn't happen. Maybe we'll be the first to find it."

"We?" Brian said. "What do you mean, we?"

"I'm going with you," she answered with a grin. "You need an anthropologist. More importantly, you need my phone. You have no choice, my friend. Lynne Parker is suddenly a part of your team."

ANCIENT

"Shit. You can't do that. In the first place Tomas will never allow it. In the second place from what I hear, that mountain's no place for a woman."

"Oh really? And it *is* the place for a New York Fifth Avenue gallery owner? Get real, Brian. I've been to the top twice. Between Arthur Borland's trip and mine there are three trails that we know aren't the right ones. That will help narrow things down. I'm also in way better shape than you are and I'm pretty low maintenance. You don't strike me as a chauvinist, so what is it that bugs you about my going? Are you afraid you'll want to get in my pants? Is that it?" She smiled mischievously.

Brian answered sternly. "My girlfriend is tied to a table naked in the jungle somewhere. I don't think getting in your pants is part of my agenda."

"Sorry. That was insensitive. I'm just trying to loosen you up a little. It sounds like Tomas wants you to find the lost city and it sounds like he'll keep Nicole alive if you do. I'll help you. Even with no hanky-panky between us. Unless we decide otherwise, that is."

She handed him the cell phone. "To use this phone, there's a magic phrase. The phrase is, 'Yes, Lynne, you can come along.' Say it."

He couldn't help but smile. "Yes Lynne, you can come along."

Yesterday Brian got the phone number of the San Ignacio Inn from Sam and memorized it.

"Do you get a good signal up here?"

"Off and on, actually. It's the Guatemalan phone company so sometimes it's great, sometimes it's nada. You have to try and keep trying. Just dial 00 first then the area code and number."

The phone showed one bar of signal. He typed in the number and heard nothing.

"It isn't working."

"Give it a minute."

In a few seconds he heard a steady hiss then the phone ringing on the other end. The faint sound went in and out and he could barely hear it. Since it was almost midnight he didn't expect to reach anyone but he would leave a message for Odette.

The call dropped before it was completed. "Dammit." Brian's frustration turned to desperation. "I have to try again. Dammit. I have to get through."

"Let me try," Lynne said. She took the phone and redialed. Before it connected she glanced at the open doorway behind Brian, a startled look on her face.

Brian whirled around and saw Tomas.

"Are we having a little chat? It looks like someone is trying to make a phone call. How naughty of you both. Lynne, I thought you understood that Mr. Sadler here is not a nice man. He's a criminal actually, and certainly not worthy of your aid and assistance."

Lynne kept the phone to her ear. She heard rings and then an answering machine. If Tomas continued talking she could shout a message into the phone. Instead he looked at her and said, "Put down the phone, Lynne. Right now."

"One sec."

"*NO* secs, Lynne." He grabbed the phone from her. He glanced at the number on the screen and ended the call.

"Who are you calling in Belize, Lynne? Do you have friends and family there? People you like to call in the middle of the night?"

Suddenly Lucky appeared in the bedroom doorway behind Lynne, awakened from the sound of Tomas' voice.

ANCIENT

"What are you guys doing here?" he said angrily. "Lynne, are you OK?"

"She's fine," Tomas answered. "She was trying to help Brian make a phone call. I don't know what that was all about but I've told you both Brian isn't the type of person a nice girl like Lynne should be helping." He put Lynne's phone in his pocket and turned to leave.

"Give her phone back to her." Lucky said.

"Tomorrow morning. For now we need to all get some sleep."

"Give it to her now."

Tomas took out the phone, quickly removed the back case and battery and took out the SIM card. He threw the phone on the desk and said, "For now, no calls."

Lucky started toward him but Lynne held her arm out.

"Not now. Let it go. We'll settle this later." Lucky glared at Tomas as he walked out.

"Is there another phone?" Brian asked. "We were so close but I want to call in the daytime when someone will answer. I have to find out if they've heard anything from Nicole."

"There are no other phones," Lucky replied. "The two Belizean workmen don't have one so if you don't either, that's it."

Lynne said, "Be patient, Brian. I'll help you figure something out soon. Trust me." Turning to Lucky, she said, "I'm going with them tomorrow. Up the mountain. I may be able to help figure out where Jack Borland's ancient city is located."

Late that night Brian lay in the bunkhouse half asleep, the snores of five other men all around him. At one time he dreamed he saw Lynne come through the doorway and go to the back of the room where Tomas slept. He spent the night wondering why she would have done that. Or if she even had.

Most of the next day was spent on logistics. The group calculated how long it would take to reach the summit. Lynne's recent experiences were helpful – she told them it had taken four days.

Tomas seemed preoccupied all day. He spent most of his time sitting in a chair under a tree, lost in thought. In the afternoon a rain shower briefly cooled things down but fired up the humidity afterwards. At five Alfredo, who had become the de facto boss of the Belizean workmen, declared the party ready to go. They all sat down for a rum and Coke. Lucky joined them but Lynne never appeared.

A half hour later she came out of the office toting a backpack loaded to the gills. She dropped it with all the other packs lined up ready for departure in the morning.

Tomas snarled, "What do you think you're doing?"

"I'm going with them."

"No, you absolutely are not."

Lynne's pleasant demeanor vanished. She whirled around and replied, "Listen Mr. Rodriguez, or whatever your name is. Get off my back. This is a free country. Maybe not the good old USA, but nobody's telling me I can't go where the hell I want to go. I *am* going with them. Period. End of story."

"And what possible interest could you have in climbing that mountain another time? I know you're an anthropologist but you've tried twice before and failed."

"This is none of your business. The mountain doesn't belong to you. It doesn't belong to me. You're leaving tomorrow. So are we. And there you have it."

ANCIENT

She turned around, cinched the straps of her backpack then headed to the icebox to fix a drink.

Tomas' phone rang around eight pm and he talked for twenty minutes. Brian watched Tomas mostly listen. When he did talk, it was in whispers. Once the call ended Tomas walked to the bunkhouse, stripped to his shorts and went to bed. The others followed within fifteen minutes. They needed a rest before the arduous climb tomorrow.

The alarm on Tomas' watch went off at five am. He roused the men and Alfredo started coffee. The sun was still behind the mountain but the darkness was quickly transforming into a half-light of dawn.

The men shaved and used the very basic outdoor shower. It was nothing more than a low partition wall to stand behind and a large plastic bag of water tied to a tree limb overhead. A hose attached to the bag could be turned on and off by the user. As crude as it was, the shower was much appreciated by every visitor to Jaguar's Call. Lynne appeared around six and waited until the men finished showering. She was amused to see the guys sneaking glances as they prepared the packs. She hung her t-shirt and shorts on the shower wall. The shower had been constructed for men so the modesty panel only reached to one's navel. There was literally no way to keep a woman's breasts from showing to anyone who cared to look. Immodest as always, Lynne stood tall, raising her arms high as she washed her upper body. The men enjoyed the view and the beautiful woman showering naked five feet away.

After a light breakfast everyone loaded up. Alfredo and one of the other Belizeans went in front followed by Brian, Sam and Lynne. The other workman was in the rear. Lucky kissed Lynne deeply and said, "Break a leg!"

Lynne laughed. "I sure hope you mean that in the show business connotation. Breaking a leg isn't something I really want to do up there on the mountain!"

Tomas and Lucky watched them walk into the jungle along the same trail both Jack Borland and his son Arthur had used.

There wasn't a moment of silence as they walked along the narrow trail. Spider monkeys howled and barked in the trees above them, infinite varieties of birds called their tunes and insects made a high-pitched buzz in an orchestral nightmare of sound. It would have been hard to talk to each other so the group didn't say much as they climbed. The packs were heavy, the path was frequently overgrown with roots and vines and with the humidity they were quickly drenched in sweat.

They were slowed by having to clear the trail so often. Each time they reached a clearing they had to spend time ascertaining where the trail went next. But they moved upwards all day.

At five Alfredo said they must stop and make camp before daylight faded. As the tents were erected Alfredo and the two workers built a campfire and the guide began cooking. From now on Lynne and the five men would eat MREs, an acronym for "meals ready to eat" which are a variety of packaged foods used by the Army. Although nutritious and filling they aren't gourmet fare but they serve a purpose because they are lightweight and don't take up a lot of room.

Brian sat next to Lynne. "Back at camp you said you'd help me later. Got any ideas how we can find out anything about Nicole?"

ANCIENT

"Sure I do, Brian. You can use my phone." She reached in her backpack, pulled out an iPhone and handed it to him.

Brian looked at her, eyes wide with surprise. "You had two phones all along?"

"Yep! Doesn't every resourceful anthropologist who comes to the jungle? What if one gets dropped in the river or snatched by a spider monkey? Or some jackass disables it by taking out the SIM card? You always need a backup plan. Now whether it'll work is another thing entirely. I did charge it up but the battery will run down eventually. I'm going to keep it turned off most of the time because it's the only contact we have with the outside world. My experience last time I climbed was that as you go higher there are patches when it works fine but most places where it's dead as a doornail. Don't ask me how my phone can drop calls on Sunset Boulevard in L.A. but yet I can use it in Guatemala on a mountaintop. It's a mystery of modern technology."

Brian motioned Sam over and showed him the phone. "Try to call Odette."

Sam held the phone to his ear. "It's ringing." After a minute or so he said, "This is Sam. Put Odette on the phone." He looked at Brian. "The reception is pretty bad but for now it's working."

Brian leaned forward with eager anticipation as Sam said, "Hey, baby. I don't know how long we're going to have a signal so let's talk fast. I'll call you back every day at five if I can get a signal. First, has anyone heard from Nicole?"

Brian began feeling lightheaded as Sam listened in silence for a long time. "OK, we'll talk about that again in a minute but let me tell you about us right now."

He glanced at Brian and said, "She's OK. She's there and she's OK."

"Thank you, God," Brian said, slumping. "I just was so afraid she was going to die." He used his sleeve to wipe his face as he unashamedly wept tears of relief at the good news.

Sam told Odette what had happened to them and where they were. He told her about the man with the pencil mustache who said he was Tomas Rodriguez, his threat to kill the farmer and his wife, the loss of their phones and that Tomas was on his way back down the mountain. Then he listened to Odette talk for another minute or so. At last he said, "This Tomas guy is undoubtedly the person who kidnapped Nicole. So make sure she stays safe. Hide her somewhere outside the hotel. If I know this creep he'll waste no time trying to find her. He has to be coming there."

Lynne pointed to her watch, indicating he should watch the usage on the phone. "I need to go to save battery, darling. I'm so glad to talk to you and I love you. Keep safe and see if you can arrange for Nicole to be there tomorrow. If we get through, Brian wants to talk to her." Sam disconnected.

Brian was excited but apprehensive. "Tell me everything," he said to his friend.

Sam told him Nicole had been kidnapped, killed a guard, escaped to Melchor, been rescued by the U.S. Embassy and was back at the hotel, desperately worried about Brian. She was upstairs in her room during the call and there was no time for Odette to get her.

Brian was impressed. "My God! I knew she was resourceful, but hell – she sounds like a Green Beret!"

ANCIENT

Sam continued. "She's still in danger, as we know. Odette said she'd tell Nicole right now about the kidnapper likely coming back to San Ignacio. I think Tomas believes he has to take her hostage again to get us to cooperate. Odette also said Nicole's been in contact with Randall Carter at her office – do you know who he is?"

"I don't know him personally but I know he's the senior partner in the firm and one of the wealthiest men in Dallas. He might be able to help her."

"The plan is we call every day at five and hope we can get through."

He handed the phone to Lynne with a promise to keep every call very short. Minutes were precious with no phone charger.

That night was the same as the others they'd experienced on the mountain. They set up perimeter security and took turns on watch. Brian, Lynne and Sam slept in pup tents while Alfredo and the other two men lay on pallets on the ground. The noise was everywhere but each night sleep came a little easier. Brian compared it to Boy Scout camp when he was a kid. You had to learn to block out the extraneous noise to fall asleep.

Sometime in the middle of the night everyone woke as one when they heard the watchman utter a loud shout. As they rolled out of their tents they saw a five-foot snake on the ground, its head neatly severed from the body by a blow from the Belizean's machete.

"Mexican python," Alfredo told the group. "It's not poisonous but they can inflict a nasty bite. Usually they eat iguanas or rodents but we're better safe than sorry."

BILL THOMPSON

The next day was an arduous repeat of the last. They started out early and made good time as they climbed. By noon the heat made it feel as if they were wearing blankets. Every step was a chore. When they stopped for lunch Lynne and Brian sat next to each other, away from the group. She consulted a small journal.

"I made a lot of notes the other times I climbed this mountain so I wouldn't make the same mistakes again. In about a hundred yards we should come to a tree where I notched my initials and an arrow. From there I have a suggestion on where to go next."

Brian replied, "We need to find an ancient stone stairway that's very wide, very tall and leads to a narrow passageway between two cliffs."

"What?" Lynne shouted. "How the hell do you know that? Dammit, Brian! We're all on the same team here. Share your information with me. I've done this trip twice before. I need to have everything so we can find the ancient city. That and Jack Borland too."

He laughed and said, "Ease up! How good is your sixteenth century Spanish?"

He pulled the manila envelope from his backpack, removed the copy of Governor Alvarado's letter and handed it to her. He also had the English translation of the letter but he kept it to himself. He wanted to see if this college professor was as smart as he figured she was.

"My ancient Spanish isn't as bad as you might think." She began to read the letter as she munched on trail mix. "Don't say anything for a minute. Let me see if I can get the gist of this."

In a few minutes she said, "Holy shit! It's a damn good thing you showed this to me now. We

ANCIENT

know exactly what we're looking for. We have to find that stairway. What else do you have?"

"That's all for now."

She lashed out at him. "This may seem like a cakewalk to you buddy, but my life and my career are at stake here. My time on this mountain's running out and I have to go back to the real world before long. I'm a damned teacher at UCLA and I need something to put me on the map or I'll be stuck as a second rate professor the rest of my life. I want to be an explorer. I want to discover new things. I'll never get the funding to do things like that unless I make an impact."

Calmer, she continued. "The English profs have to publish or perish, you know? They have to write books or get relegated to being someone's assistant. It works the same way in anthropology except we're expected to mount expeditions, spend some foundation's money and come home with the glory. We have to be on the same team, Brian. We're looking for the same thing for different reasons. We both want to find an ancient civilization. You want to find Jack Borland and maybe some gold. I want to find the Mayan city itself, to know how these people functioned. Help me and I'll help you. Any way you want. What else do you have to show me?" She put her hand on his leg.

Brian pulled away. "What're you doing?"

Lowering her voice she said, "Just being the red-blooded American girl I am. I'm not an anthropologist a hundred percent of the time. Are you a stuffy antiquities guy all the time? I don't think so. I bet you like a little action as much as I do."

"Lynne, you know that I'm involved with Nicole and she may still be in danger. What kind of guy would I be if I just hopped in the sack with you?"

She pulled back, indignant. "Hey, mister. Did anybody say anything about hopping in the sack? I don't think so. I'm just interested in playing around a little. What we do after dark isn't anybody else's business."

"I think you're more interested in doing whatever it takes to get me to tell you everything I know about Captain Jack Borland's expedition. And like I said earlier, that's all I'm telling for now." He stood, stretched and rejoined the others.

"About ready to get moving again?"

They donned packs and started walking. Brian could feel the rarified air – it was harder to breathe at this altitude and the hiking made him wheeze. He saw Sam struggling as well.

"How high are we?" he asked Alfredo.

Looking at his altimeter wristwatch, Alfredo said they were above six thousand feet and therefore had about two thousand more to go.

"We can slow things down so no one gets sick. If anyone wants to rest just say so."

For half an hour Lynne had been scouring the jungle for the marked tree that would show she had been here before. Finally they came to a fork in the trail, both paths ahead barely visible because of overgrowth.

Lynne yelled for the group to stop, dropped her backpack and pulled brush aside. Notched into a tree were the initials LP and an arrow pointing to the left.

"OK. I went that way and there's nothing there." She asked Alfredo to ask the two Belizean guides which way Arthur Borland had gone. The guides agreed they had also gone to the left. They all agreed the left trail wasn't the correct one. They took the trail on the right.

ANCIENT

They hiked for four hours, taking regular breaks for rest and water. It was obvious no one had been on this trail in some time – the workers walked in front of the others removing vegetation, vines and small trees. They lost the path completely now and then only to look further and pick it back up. Lynne walked the edge of the trail, peering into the undergrowth to try to find some sign of an ancient staircase. The sun was setting when she finally saw something.

Directly in front of them the trail took a sharp turn to the left. "Guys, come over here. Look at this. The trail's been cut with a dogleg to the left right here. Know why the natives did that? Because they couldn't go straight any longer. Any idea why not?"

Brian threw out a guess. "Because it's easier to go up a winding trail instead of one that goes straight up a mountain? That'd be some tough climbing – most people would rather take a switchback than go straight uphill, especially at this altitude."

"I don't think that's the answer. I think the natives hit a dead-end. It was too hard to continue to clear undergrowth on the straight path so they turned. This is the first real dogleg we've seen on the entire trail. Something's different here – let's see what it is."

She asked the workers to clear some brush and in a few minutes they found three stones perfectly aligned in a row. There was a second row above that set. As Mayan stairs tend to be, these were very tall. Everyone dropped packs and the three guides began hacking in earnest. The straight line of stones continued both to the sides and upwards.

BILL THOMPSON

"This is definitely man-made," Lynne said quietly. "It's possible we've found our stairway. This may be the very place the letter talks about."

ANCIENT

CHAPTER FOURTEEN

They set up camp along the trail next to the stairway since it was too late to begin clearing it. Everyone was excited - they had that renewed sense of energy that comes with discovery. Alfredo and the workmen chatted quietly as they smoked pipes. Sam rummaged through his pack and came up with two bottles of warm beer. He brought them out and everyone had celebratory swigs, passing the bottles around like champagne.

Brian said, "Lynne, I need your phone again."

She took it out, turned it on and handed it to Brian. "You're not the only one who needs something. Keep that in mind when I ask you to pay me back."

He looked at her quizzically but she just laughed and walked away.

Sam dialed the number and handed the phone to Brian. "You can talk this time. They know we're calling now so Nicole should be on the line too." For once the connection was clear.

Odette answered on the first ring and he asked to talk to Nicole.

"I'm so sorry but she's gone. She talked to her boss this morning. She told him the kidnapper was most likely coming for her so he insisted she fly home. I took her to the airport in Belmopan at noon and she caught the Tropic Air flight to Belize City. She was booked on the nonstop American flight to Dallas that left a half hour ago.

"She said you'd want to talk and she does too but don't waste your phone battery. She said she loves you and she'll call me if there's anything urgent she needs to talk to you about. She asked you do the same. If either of you has something urgent I'll relay it or set a time for you to talk."

Nicole would call Collette Conning at Brian's gallery and let her know that he was going to be gone longer than he had expected.

"Nicole said if Collette needs anything she'd let me know."

Unwilling to waste precious minutes, he thanked Odette, handed Sam the phone and told him Nicole had gone home. Lynne perked up when she overheard.

Sam cautioned his wife. "Be careful. That guy Tomas will be angry when he finds out she's gone. And Odette, he's been in our hotel. He took some papers from Brian and Nicole's room. Keep your eyes out for him. Take care of yourself." He disconnected.

Brian felt responsibility for his old friend. "I'm sorry you guys are in the middle of this. I hope Odette stays safe."

"Don't apologize for one minute. Odette's a scrapper. She's been independent her whole life and she knows how to handle herself. You'd better worry about Tomas if he decides to take her on!"

Lynne patted Brian's arm. "I'm glad Nicole's going back to the States. She'll be safe and that should make you feel better." She flashed a smile and walked away.

ANCIENT

"What's up with you two?" Sam muttered. "She's suddenly your best friend."

"She knows I have information and I'm not willing to give all of it to her."

"That might be your intention but from what I see, I'd say she's willing to give you anything *she* has to get it."

"I can handle her, Sam. I'm not interested."

"You may be able to handle her, buddy, but if you tell me you're not the least bit interested in a female who looks and acts like Lynne Parker I'd say get your testosterone checked. She's hot as hell, Brian. And you know what happens in the jungle stays in the jungle," he smiled. "Know what I mean?"

Brian didn't smile. "No, Sam, I *don't* know what you mean. I presume you're kidding." He stopped as Lynne came back over and asked to see the letter written by Governor Alvarado. She read the part about the stairway, confirming it was ten varas wide and thirty long.

"How long is a vara?" Brian asked.

"A vara is a Spanish measurement used in the sixteenth century. It's roughly three-fourths of a meter or about two and a half feet. Doing the math, the stairway Cortes saw was maybe twenty-five feet wide and at least eighty to a hundred feet high. So what we're looking for is very tall."

Around nine they retired to their tents. The man on watch was responsible for keeping the campfire burning; its firelight flickered against the canvas of the tents. The humidity and temperature were still sky-high so Brian lay naked on top of his pallet. His tent flaps were open but the screens were zipped shut. That way he could catch a breeze without getting eaten by bugs.

BILL THOMPSON

He thought about the stairway Lynne had found. Tomorrow would be an exciting day – hopefully the start of this trip's real purpose. And it was all easier now that Nicole was safely home. He could concentrate on his goal. Maybe in a few days they would have the answer to Captain Jack Borland's disappearance. And maybe a key to the ancient Mayan civilization. He drifted into slumber thinking of a stairway to a city high in the clouds - another Machu Picchu but this one in the rain forests of Guatemala.

He suddenly woke up, aware that he wasn't alone. The pup tents weren't big enough for two adults to sleep side by side but they were roomy enough for close company. Startled, he looked up and saw Lynne Parker sitting cross-legged next to him, looking up and down his body approvingly. She was naked just as he was. Her breasts were beautiful in the half-light of the flickering embers, he casually thought.

"What are you doing?" he whispered, trying to cover himself with a flap of his sleeping bag.

"Nice to see you too. Glad someone else sleeps in the nude with all this heat."

"Lynne. What the hell are you doing?"

"Come on. I thought you were a smart guy. Can't you tell what I'm doing?" She moved the cover away and put her hand on his penis. It jumped to life immediately but Brian jerked it away.

"Look, I can't do this."

"Part of you looks like it can do this." She put her hand back on him. He grew harder as she held and squeezed it. He took her hand and roughly pushed it away.

"I am *not* going to do this. This isn't right."

ANCIENT

"What isn't right? Are you married? Am I? Are we tied down to one person? Have you and Nicole ever had dates with other people? We're adults, Brian. I'm not hooking up with you for life. I want some fun. This stuff happens. And I want it to happen with you." She took his hand and put it on her breast. He pulled it away immediately, feeling guilty with Nicole so far away.

"Lynne, any man on earth would be dying to sleep with you. You're beautiful and sexy as hell but it isn't right for me. I can't do this. I can't do it to Nicole."

"OK, Mister Honorable Guy. I didn't know guys like you still existed. I was just looking for a little fun. Nothing more, nothing less. Don't read a lot into it. I'm a red-blooded American girl and you're a red-blooded American guy and we're both out here in the jungle. I'm attracted to you. That's all I can say. I was looking for fun. Obviously you're one of those men I don't see very often. A loyal, faithful one!"

She crawled out of his tent and walked five feet to hers. It was nearly midnight and the only other person awake was the watchman, one of the Belizean workers. He had seen her walk naked into Brian's tent. He smiled approvingly as he now watched her return. She glanced at him and smiled back, unconcerned about her nudity.

I bet that was fun for Brian, the watchman thought to himself.

When Brian awoke it was dawn. He pulled on a pair of shorts and crawled out of his tent, smelling coffee brewing on the campfire. He saw Lynne standing nearby, holding a water bottle and with a toothbrush in her mouth. She was dressed in her signature t-shirt and shorts. She gave him a little wave and he nodded back.

Sam popped his head out of his tent. "Morning. Did you sleep OK?"

"Uh, yes." Brian wondered if Sam had heard them talking last night. "How about you? Ready for the adventure today?"

"Ready, buddy. I'm excited about all this. Alfredo, come over here a minute. I thought about something last night. What requirement do we have to report archaeological discoveries?"

"Same here as back in Belize. As soon as we discover something significant, whatever that means, we have to notify the Department of Archaeology. Work has to stop until they come out and investigate."

Sam replied, "Yeah, and it might take years for them to come out. I know a guy who found a tomb on his property along the Macal River near San Ignacio. He obeyed the law and called the authorities. They haven't been out there yet and it's been two summers. If word gets out about his find, my friend's afraid looters will show up. Word actually *always* gets out because the people who work for the Archaeology Department don't make any money. Passing along a little tip here and there about hidden treasure can supplement your income pretty well. There are so many Mayan things buried in Belize and there's so little money to properly conserve anything. That's why nobody ever follows the rules. If you notify them it takes forever."

Alfredo added, "Here there wouldn't be much of a problem so long as we didn't find something really significant. But for instance if we find an ancient city like we're looking for, then it would be no bueno if we hadn't reported it as soon as we knew we were on to something big.

"Here's my suggestion. Until we come across something important, there's no reason to notify them anyway. Let's see how things go and if we stumble across the find of the century, we call the authorities and let them take over."

Lynne overheard the end of the conversation and said, "The Ministry of Culture governs archaeology here in Guatemala. They try to protect from looters, but it's impossible in remote places like this. If we found something the country itself would be better off if we kept exploring, properly mapped our finds and brought our treasures to the authorities instead of waiting for them to get around to coming out here. I guarantee you word would get out because our workers would talk. Then looters would come and by the time the government got to the site nothing of value would be left."

"So do we agree it's better to ask forgiveness than permission?"

"Absolutely," Lynne smiled. "Always."

Alfredo agreed. "Works for me. I need to get packets so the men can eat and get to work on that stairway." He told everyone to leave their camp intact in case they needed to spend another night here. No one knew how long it would take to clear a path up the staircase or what was next.

Alfredo and the Belizean workers used the three machetes they had, clearing dense vines and small trees that had grown up between the stones of the staircase. Brian tried to see how wide the stairs were but had to give up. He could see about four feet but presumed they continued on deep into the jungle since the letter described them as about twenty-five feet wide. Without a knife he couldn't clear enough foliage to see how far they went.

For three hours the men worked on the stairway, cutting a swath about two feet wide so the group could ascend. The tedious work stopped mid-morning when clouds built up overhead. Suddenly the daily rainstorm dumped several inches of water on them. Everyone retreated to tents to wait it out without getting soaked. Half an hour later it was over and the men were back at work.

Lynne fixed lunch so Alfredo could keep working. Afterwards she said, "Brian, let's see how their progress is going." She walked over to the stairway and looked up. A sort of tunnel had been cut through the thick growth. "Come on! Let's go up."

Brian followed her. The heat inside the carved out tunnel of undergrowth was unbelievable. It was like an oven. He counted the steps up the narrow passage. The men had excavated ten very tall rows of steps that extended up nearly twenty feet.

Lynne said, "It obviously goes on and the letter says it's maybe eighty feet high. If these are the right stairs we have a long way to go."

"How could these not be the right stairs?"

"Easy. You've been to other Mayan sites like Tikal or Palenque. There's never one stairway – there are dozens. Some go up the sides of tall temples, others lead the way to plazas or ceremonial areas. If this were the only stairway in this area I'd be surprised. I just hope to hell this is the right one."

Suddenly she turned, her face inches from his. "Did you sleep well last night or were you a little frustrated?"

"I slept OK. I wasn't frustrated. I just can't betray Nicole."

ANCIENT

She laughed. "A little fling in the jungle never hurt anyone. Who has to know?" She nudged past him in the narrow tunnel of vines, starting back down. "See you again sometime."

As they descended another brief downpour came and the humidity rose exponentially. Back at camp Lynne said, "I'm hot as hell and my shirt's drenched." She nonchalantly pulled her t-shirt over her head then walked to her pack, knelt down and retrieved a dry one. Sam looked at Brian and raised his eyebrows, smiling appreciatively at the gorgeous woman naked from the waist up who was casually changing clothes in front of everyone. Alfredo glanced at her too but continued gathering rainwater from a plastic bucket to refill their water bottles.

Work continued until four o'clock when Alfredo called a halt. There were twenty-two rows of excavated steps leading up the mountain. The stairway was visible only through the two-foot wide tunnel the workers had cut upwards through the vines. Lynne went up first - Brian held back and let Sam go next. He still wasn't certain what Lynne's plan was but he was pretty sure it wasn't just a fling in the jungle. She looked like a girl who knew what she was after and how to use her numerous attributes to get it. What she was selling, he wasn't buying.

Promptly at five Lynne dug out her phone and turned it on. Handing it to Sam she said, "You've got 83% battery. You might think about making your calls every other day. How about you tell her to stand by every day at five just in case, but not to expect a call except every other day."

Sam agreed and placed the call. Today it took three tries before he got a connection and even then the signal was faint, fading in and out. Odette answered on the first ring and told him she had spoken with Nicole who said she was fine and so was the gallery. She sent her love to Brian. Odette said things were good in San Ignacio – she hadn't seen the mustached man around town and had heard nothing from anyone about him.

Odette understood that Sam would call less often, and they were saying their goodbyes when the call abruptly ended. "Signal's lousy up here," he said to Lynne. "I could barely hear her." He looked down at the phone. "I used four percent of the battery on that call – it's at 79% now – so we can calculate pretty well how much juice a call takes. We have to be careful."

Later Sam told Brian what Nicole had said – when he mentioned that she sent her love Brian looked down, glad that he had done the right thing about Lynne. He had resisted her even though he had seen her naked more than once on this trip - including in his tent. And he had been aroused. After all this time away and with a woman who looked like her, what man wouldn't be, he rationalized. He had new resolve – he wouldn't let things happen with her. Even though he knew she'd try again.

The guides had slaved in the oppressive humidity all day; they were asleep before dark. Guard duty for them was begin at three am and only in one hour shifts so they could get a good night's sleep first. The others would take two-hour shifts; Sam, Lynne and then Brian.

At one am Brian was sleeping soundly but he sat up abruptly when Lynne tapped him on the leg.

"Better quit sleeping naked," she laughed. "If a mosquito bites you in the wrong place it could hurt."

ANCIENT

Ignoring her comment, he pulled on his shorts, t-shirt and shoes. "Anything happening out there?"

"Nothing. I'm beat; I'm going to hit the sack."

She undressed outside her tent. When he saw what she was doing he turned away but then he looked back, watching her take off everything she wore, admiring that perfect body. She turned suddenly, smiled at him and crawled into her tent. He was ashamed for looking but once again he'd become aroused watching her.

Next morning the work began early in an attempt to beat the afternoon heat. The opening was wide enough for only one man to use a machete, so two hacked through brush all along the bottom of the stairway while the third moved up.

Shortly the worker from the top came down and spoke with Alfredo, who told the others, "We have a problem. He has reached the top of the stairs. If the measurements in the Alvarado letter are correct, it's far too short."

Within minutes the other worker reached the end of the stairway horizontally. It was time to measure.

Alfredo ran a tape up while Brian held the other end. Finally he called out, "I'm at the top."

"Fifty-one feet."

Back on the ground, Alfredo took the tape and they measured lengthwise. "Twelve feet," Brian said.

Lynne was disappointed. "Shit. This isn't the right stairway."

Brian was more positive. "The fact that there's a stairway at all is a plus. We're clearly in a city. There may be something else at the top of the stairway. Or this may be the right one, just smaller than the Spanish Governor said. After all, he wrote that letter years after he was actually here. Maybe he didn't remember – or maybe he exaggerated so the King would be impressed."

"You're right. We need to do more work here. We need to see what's at the top of the stairway. Let's see if we can find a narrow portal of some type then a plaza with a building in it. I guess we need to think positively. Right, Mr. Sadler?" She smiled.

"Right, Miss Parker." Surprising even himself, he smiled back.

Sam looked at Brian and raised his eyebrows. "If you two are finished, can we get focused again?"

Fifty feet above the trail at the top of the staircase, there was less foliage so the workers could clear faster. By noon they had cleared what they could now see was a flat surface.

Everyone clambered to the top and saw tall mountains soaring a thousand feet or more everywhere they turned. It was an awe-inspiring sight. The temperature and humidity this high above the jungle floor were noticeably lower too.

Sam asked, "Do you see any evidence of a building or ruins?"

Lynne shook her head. "I'm planning to spend the afternoon up here. I didn't see anything yet but I want to walk every inch of this platform. Keep your fingers crossed."

They went down for lunch then everyone climbed back up the narrow passageway. Alfredo and the workers finished clearing brush and low scrub while Brian, Lynne and Sam combed the almost-flat area the men had cleared.

Shortly Alfredo called out, "Come over here, guys." The men had found a second set of steps leading back down.

ANCIENT

Lynne was thrilled. "This pretty well cinches it. We're on top of a temple, I think. Let's measure the distance between our two stairways then keep clearing the underbrush. I think this expanse of flat ground we're standing on is the top of a four-sided temple. If I'm right, there will be a stairway on each side."

A half-hour of final clearing proved her right. They were standing on a pyramid, the top of which was a twelve-by-twelve foot square.

"Each side is exactly five varas," Lynne calculated. "That's exactly what we'd expect from Mayan builders. It doesn't match at all the description in the letter Jack Borland had, but regardless it's absolutely incredible. This is an undiscovered temple in a forgotten city. In the middle of this platform there'll be an altar or a round stone – maybe even the foundation of another building. The Maya always put something on top of their temples."

The men removed all the growth, their machetes making ringing sounds as they struck stone.

"Mira aquí!" one yelled at last. *Look here.*

There was a rectangular piece of stone that rested six inches above the surface. It was roughly two feet long and four feet wide. They brushed away dirt with their hands and saw faint carvings.

"My God, this is beautiful," Lynne said as she moved her index finger slowly over the grooves.

Brian asked what she thought it was.

"It's Mayan for sure – probably a stela. It's completely consistent with carvings I've seen at Tikal, which isn't that far from here. We're definitely standing on top of a Mayan temple. The carvings probably represent a god – I'd have to spend some time on these before I could tell for sure - but that would be my guess. We're probably the first people to see this in a thousand years."

She pulled out a camera and took dozens of pictures then she marked the GPS coordinates with her phone.

She told Brian, "If we're actually in a Mayan city I couldn't have asked for more. With the jungle covering everything so completely it's impossible to know how big this place is. We could be in the middle of a temple complex that has dozens of buildings. I hope we can find the building that Cortes found - the one Jack Borland was looking for - but for me, if we found nothing else this one structure is worth it all.

"There's something that's been bothering me but I think I understand it now. The stairway in the letter is different. It's not on the side of a temple like the ones here. It's a real set of stairs that leads to something - a passage in a cliff, maybe. But we won't know exactly what it all means unless we find it. Even though the Mayans built some huge cities, most of their settlements were only a square mile or two in size. I think the stairway mentioned in the letter is in this area. We already know they built a building right here and I figure the rest can't be far away. If this is a lost city, this is huge."

ANCIENT

CHAPTER FIFTEEN

Alone in her office, Nicole thought about what she'd been through. She was fortunate to have a boss whose personal involvement in her welfare had brought her safely home. Even more, Randall Carter had arranged temporary security for her. A guard accompanied her twice a day for the five blocks to her home at the Ritz-Carlton. That building was under heightened security as well.

Thank God for Randall Carter.

Two days ago when her plane from Belize arrived in Dallas, an airline representative came on board, instructed the passengers to remain seated for a moment, and ushered Nicole off the plane ahead of the crowd. She was whisked to an unmarked VIP lounge inside the security area. One person was waiting Randall Carter.

"Mr. Carter, thank you so much for helping me. I had nowhere else to turn when I got away from the kidnappers. Thank God you helped me."

"No thanks are necessary. I was pleased to be of assistance and I'm so glad you're safe and back in the USA. I know you're tired and as soon as the airline rep retrieves your checked luggage we'll be out of here."

BILL THOMPSON

For a fleeting moment she wondered how Randall Carter had gotten through security without a boarding pass. Since 9/11 it had become virtually impossible to do but she also knew that here in Dallas there was nothing he couldn't accomplish. Tom Horton, the president of the parent company of American Airlines, was Randall Carter's neighbor in exclusive Preston Hollow, as was former President George W. Bush. People like Carter had power others could only fantasize about.

"Thank you for coming personally to meet me. That was kind of you but you didn't need to do that. I could have caught a cab home."

"Not a chance, Nicole. My goal today is to get one of Carter and Wells' best legal minds back home and back to work, safe and sound." He told her to take as much time off as she wanted. He offered a counselor in case she wanted some help getting over the terrible ordeal she had been through

She thanked him for his concern and took the name of the therapist even though she didn't expect to visit him.

After only one day off she forced herself to get back into her job, mainly to stop obsessing about Brian. Carter would keep her up to date on the search for her kidnapper. She knew Brian and Sam were OK although with limited battery life she couldn't talk to him.

This morning she'd prepared the defense of a Dallas oilman who was accused of killing his wife. It was the first murder in five years in the posh community of University Park and there was no doubt the man had actually committed the murder.

The problem was that it was actually the wife who had paid to have her husband killed while she was playing bridge one afternoon. The gunman, not the sharpest pencil in the drawer, got his money up front but unfortunately misunderstood the timing. He used the wife's alarm code to enter the house, walked into the husband's study and was holding a gun to his head when the wife came home from her bridge game. The gunman wasn't supposed to be there – the wife heard a noise in the study, opened the door and her husband used the confusion to grab the gun. A wild shot was fired as the men struggled. The wife collapsed at the study door, fatally wounded. Police responded to the alarm call, the gunman ran, and the husband was left holding the weapon. He was charged with murder. The police thought there was no gunman at all - it was just a husband and his now-dead wife.

The defendant's money was spread all over Dallas seeking information about the shooter. Finally someone came forward. He told a story about a guy in a bar who bragged that he got twenty grand for a murder he didn't even have to commit since the intended victim accidentally killed the wife who'd ordered the shooting in the first place. This news didn't convince the DA's office so a date was set for the oilman's murder trial. Nicole was certain the case would be dismissed but she had to prepare on the off chance it wasn't.

Nicole's assistant knocked softly on her office door and stuck his head inside. "Miss Farber, Mr. Carter would like you to join him at the Petroleum Club for lunch at 1:30. He has a new client he wants you to meet. You're free then; may I accept the invitation?"

"That sounds great. Tell him I'll meet him there. Who's the client?"

"He didn't say. Mr. Carter will have a driver pick you up downstairs. Security will take you from here to the garage."

She smiled. He was still looking after her welfare. She was blessed to work for Randall Carter.

A little after one pm she and a guard took the elevator to the garage where she was handed over to the driver of a black Mercedes sedan.

"Shouldn't take long at all," he said. "Traffic's pretty light even though it's the lunch hour."

They went down Pearl Street and turned on Ross. The driver entered an underground parking lot, found a spot and accompanied her to an express elevator going directly to the fifty-fifth floor of the fourth tallest building in Dallas. When she stepped off the maître d' welcomed her.

"Good afternoon, Miss Farber. Mr. Carter and his guest are waiting for you in the bar."

She walked into the expansive lounge and saw Randall Carter wave. As she walked across the room she looked at his guest, a strikingly handsome man maybe in his late sixties. *He looks familiar,* she thought. He was dressed in a dark pinstripe suit she guessed might be from London's Savile Row. She knew Randall Carter had his suits custom made there and this man's taste appeared equally impeccable. He wore a starched white shirt with simple gold cufflinks and a red Hermes tie. As she reached the table both men stood.

"Nicole, I'm glad you could make it. I want you to get to know our new client. He was particularly interested in meeting you." She smiled at the man and he held out his hand.

"Miss Farber, it's a pleasure. I think we have a mutual acquaintance."

ANCIENT

"Thank you. Good to meet you too. I'm afraid I didn't get your name."

"I'm sorry – my fault. Unfortunately many people know me on sight! It's refreshing to see you're not one of them, so forgive my rudeness. I'm John Spedino."

The shock was evident on Nicole's face. "Are you all right?" her boss said. "You look as though you've seen a ghost. Have you two met before?"

"Please be seated, gentlemen," Nicole responded, instantly regaining her composure. "No, I haven't met Mr. Spedino but I think you know my friend Brian Sadler."

"Yes, Brian and I have met a time or two. I am a big fan and an occasional customer of his gallery. Please send along my regards when you talk with him next. I understand you and he had a distressful trip to Central America recently."

"How, uh, how do you know that . . ." Nicole stammered as Randall Carter smiled and raised his hand.

"John's a good friend. I hope you don't mind that I shared with him about your misadventure in Guatemala last week. It's an incredible horror story but one with a good ending, thank God. And Brian's continuing search for Captain Jack and the lost library of the Maya – that's a fascinating tale!"

Nicole attempted a half-smile and sat. She had always made a point of separating her personal life from her job. She considered herself a private person and she was uncomfortable here, especially given her employer's decision to relate her story without asking her in advance.

They ordered lunch and Carter turned the conversation to the matter at hand. "As you may know, Nicole, a couple of years ago John Spedino was convicted of fraud involving a public company called Bellicose Holdings. I think you're very aware that Warren Taylor and Currant was the investment banking firm here in town that took Bellicose public. You also know it shut down over the negative publicity surrounding the fraud. Your friend Brian was a broker there at the time the Bellicose public offering occurred."

Nicole listened intently.

"Mr. Spedino's previous counsel convinced a judge to grant a new trial on the grounds that the president of Bellicose Holdings, Francois Rochefort, perjured himself to avoid jail time. Rochefort's a convicted criminal - he served ten years in a French prison for fraud. Mr. Spedino has told me he had nothing to do with any of this. The U.S. Attorney has been trumping up charges against John Spedino for years and until this Bellicose matter their success rate was zero. John has never had a conviction for anything and he has assured me he is guilty of nothing now.

"Our firm has been retained to represent him going forward. Our goal is to resoundingly prove to the prosecutors that they have nothing to gain from a new trial. We want to convince them that Mr. Spedino will never go back to prison for anything involving Bellicose or Francois Rochefort because he's innocent. But if the U.S. Attorney insists on filing new charges we will put on his defense. I want you to be the lead attorney on this one, Nicole. It would be a personal favor to me if you would handle it."

John Spedino leaned forward in his chair and touched her sleeve lightly. "From what Randall tells me you're the top criminal lawyer at Carter and Wells. That says a lot, Miss Farber, and I'm pleased

ANCIENT

that Mr. Carter and I have selected you to handle my case. I'm putting my future in your hands and I'm confident you're exactly the right person for me."

BILL THOMPSON

ANCIENT

CHAPTER SIXTEEN

The morning after the group had found the temple they were breaking down their campsite. Lynne was already up on top examining the jungle around the ancient structure. Since the jungle always hid ancient buildings, they often looked like nothing more than tall mounds. She held a compass, turning in each direction as she looked for a structure taller than the one on which she was standing. It should be nearly a hundred feet high and it might or might not have the ruin of a building on top.

By the time she descended the men had finished loading and the backpacks sat in a row, ready to be hoisted and carried.

"Did you see anything?" Brian asked.

"Maybe. It's hard to tell with so much growth and so many trees but I think there are at least two or three tall structures within a half-mile of here. Let's keep moving."

A half hour later Lynne stopped, glanced at her compass and held up her hand. "We're going the wrong way. We need to be going there." She pointed into a tangled mess of trees and vines.

BILL THOMPSON

The three of them waited on the trail as the workers and Alfredo hacked into the brush. After an hour the men had cleared only fifty feet.

By mid-afternoon thunder boomed ominously. They quickly set up one tent and threw their stuff inside, barely making it as the daily rainstorm came, torrential but brief. Alfredo ran here and there, pulling open the portable shower bag and setting out cook pots to catch the rain. Within ten minutes it was all over and there was plenty of water.

They were all sopping wet and sky-high humidity was like a furnace. They'd been together long enough by now that no one gave nudity a thought. Everyone peeled off soaked clothes and wrung them out. Sam glanced at Lynne; she grinned and said, "Hey, you've seen one set, you've seen them all. Right?"

"Not necessarily true," Sam muttered under his breath to no one in particular.

Refreshed and clean, everyone hung wet clothes on branches, dug through their packs and donned dry clothing.

Brian and Sam leaned against a tree, catnapping as the workers cleared the trail. Lynne made notes in her journal. After a couple of hours they heard Alfredo's muffled voice.

"Hey guys! Come see this!" They walked a hundred feet down the new trail until they reached the workers.

"Esta otra escalera!" one of the men said, pointing forward.

Alfredo translated. "They've found another stairway."

Where the men had cleared Lynne saw three steps. They had worked horizontally instead of going up like last time.

ANCIENT

Her voice quivered with anticipation. "Let's keep clearing and see how wide this baby is."

As the workers cut and chopped Lynne consulted Captain Jack's letter, both the original and the English translation.

"Cortes says the stairway is twenty-five to thirty feet wide and seventy-five to ninety feet high. We're looking for stairs that lead to some kind of narrow passageway or aperture, through which we should find a small flat plaza."

It didn't take long to finish. Alfredo said, "We've completely cleared the stairway sideways. It's about eight meters wide."

Lynne's head shot up. "Eight meters - twenty-four feet! Let's measure."

Sam took one end of a tape and walked to the far end of the rock stairs.

"Ready!"

At the other end she pulled the tape taut and measured. A minute later they heard, "Bingo! It's twenty-seven feet. Exactly ten varas wide."

The workers set up camp, showered and rested while Sam worked on dinner. This was the day for a call; Lynne passed over the phone at five.

Sam and Odette spoke very briefly, then he told Brian, "Nicole wants you to call. She says there's no emergency and it won't take long but she'll be standing by every day at this time until she hears from you."

"OK. I'll call her now but I'll make it quick." The phone's battery registered 64%, lower than Brian would have expected since two days ago it was nearly eighty. It must have drained from Lynne's taking so many pictures of the ruins, he thought to himself.

BILL THOMPSON

He walked away from the others and dialed her number. The ring tone was faint but she picked up right away.

"Brian, are you OK? I know we have to be brief but just tell me nothing's wrong. I've had a feeling something isn't right and I just want to hear things are good."

Even though nothing really happened with Lynne, Brian felt like a liar as he assured Nicole things were just fine. He said they'd found a temple and maybe were in a city, but were still looking for Jack Borland's staircase.

They talked about Tomas. Brian told her how much the mustached man knew about her.

"He was the one who kidnapped me!" she responded. "He took you and Sam too?"

"Yes, but we're all safe for now. We can't spend any more time talking about him. We have to conserve this battery. Just be careful, baby."

"The firm's providing security for me. I'm more worried about you – he's probably still right there in Guatemala."

She changed the subject. "Brian, here's why I called. Please be calm. Today Randall Carter introduced me to a new client I'm going to be representing – John Spedino."

Shock and revulsion coursed through him. "Spedino's in Dallas? I thought he was in jail for life."

"He was granted a new trial. He claims Francois Rochefort committed perjury and Spedino himself wasn't involved at all with Bellicose Holdings. Long story short, I have no way out of this unless I quit the firm. Being the newest and youngest attorney ever elected partner, that's not something I'm willing to do. I talked to Mr. Carter - it was his decision to represent Spedino and I can't question that. I told him I wasn't comfortable representing a man with whom you'd had an involvement but he told me I'm the best and it would be a personal favor to him. What can I do, Brian? Tell him no, when the man just got me rescued? You know how this works. It doesn't matter if our clients are guilty or not. Everybody's entitled to a lawyer - we represent them regardless. You also know my success rate is the best in Texas. It makes sense why Mr. Carter assigned me to this case."

Brian was furious. "Bullshit! Do you know how dangerous he is? He's *Mafia,* Nicole. He's the godfather. Don't you get that? They call him Teflon Two – he's the same kind of guy John Gotti was. You know all this already. There's nothing this guy won't do or hasn't done. Don't be deceived by how he looks or how he talks. He's as smooth as silk. What the hell do you think you're doing . . ."

She interrupted brusquely. "We don't have time to go through this now. I appreciate your concern but I'm a big girl. I'm not marrying this guy – he's my client. I think I can handle it and by now I'd hope you think so too. So you concentrate on your job and I'll do mine."

Her curt attitude frustrated him. "This is different. You don't have any idea what you're getting yourself into. Or what you may be getting *me* into."

"Sorry, Brian. I hate to interrupt just when you're getting into your 'fatherly advice' mode but I've had enough. I hope you find what you're looking for out there in the jungle. If I need you I'll call Odette and you do the same. I love you." She disconnected.

Brian glanced at the battery life remaining - 60%. He clicked off the phone and gave it back to Lynne. She reached inside the flap of her pup tent and stuck it on top of her pack.

BILL THOMPSON

By dusk everyone had settled into tents for the night. The Belizean workers were exhausted and their snores added to the din of the jungle. Watchmen were assigned to shifts as usual.

Around midnight the person on watch quietly took Lynne's phone from her tent. A call was made – in whispered Spanish Tomas got a progress report and learned that they may have found Captain Jack's stairway. Tomas barked instructions and hung up. The entire call took one minute; the phone was quietly placed back into Lynne's tent as everyone slept soundly.

ANCIENT

CHAPTER SEVENTEEN

The man with the pencil mustache who called himself Tomas Rodriguez walked briskly through the lobby of the Westin Hotel in Guatemala City past a bar bustling with noisy tourists. He went directly to a bank of telephones in a quiet area behind the concierge desk.

He spoke in rapid Spanish. "I'm calling to give you a report, boss. They've found a temple but it's not the right one. They uncovered another stairway today but it's too early to tell if they're on to something. I'll hear more as things develop although cell phone service is not good up where they are. In the meantime what else should I do?"

Tomas listened for a moment. "I understand."

He used an international calling card for another call. This time he spoke in English.

"This is taking far longer than you said. Are you in contact with the expedition?" The answer angered him.

"That's not acceptable. You have a major problem, and you've made it my problem. Time is running out, my friend. This had better work – if these people are on a fruitless mission and return empty-handed things will be very bad for you. Do you understand? My people want this matter wrapped up in ten days. Ten days. No more excuses, no more stalling for time."

Tomas laughed as he left the building. This fool couldn't control the timing and Tomas knew more about what the expedition was doing than this guy did. Tomas merely wanted to keep him on his toes. A scared man is a submissive man. And this one was scared. That was certain.

About fifteen hundred miles east of Guatemala City, Arthur Borland's phone rang. Hands shaking, he reached in his pocket as the man across the table said, "I'm sorry Lord Borland, but you can't use your phone here. Just step away from the table and I'll hold your place."

When that call ended Arthur called Bijan Rarities in New York. Collette Conning answered.

"This is Arthur Borland. I was wondering if I could get an update on Brian. Have you heard anything lately?"

She told him what she knew and he said, "I'm glad to hear things are progressing there and I wish them well. I mentioned to Brian that my mother is ill and I'm afraid things have taken a turn for the worse. My wife and I are at her house, sitting with her day and night. I've just stepped out of her room to make this call. I fear her time is short. She's asking every day for news about my father so if you talk to Brian please let him know time is of the essence. If we can get some answer as to what happened to Captain Jack it will ease my mother's final days immensely."

Collette assured him she'd pass along the message.

ANCIENT

Far from his mother's home in England, Arthur strode back across an expansive room, the sounds of bells clanging and coins dropping into metal pans all around him. He took his seat at the table. With a smile the dealer said, "Just in time, Lord Borland. I've finished shuffling and we're starting a new hand."

A pit boss put a slip of paper in front of him and leaned close. In a whisper he said, "Just sign the marker, my Lord. We've worked everything out and increased your credit limit." The dealer then moved ten thousand dollars in black chips to Arthur's place at the table and said, "Better luck, sir."

BILL THOMPSON

ANCIENT

CHAPTER EIGHTEEN

When Nicole arrived at the office the next morning Ryan was waiting. "Mr. Carter would like to have a word with you."

She closed the door and called her boss. He told her he was moving her caseload to other attorneys so she could concentrate on John Spedino's defense. "This is a very important client and I want both your expertise and your full attention on his case."

"I can handle more than one case at a time," she snapped curtly.

"Of course you can, but for now I'm asking for full focus on this one. He'll be in your office at ten to get started."

She pushed for more information. "He's a different sort of client than Carter and Wells typically represents, correct? Hasn't he been compared time and again to John Gotti? Hasn't he been called the country's most notorious, high profile mobster? I know you personally made the decision to accept him as a client and that's your prerogative, but I just want to be sure we know we're representing a guy who's been accused of everything in the book, including murder."

Carter's voice was firm. "Accused, yes. Convicted only once and now that's been overturned. Trust me, Nicole. I know what I'm doing. I don't treat this firm's reputation lightly. Every American is entitled to the best attorney he can afford, John Spedino included."

Afterwards she struggled to understand what was going on. Spedino must be paying the firm an incredible fee because he absolutely wasn't their kind of client. She didn't know why Randall Carter was pushing so hard but she owed him a huge debt of gratitude. She also was in no position to question the senior partner in the firm.

Precisely at ten her assistant advised that Spedino was in the waiting area. Ryan ushered him in and she gestured to a couch. "Have a seat and let's talk."

As she pulled a chair closer Spedino said, "Why don't you sit on the couch by me? Sometimes I don't hear as well as I should and I don't want to miss anything." He patted the cushion and she moved over, legal pad and pen in hand.

He continued, "Before we get to business, tell me about your trip and the kidnapping. I think it's amazing how you escaped and it's fortunate you were rescued. Randall is a very resourceful man, I understand. It's good to have friends in high places."

"It sounds as though you already know my story."

"Not really. Randall told me bits and pieces but I asked him to leave the details to you. I'd rather hear the story first-hand."

She spent nearly an hour telling John Spedino what happened, beginning with her kidnapping at the cave entrance. She explained how she was held prisoner in a remote camp in the Maya Mountains of Guatemala and gave a vague description of her escape, omitting the detail about her killing the guard. She told him that Randall Carter had arranged her pickup in Melchor de Mencos just in time to avoid her being taken hostage again by the same man, who apparently had also kidnapped Brian and two others.

"Brian says he calls himself Tomas Rodriguez. Who knows if that's his real name?"

ANCIENT

"I may be able to assist Brian in his problems with this 'Tomas.' I too have friends in high places. Please write down every detail you can recall about this man, his mannerisms, dress, appearance, inflection of voice – everything, and I will make an inquiry."

"I don't know if that's what Brian would want me to do. But I do appreciate the offer."

"Nicole, you are going to be of immense help to me. I can feel it already. I can only hope to repay you in some way other than the enormous fees Randall has prepared me for. Let me do this small favor to help both you and Brian, two people whom I have come to admire."

She promised to think about it and then shifted the conversation to his earlier conviction for fraud. She took notes and studied his body language to see what kind of witness he would make on the stand in a courtroom. She caught herself wandering. *He's charming, polished, erudite – slim and trim, obviously exercises – but if you believe the stories, I'm sitting next to one of the most dangerous men on earth.*

At 12:30 she suggested they take a break. "May I buy your lunch?" he asked.

She declined, saying she needed the hour to catch up on calls. "I'll see you back here at 1:30."

Spedino spent the afternoon answering hundreds of questions as quickly as she tossed them out. He explained why the government might think he had an involvement with Bellicose Holdings but assured her that the evidence against him was purely circumstantial. He told her it was Francois Rochefort's testimony that had convicted him but that Rochefort was himself a convicted felon. As her boss had done, Spedino reminded her that he had often been charged with crimes but until now he had never been convicted of so much as a traffic ticket.

"So if there were another trial do you think the government would use Francois Rochefort as their star witness again?"

"I have no idea," Spedino replied evenly. "I hear the man has disappeared. Maybe he's in the Witness Protection Program – I wouldn't know about that – but if he has chosen to drop out of sight then perhaps he would not be a thorn in my side the next time." He forced a smile. "Sometimes things work out for the best."

His answer gave Nicole goosebumps.

She wrapped it up at six. She handed her assistant the pages of notes she'd taken, asking him to log everything into the computer for cross-referencing.

Spedino stood and stretched. "I know your boyfriend is deep in the jungle somewhere. To avoid having both of us spend dinner alone, would you join me? I'd enjoy very much getting to know you better."

Somewhere in her head alarms went off but she attributed her feelings to Brian's caution about Spedino. She was just stubborn enough to prove she knew how to handle herself, so she accepted.

"Where are you staying?"

"I'm at the Ritz-Carlton just down the street."

"What a coincidence. I live in the residences just around the corner."

He smiled. "I have found in life that there are few coincidences, Nicole. Do you have a car here in the building?"

Few coincidences? Did he stay at the Ritz so he could be near her? Surely that wasn't what he meant?

Let it go, she told herself. *Don't overanalyze.*

She said she was walking and he asked to join her. She agreed with the admonition, "I have to warn you that I'll have a security guard with me. That's Mr. Carter's way of ensuring I don't get snatched right off McKinney Avenue and whisked back to the jungle!"

She stopped at the hotel entrance and they agreed to meet in the bar an hour from now. Nicole and her escort walked around the corner to the Residences where he dropped her off.

As she walked into the Ritz-Carlton she saw John Spedino sitting on a couch sipping a martini.

ANCIENT

"Sorry I'm a little ahead of you," he said as she approached. "I made a couple of calls then decided to come on down. I was excited at the prospect of an evening with a lovely southern lady!"

She grinned self-consciously. *My God, I'm acting like a schoolgirl!*

"Come sit next to me." He scooted over and made room.

"I'll sit over here, Mr. Spedino. I think you can hear conversations just fine. I think you use that line to get close to women."

He laughed heartily and said, "I'm afraid you're right. It's one of my biggest weaknesses, beautiful women!"

When her Cosmopolitan was delivered they toasted, then he said, "I've been thinking about our discussion this afternoon. Not about me but about you and Brian. I'm certain I can help convince this Tomas Rodriguez to back off, and perhaps I can also find out for whom he is working. I can make Brian's problem - and yours - go away."

"How can you be certain? He's in Central America."

"I've developed a wide network of associates around the world in many years of business dealings. I'd like to make a few calls tomorrow to see what we can turn up but I want your OK first. I hope you don't think I'm interfering nor is this is a quid pro quo. It's enough for me that you will be representing me should the government foolishly decide to press on with this case. To be frank, money means nothing to me – I have been blessed with plenty. So I prefer to return favors by helping than by spending money.

"I would do anything to help a friend. I have always thought highly of Brian and now I think very highly of you as well. How good a friend would I be if I refused to help when I knew I could? And how good a friend would you be not to help Brian? You would do anything to protect him and I certainly understand that. I'm glad that I am able to assist you both."

"I'll think about it," she said at last. "You're very convincing, Mr. Spedino . . ."

"Since we're friends please call me John."

"John, I'm not sure Brian would want anyone else involved in this. I'll ask him next time we speak."

They finished a drink and she excused herself to use the restroom. Spedino ordered another round, moved her drink close to him for a few seconds and passed his hand over it. Then he replaced it on her side of the table.

Returning to the table, she saw the second round. "I'm not much of a drinker, especially two Cosmos. Usually I switch to wine, especially if I skipped lunch like today." She sipped the drink slowly.

"I'm happy to order you something else if you want but remember that your condo is just around the corner. If worst comes to worst I'll make sure you get home safely."

Assuring him she was fine, she lifted her Cosmopolitan and took another drink. "I have a question, John. A couple of years ago when you first went to prison, a man approached Brian and me one day when we were at lunch in London and said you wanted a million dollars for a cheap imitation of the Declaration of Independence. The document was a cheap imitation but the man said David Cardone had sent him on your behalf. What was that all about?"

"I heard about that myself. That was Cardone's way of trying to harm my reputation with Brian. He took over some of my business interests when I went to prison, as you may have heard. He had been my friend but once I was imprisoned he changed. He took control of many things that were far beyond our agreement and I am still trying to straighten things out. Suffice it to say that David Cardone has harmed me greatly. Paybacks come when one least expects them.

"As I said earlier, I have plenty of money. I had no need to press Brian to give me a million dollars. After all, the Bethlehem Scroll ended up exactly where I wanted it."

ANCIENT

She felt an unusual sense of euphoria as she listened to him. "So Cardone's not the big bad godfather he thinks he is," she said, flashing a huge giddy grin.

That was a strange thing to say, she thought hazily.

"No, Nicole. I am."

Did he just say that? She sipped her drink as her brain struggled to process what he was saying. She was getting mellower by the minute, enthralled by this charming man. She knew she was half his age but decided a man like Spedino probably would have no issues in the sex department.

What? What am I thinking?

He smiled and patted the seat next to him. "It's time to sit on this side." She smiled back, came around and sat very close to him - closer than she had intended. She suddenly felt very comfortable in his presence.

He asked, "Do you want a third drink or should we go to dinner?"

She spoke lazily, finding it hard to put her thoughts into words. "I think a third drink would be dangerous at this point. Want to go to my place? I could make us a nice quiet dinner."

What? What did I just say?

"Oh sorry. I didn't mean to say that. Where did that come from?" She stumbled with the words but he patted her knee reassuringly. She looked down; his hand was higher on her thigh now but suddenly it wasn't a problem.

"If you're not in the mood to spend time in a restaurant then I'd be happy to see you home safely. And if you'd like to eat at home that sounds wonderful to me. Whatever works for you."

She held his arm tightly as they walked to the residences. The doorman was away from his post so she unsuccessfully tried twice to enter an access code. Finally she told the godfather the number. He entered it, held the door and helped her into the elevator. Her head was in a fog as the car ascended and she fumbled in her purse trying to find her key.

277

BILL THOMPSON

"Wow, those drinks really hit me. I guess I should have gone to lunch with you after all and gotten something on my stomach."

She handed her purse to him; he pulled out her key and opened the door. Inside, he walked to her expansive windows and said, "What a spectacle. Dallas at night. I think this city has one of the most wonderful skylines of any in America. The architecture is unbelievable."

Nicole didn't hear him – he turned and saw she was no longer in the room. He walked to the door of her bedroom and saw her clothes thrown on the floor. In the half-light she lay sprawled on the bed in her bra and panties. He sat on the bed next to her, running his hand up and down her leg, higher and higher.

"Umm, Brian," she mumbled. "Get undressed and get my panties off." Her eyes were closed and she had a small smile on her face.

John Spedino took his time. He took a video recorder from his jacket pocket. He hung his jacket and trousers carefully in her closet and removed his shirt, t-shirt and boxers. His socks were last. He walked to her bed, set the small device on her nightstand, turned it on and said, "Nicole, I want to help Brian by finding out everything I can about this Tomas Rodriguez. Tell me that's fine with you."

"Yep," she murmured. "Thass fine with me."

"Now roll over."

She obeyed and he unfastened her bra. She rolled back over and said, "Brian, pull down my panties. I want you . . . inside me." Her words came slowly and her eyes stayed closed.

"I want you to say *my* name, Nicole. I want you to tell John Spedino to get inside of you."

She mumbled, "John Spedino, take off my panties. Get on top. I want you inside of me." He removed her underwear and sat next to her on the bed, running his hands up and down her flawless body, missing nothing. He filmed her as she lazily moved her hand to his manhood, wrapping her fingers around it.

ANCIENT

"Wow, somebody's BIG!" she murmured, half asleep. She spread her legs wide apart. "Kiss me all over," she whispered.

An hour later he made sure Nicole was sound asleep, retrieved the recorder, dressed and let himself out of her condo. He took the elevator down and walked around the corner to the hotel. He had a glass of wine in the bar then went upstairs to bed. After he checked the video he turned off the nightstand lamp. He had everything he needed.

BILL THOMPSON

ANCIENT

CHAPTER NINETEEN

Nicole awoke with sunlight streaming into the windows of her bedroom. She squinted at the light then winced as she felt what seemed like little hammers beating inside her head. She glanced at the clock. It was 8:25!

My God, I have to be at the office in thirty minutes!

When she stood up she felt dizzy and nauseated. She saw last night's clothes tossed all over the floor.

What the hell happened?

She remembered going to the bathroom at the hotel, coming back to a second Cosmo and then things began to fade.

How did I get back to my house? What's going on with me?

She took two aspirins, stood in a hot shower then called the security guard who was to meet her downstairs, telling him she would be a half hour late. She called Ryan and told him to make John Spedino comfortable until she got there. Then she tried to retrace events to figure out what happened last night. She couldn't show up at the office and ask her client how she got home. That would be ridiculously immature, like the morning after a college frat party.

Part of me wants to think I got drunk because I hadn't eaten anything. Another part of me is getting really nervous about what else might have happened.

BILL THOMPSON

Brian warned me about John Spedino. But surely he had nothing to do with this incredible hangover!

An hour earlier, Spedino sat in his room at the Ritz-Carlton and made a brief phone call, initiating a search for information about Tomas Rodriguez. Then he had a light breakfast downstairs and walked to Nicole's building. Ryan put him in her office and gave him coffee.

Twenty minutes later Nicole and the security guard walked in. Her head throbbed but she tried to ignore it.

"Good morning, John. Sorry I'm late."

"Good morning. I trust you slept well."

"Yes, thanks. And thanks for the evening. I'm afraid I may owe you an apology – I know we planned dinner but I don't think I was very good company."

"On the contrary. Think nothing of it! I assure you I enjoyed your company immensely. And hopefully you enjoyed mine as well. You seemed to be having a good time." He smiled broadly and she wondered exactly what he meant.

Drop it, she said to herself. "OK then. Let's get down to business."

ANCIENT

CHAPTER TWENTY

As the sun rose in the Guatemalan rain forest six adventurers crawled out of their tents with a heightened sense of enthusiasm. Even the two normally stolid Belizean workers were smiling and talking quietly.

"They're excited to see what lies up the staircase," Lynne said.

Brian was surprised. "I didn't realize you spoke Spanish. I know you translated that ancient Spanish document, but you're a linguist too? My what talents you have."

"Why thank you, sir. If you're going to spend time in Central America it's good to know Spanish. I'm pretty fluent - I can handle a conversation if I have to."

Brian looked at Sam. "How about you? How much Spanish have you picked up in all your years in Belize?"

"I'm like Lynne. I know enough to talk to the people who work for me at the hotel and to get by. I can speak and understand it pretty well. Odette can too – it's just something that comes with spending time down here."

Since Lynne knew what they were looking for, she asked Alfredo to cut a swath up the stairway. "It might take a few days but the opening has to be big enough for us to easily walk through. Tell them to take their time and don't push it. It's hotter than hell in there and we don't want anyone getting sick from heat prostration."

The process took two days; the men stopped every couple of hours for a smoke and lots of water. Since there were no extra machetes Lynne and the guys couldn't help, so they stayed at the campsite killing time while they waited expectantly.

At five Lynne handed the phone to Sam. Brian said, "Can I see that a sec?"

Sam passed the phone to Brian – he saw the battery was at 52%. Only two nights ago it had been at sixty. Furrowing his brow, Brian handed it back.

"What's up?"

"I don't know. This is weird. I know you took pictures the other day and I accounted for that. Your phone is losing power faster than it should be assuming it's turned completely off between the calls we make."

"It is. Maybe it's just the iPhone. They're quirky."

"Yeah, maybe it is." He listened as Sam tried the call once, then again.

"No signal. I guess we're lucky this is the first time that's happened."

"It goes in and out," Lynne reminded him. "Try it again in ten minutes."

This time it worked. He spoke briefly, disconnected and handed the phone to Brian.

"Collette asked that you call."

His assistant passed along Arthur's report that his mother was dying. "He sounded so despondent. Please let me know as soon as you find out anything – you may be his only hope."

Brian discussed Arthur's call with the others and decided it would be heartless to get anyone's hopes up until they had something concrete to report.

Before he handed it back, he glanced at the screen. "Fifty percent battery. Hope our trip ends before the phone dies."

ANCIENT

Immediately after dinner the exhausted workers went to bed. Lynne and the guys took the watch duties to allow the Belizeans a night off.

The next morning Lynne took Alfredo into the jungle down the newly cut trail. She climbed the stairway and they measured.

"Eighty feet," he called up to her.

Back at camp Lynne gave the workers a pep talk. She figured the top wasn't far away. "Let's keep the same steady effort today and maybe we can find what we need." The men went to work.

Within an hour Alfredo came back with good news. "We are above the trees now. At this height the staircase is covered in grass and low vegetation but you can see upwards because the treetops are below us."

The three excitedly snaked through the vine-covered tunnel up nearly ninety feet. Toward the top they popped out into bright sunlight and saw the two workmen sitting about ten feet above them on the stairs, smiling broadly.

"Esta es la parte superior," one said as he patted the ground next to him.

Lynne let out a war whoop. "They're sitting on the top!"

Like before, the mountains towered majestically around them. The platform where they stood was covered in grass and waist-high vegetation, nothing like the dense growth they'd come through. Below them a mass of green jungle extended for a hundred miles in every direction.

"This is more like it," Lynne murmured. "Guys, this isn't a temple. It's the plaza at the top of a stairway that the Mayans cut into the side of this mountain. So far everything matches the description in the letter."

Brian pointed to his right. "Look at that!" A hundred feet away a crevice cut into the side of a mountain.

The aperture was wide enough for only one person at a time to pass through and It was full of scrub brush. As the workers cleared it, Lynne complained, "I feel like a kid at Christmas when someone else is getting to open presents and I have to wait. I want to see what's on the other side!" They all agreed it was hard to be patient even for only fifteen minutes.

When the workers came out they were smiling broadly as though they had a secret. Lynne and the others scrambled through. The passage was only thirty feet long; it opened onto a broad flat expanse of grass ringed by ten thousand foot mountains. They stopped in their tracks and looked at what stood in front of them. There was an ancient stone building with a dark doorway in its middle and statues on either side depicting enormous crouching jaguars.

"Those are the protectors," Lynne said reverently. "The Mayans put them here. We've found it."

ANCIENT

CHAPTER TWENTY-ONE

By mid-afternoon Nicole was struggling. Her head nodded occasionally as she vainly tried to make notes of their discussion.

Finally Spedino said, "Let's stop for today. You seem tired. I was hoping you might join me for dinner this evening and if you feel up to it I would enjoy that very much."

"I apologize for this afternoon. I guess I didn't sleep as well last night as I thought. Thanks but no, tonight I'm going to stay in so I'll be ready for our meeting tomorrow. We only have a couple of days left before you leave, right?"

"Yes. I'm going back to New York on Sunday so we only have tomorrow and Saturday. I don't mind working on the weekend if you don't."

She assured him weekends were part of the routine. After agreeing to start at nine tomorrow, she showed Spedino out, shut the door and collapsed into her chair. She was physically drained and mentally exhausted. And it was only three o'clock. Still clueless about last night, she packed her notes into a briefcase and buzzed Ryan to call the security guard to accompany her home, saying she wasn't feeling well.

When Spedino arrived at the Ritz-Carlton the message light was blinking on the phone in his room. His life would have been much simpler had he chosen to use cell phones like everyone else did, but

BILL THOMPSON

John Spedino didn't trust the technology. He knew it was possible to intercept calls, to see numbers called and received and to record conversations. His calls were sensitive to say the least, and he decided long ago that he'd stick with landline phones.

He listened to the message then pulled a small PDA from his pocket. Every entry in the device was encoded and he quickly scrolled to the information he needed, picked up the hotel phone and placed a call to Guatemala.

"You know who this is. I will be there on Sunday afternoon. I want to talk to Jorge Arocha face to face. Arrange it for someplace quiet – you know what I mean? You never know how this meeting might end." He listened a moment and replied sharply, "I don't care what it takes. I don't care how important he thinks he is. *I* decide when we meet. And you will make sure he's there." He hung up.

He arranged for his Gulfstream G350 to depart Love Field at 9:30 Sunday morning then called his limo driver. Before five he was sipping a dry martini at Al Biernat's Steakhouse. The unique bar there was one of his favorites when he was in Dallas and Al knew him by name. Never mind that Al had a reputation for knowing *everyone* by name. It suited Spedino just fine.

By the time Randall Carter arrived John was on his second drink.

"How'd it go?" Carter asked. "Did Nicole grill you until you couldn't take any more?"

"We stopped early today. I think she had a bug and she wasn't feeling well. I'm sure tomorrow morning she'll be back in good form. Let's get down to business." He dropped his voice to a whisper. "How's my mortgage brokerage operation going? Are we still making money?"

"It is indeed," Carter responded quietly. "The nominee shareholders in Antigua are holding regular board meetings and I've attended every one on behalf of the Panama trust which owns the company's shares. You should have received last month's financials by now – have you been getting them every month?"

Spedino affirmed that he had.

Carter continued. "The company is really growing, John. In fact I worry about how big it is. I know you wanted it set up as an offshore corporation but I have to advise you again that the avoidance of U.S. taxes is one thing – that's a good business practice. The *evasion* of taxes is another thing entirely. This company has U.S. owners. You know it and I know it too. As I told you when we set it up, you need to file a U.S. income tax return."

Spedino smiled and patted his attorney on the arm. "John, I'll never presume to tell you how to practice law. You run your business and I'll run mine."

The topic of conversation turned to football as the two men were seated at their table for dinner and a fine bottle of Bordeaux wine.

BILL THOMPSON

ANCIENT

CHAPTER TWENTY-TWO

By the time they wrapped things up on Saturday Nicole felt comfortable that his case was under control. She had probed into his past, knowing there were parts he had chosen to gloss over. There had been others where he frankly admitted strong-arming his way into or out of this deal or that.

"I've done things of which I'm not proud," he said to her at one point. "I'm sure we all have. But I have beaten the Feds over and over. This trumped-up fraud charge is a figment of the imagination of Francois Rochefort, a man whose criminal record is well documented. As usual, the government has cast a wide net and caught the wrong fish. They have no evidence other than a felon's testimony. With you as my counsel, I'll be fine."

She walked him to the elevator and he asked if she'd like company on her walk back to the Ritz-Carlton.

"No thanks. I'm staying a while longer to get my notes ready for Ryan to compile on Monday."

"I'd appreciate it if you'd ride to the airport with me tomorrow, Nicole. I'm leaving early - I have something to show you and I promise I'll have the driver drop you back home in plenty of time to have the rest of your Sunday to yourself."

That was a simple request. Why not?
"Sure. I'll be happy to do that."

BILL THOMPSON

At eight-thirty Sunday morning the sedan swung into the driveway of Nicole's building. She slipped into the back seat next to John.

"You look wonderful," he said, admiring her white sleeveless blouse and shorts. "It's a short ride. We're only going to Love Field."

She was surprised, since that was the smaller of the Dallas airports.

"Since you're going to New York I figured we were headed to DFW."

"I am going there but I'm flying private today. I'm leaving from the business jet terminal. And I must confess that I had an ulterior motive for asking you to come along today."

She looked at him quizzically as he continued. "Your reputation is unmatched and I've come to respect your work very much in the few days I've been with you. I want to retain you not only to be my primary attorney but also I want to hire you. I want you to be my consigliere, my confidential advisor and counselor from now on in virtually every aspect of what I do. You would continue your blossoming career with Randall Carter's firm and you would of course represent other clients but my work would be the primary focus of your time. I think you have a brilliant mind and I want you on my team."

Her skin grew suddenly clammy and cold. *Holy shit. What's this all about?*

"John, I'm flattered that a person of your stature and business acumen would even consider me for such a position. But I'm quite happy doing what I do and I'm not qualified to serve as an advisor to a corporate kingpin like you. Although I appreciate your interest in me, I have to pass. I don't think Randall Carter would allow me to split my time; he's got big plans for me and so do I, frankly!" She laughed a little more nervously than she would have liked.

"Don't sell yourself short. I can teach you everything you need to know. I can be a really persuasive man, Nicole. You'll earn at least half a million dollars a year more than you do now, tax free and well insulated from the U.S. government if you'd like it that way. You'll see places and do things you have only imagined. And leave Randall Carter to me. I guarantee he will be very satisfied with this arrangement. It will be profitable for him as well as you. That will not be an issue."

She laughed. "I'm certain any person acting as consigliere to you would experience a world unlike the mundane one the rest of us live in. But really, I'm happy doing what I do. Thank you so much for the offer but I have to decline."

His voice turned hard and she instinctively leaned away. "You force me to play all my cards. I had hoped to convince you on my own that my offer was something you would enjoy." He pulled a small black device from his inside jacket pocket, turned it on and handed it to her.

Shivers of fear coursed through her body as she looked at the screen, seeing herself lying on her bed in her underwear. "John Spedino, take off my panties. Get on top. I want you inside of me." She saw herself doing things to him of which she had absolutely no recollection - things only she and Brian had ever done together.

She screamed, "You damned bastard! You drugged me! My God, I should have listened to Brian. You're totally evil. Are you crazy? You can't get away with this!"

"Please don't be naïve. Please don't tell me you've never had a fling before – a one-night stand. It meant nothing. To anyone but Brian, that is. And I don't intend for another soul to ever see this recording. It was just my way of creating a lasting memory of a beautiful girl who was willing to perform for me.

"Now I'm going to ask you once again to reconsider my proposal. This tape is one thing if it's just between you and me. To the outside world, on the other hand, it shows a woman who lacks good judgment, one who can be compromised. In short, it could suddenly and completely end the career of one of the top legal minds in Dallas. That would be both unfortunate and unnecessary."

"What . . . what do you want?" she said in a small voice. "Why do you want to hurt me?"

"I have no desire to hurt you. In fact I want you and Brian to continue to be the two closest lovebirds in the world. Frankly, his career is more interesting to me than yours because of what I want. You see, I want *everything*. The harder something is to have, the more I seem to want it. It's a personality flaw, I suppose." He laughed the cruel laugh she'd heard before.

"Remember the Bethlehem Scroll? That was the most important artifact in the entire world. I had to have it. And then I wanted you. Look how well that worked out. From now on, you'll do whatever I ask. Anything. You'll do whatever I want. Won't you?"

The driver lowered the partition between the front and back seats as the car slowed. "We're at the hangar, Mr. Spedino."

"Fine. Pull inside and park until I'm ready. Now raise the partition. Miss Farber and I have a little last minute work to do." He looked at her. "Your first job, consigliere, is to handle a little problem I have, right here. As he began to unbuckle his belt a tear trickled down her cheek.

ANCIENT

CHAPTER TWENTY-THREE

The $30 million jet streaked through the morning skies. Instead of flying north toward New York the pilot followed the flight plan he had filed yesterday. Heading south at nearly 550 miles per hour, the plane was over the Gulf of Mexico in thirty minutes and would land at La Aurora Airport in Guatemala City in just over two hours.

Shoes kicked off, Spedino was comfortably settled in his seat reading the Sunday New York Times and sipping a cup of coffee. Although the jet could seat sixteen this one had been configured with only six passenger seats, a galley and seating area for a hostess, a restroom and an aft bedroom and master bath complete with shower. John Spedino could go anywhere he wanted, anytime he chose.

The attendant who sat in the galley read a book until she saw a small light come on. She walked to her sole passenger and said, "May I get you something, Mr. Spedino?"

"What do we have for breakfast?"

"We have cereal and fruit or I can whip up an omelet with ham, sir. Which would you like?"

He chose the fruit and settled back. Life was good and it was soon going to get even better. He needed to find out exactly what was going on with Jorge Arocha and why he chose the course of action he did. Spedino would leave Guatemala with the information he wanted. He always got what he was after.

Half an hour out the co-pilot stepped into the cabin and told his passenger they would be landing soon. They taxied to Athos Charters and the pilot disembarked. Soon a customs man walked with the pilot to the aircraft, glanced inside and said, "Mr. Spedino, welcome to Guatemala. You're cleared to disembark, sir."

The pilot escorted him to an armored SUV nearby. Within thirty minutes the vehicle pulled into an industrial area in central Guatemala City. "I was told to drop you here," the driver said in broken English. In flawless Spanish Spedino replied, "Wait here until I return. I don't know how long it will be."

He walked through a metal door in a large building. A dark, empty warehouse loomed before him, half a city block long and equally as wide. Standing just inside was a swarthy man who said, "Buenos tardes, Senor Spedino."

"Rafael. Good to see you again." They walked to an office on the far side of the building, its lights blazing through an open doorway. Sitting behind a desk was a swarthy man dressed in fatigues flanked by a pair of bodyguards.

The man behind the desk stood and extented his hand. "John, welcome to my country. To what do I owe the great honor of your visit?"

Spedino ignored the outstretched hand. "Jorge, I would enjoy the pleasantries of a conversation with you but my time is very valuable and I know yours is as well. So let's get to business. A few months ago I did you a favor. You called me and told me you had a man who owed you money – a great deal of money. His only means of payment was to find some gold sheets that the Maya had hidden hundreds of years ago. It was a crazy story, you must admit."

"Of course, but when people become enamored with the products I sell they often end up in big trouble. The crazy tales sometimes are true. I checked out Arthur Borland meticulously. You know

ANCIENT

me. I do nothing halfway. His father was lost while searching in this country for the very gold that may save Arthur from becoming lost as well. Even now as we speak Arthur is making things worse and worse for himself. He is a sick man." Jorge Arocha grinned maliciously.

"Sick because of the drugs your people sold him."

"No one forced him. You used to dabble in that business as well. Forgive me if I retain my peasant background and rely on the coca leaves for my income. I know you have become much more civilized. Look at you. A big businessman." His lips curled into a mocking smile.

Spedino's jaw tightened but his voice remained completely calm. "When you called me I gave you the name of a man – Brian Sadler – whom I thought might be able to help Arthur Borland find his gold. I was doing you a favor, Jorge. Brian Sadler is important to me. He is an antiquities dealer from New York and he is on an expedition at this very moment. But he has encountered many problems since I gave you his name. A man impersonating him in New York attacked a worker at his gallery. Then his lady friend was kidnapped and held prisoner in the jungle. Finally a man called Tomas Rodriguez took Brian and his party hostage. I'm here to find out what this is all about. Tell me right now exactly what you think you're doing."

"Ah John, you Americans are so adept at skipping the formalities which are important in another country and so eager to impose your abrupt behavior on everyone else." The man again smiled broadly but without feeling. "You should always be polite. Would you care for a cup of coffee?"

John Spedino looked him in the eyes. "I didn't come here for a lesson in etiquette. I asked you a question. Answer me. Now."

The Guatemalan's eyes turned hard and steely. "Oh, you want an answer, do you, Mr. Important Man. Well here is your answer. I have no idea what you're talking about, *cabron*. Get out of here. Who the hell do you think you are speaking to me in that tone of voice?"

"You call me a *cabron*? A *bastard*? You have one minute to live unless you start talking." Spedino gave a brief nod to Rafael, the man who had met him inside the building, and a .45 automatic appeared in the man's hand. The guards behind Arocha reached inside their coats but Spedino said in Spanish, "No, gentlemen." The men withdrew their hands and held their arms at their sides.

"John, John," Jorge Arocha said confidently, "I hope you aren't offended. I became upset with your harsh behavior because I am accustomed to our Latin way of doing things. Forgive me if I've misspoken." His cold eyes belied his kind words.

"I want answers. Who is this man Tomas Rodriguez?"

"I don't know that name."

"What name do you know him by? I have much at stake in this situation. I won't tolerate you much longer."

Unaccustomed to being spoken to in such a manner, the Guatemalan drug lord became livid. He stood and raised his voice. "You think you can scare me, John? You think YOU are the godfather here? No. You are in *my* country. *I* call the shot

Spedino said calmly, "Although it is too late for you to learn, I am going to give you a lesson anyway. I am the godfather here. I am the godfather *everywhere.* And you knew that until you decided you were smarter than I am. But you must be wary. You must trust no one. You should always respect your superiors for they can wield unbelievable power over you in seconds. Now, men." Spedino nodded to the goons standing on either side of Arocha and they grabbed his arms, pushing him down into his chair.

"Your men work for me, Jorge. They always have. You are nothing, you son of a farmer. You stupid man – you're no better and no smarter than a cocaine addict standing on a street corner in Harlem. And you want to challenge *me?* Now you will talk.

ANCIENT

You will tell me everything I ask you or I will kill you myself. Do you understand?" John Spedino stood two feet from Jorge's face, seething with fury.

For the first time today, fear overwhelmed the Guatemalan. "Yes. I understand," he said, his voice meek now.

"Why did you have Brian Sadler's associate beaten at his gallery?"

"Arthur Borland promised to give us two gold sheets as partial payment for the drug and gambling debts he owed. Instead he handed them over to Brian Sadler. We anticipated the possibility of a problem so I had hired a man who bore a striking resemblance to Sadler. I had Sadler followed from his club but everything happened too quickly. Sadler's double arrived after the associate had locked the gold into a vault. She wouldn't open the safe so he beat her but still she refused."

"Why didn't you just take Borland himself?"

"Because Borland was the key to finding the rest of the gold that his father had searched for in Guatemala many times before. This time it appeared the stories might really be true. He had tried and failed once. I checked out Brian Sadler myself. For a novice he has had great success and is a well-known personality. He had the means and the brains to find it if anyone could. I thought if I kidnapped Arthur Borland then Brian wouldn't go into the jungle. He needed to believe everything was fine."

"And why on earth, Jorge, did you kidnap Nicole Farber?"

He shouted, "I didn't kidnap her! You must believe me. I used an associate of mine, Enrique Costa. I told him to do whatever he needed to motivate Sadler to find the gold quickly. I gave him free rein and that is what he chose to do."

"So Enrique Costa is Tomas Rodriguez – the kidnapper of both Nicole and Brian."

"Yes, yes. That's him. And by the way you may think you know that woman, but she's crazy. Did you know she killed one of my men during her escape?"

Spedino laughed harshly. "I'm not surprised. She's a spunky woman. And yes, I know that woman. I know her very well." His face turned hard again. "Tell me the rest."

"Enrique has worked for me for many years. He is one of my top people in Guatemala. He took Brian, a Belizean guide and Brian's friend, the hotel owner from San Ignacio, to a remote camp in the mountains and sent them off to find the lost city of the Mayas. They say there are books there, codices of the Maya, John. It could be a discovery worth millions without even taking into account the gold that is also supposed to be hidden there. Brian will do whatever Enrique says – he thinks Nicole is still held captive. And Enrique gets regular reports from one of the people on the expedition. The latest news is that they may have discovered the Temple of the Sanctuary, the one Captain Jack was searching for."

"You are an incredible fool if you underestimate Brian Sadler. I am certain he knows by now that Nicole is no longer a hostage. Where is Arthur Borland now?"

"He's at the Cardinale Casino on the island of Bonaire. A friend of mine manages the place and I've instructed him to give Borland everything it takes for him to remain quiet and happy. So far he has purchased a lot of cocaine and lost nearly $200,000. But his credit remains good so long as I guarantee it."

"Now I am going to give you your reward for being honest with me." Spedino looked at the others in the room. "Rafael, take these two men outside and wait until I come out. Senor Arocha and I are going to have a little talk."

Shortly Spedino came out and said to Rafael, "I'm finished with him. Take care of it."

Tomas Rodriguez, whose real name was Enrique Costa, stood under the portico outside the Westin Hotel in Guatemala City. He was following instructions texted earlier by his boss, Jorge Arocha. His eyes searched arriving vehicles until he spotted the armored SUV he was looking for. The driver hopped out and opened the back door for Costa. It was dark and hard to see as he climbed inside. He said, "Godfather Jorge, what's this all about?"

"It's not Jorge," John Spedino said tersely. "Close the door."

Enrique was afraid. He had never been in the presence of John Spedino before but knew exactly who the man was. There was also another man riding in the passenger seat up front, a man he didn't recognize.

"Ah, Godfather," Costa said, his eyes showing his fear. He bowed his head. "What a pleasant surprise."

Spedino turned to the driver and said, "Go." Then he raised a privacy partition between him and the driver.

"First things first. Jorge Arocha is not the godfather. Why do you use that title to address him?"

"Because he insists upon it, Godfather. He is my boss – my jefe. I must respect him."

Spedino's voice rose. "You know who is the Godfather. Say it!"

"You are the Godfather, Senor Spedino." He lowered his eyes.

"Your boss left on a trip today. A very long trip. You will see him again before long, I'm sure. When you arrive in hell."

Costa shuddered and put his head in his hands. "I am your servant, Godfather. I will do everything you ask."

"That is correct. You *will* do everything I ask. Tell me what you know about Brian Sadler and Nicole Farber. I want to hear everything. I want to know exactly what you were told to do with each of them and why."

"Jorge told me to hold Nicole secure so that Senor Sadler would do his bidding. I suppose you know that the English lord is the one who's behind this all. He owes Jorge a lot of money and Jorge was determined to get it back any way he could."

Costa told Spedino that he and an associate captured Nicole and later Sadler and his friends.

Spedino asked the name of Costa's associate. Committing it to memory, he continued his questions.

"So Jorge told you to kidnap Nicole, strip her naked, tie her to a table in the jungle and leave some illiterate fools to guard her from whatever could have befallen her?"

"Ah, sir, not exactly. He said that I should do whatever I thought best. I was trying to ensure her cooperation and that of Senor Sadler as well."

"But it didn't work, did it? Despite all that effort she got away and killed one of Jorge's men when she escaped. Then you tried to capture her again at the border. Is that correct?"

"Yes, Senor, but she had . . ."

"Enough excuses!" Spedino shouted. "You sent Brian Sadler and five other people to the top of a mountain and you didn't even have enough common sense to go with them. Instead you left and came back to the comforts of city life. Are you an idiot? Any one of those people on the expedition, even the workmen from Belize, is smarter than you are, 'Tomas Rodriguez'."

"But Godfather, I am receiving regular reports by phone from one of the expedition members."

"And who is that?"

Costa told him.

"And why do you believe any information you learn will be correct?"

"Because I have promised that my source will reap rich rewards if the group finds Jack Borland's Ancient Library and the gold sheets."

John Spedino asked questions for ten more minutes and Costa answered every one. He told Spedino everything he knew about the expedition, its members and about Arthur Borland.

Spedino lowered the partition and told the driver to stop the SUV. He barked instructions to Rafael, who'd been riding in the passenger seat. Rafael frisked Enrique, finding a handgun and a cell phone in his jacket pocket. Spedino took both and told Rafael to wait outside the vehicle. Spedino raised the privacy barrier and said, "I wanted us to be able to talk alone, without Rafael hearing our conversation. Now that we've covered all the serious talk, I want to know something. Tell me more about this girl – this Nicole Farber. What does she look like? I hear she's really beautiful."

"Oh, Godfather, she is a beauty, a rarity in fact. Blonde, blue eyes, an ideal American woman."

"You saw her naked in the jungle, I presume. Is her body beautiful as well? Does she have perfect breasts?"

Enrique relaxed. This was going well. The old man just wanted to be titillated by stories of the naked girl.

"Yes, Godfather. I saw her naked every day. I saw every inch of her body. She is perfect, that is certain. And her breasts, they are like melons – round and ripe. She is very tan, even on her breasts. I think she must tan naked as rich American ladies sometimes do. I wanted to touch her but you know, I decided against that. But that woman - she could arouse any man for sure."

"You included?"

"Of course. I am just a man, after all! I wanted to do far more than touch her, if you know what I mean. But I restrained myself!" He grinned. "I can do more than tell you, Godfather. See for yourself!"

Tomas pointed to his phone. The Godfather handed it over and the man thumbed through to the picture of Nicole tied naked to the table. He grinned as he passed the phone back to Spedino.

The old man will really like this!

He looked at the picture impassively. "Did your men get a good look also? Did they get to see her spread out like this? And did you let them touch her?"

"Oh yes. And I gave strict instructions that they could look all they wanted but not to touch!"

"And when you left each evening how did you ensure that order was obeyed, Senor Costa?" The godfather smiled at him.

"I could only hope they could restrain themselves as I had done," Costa laughed, even more confident as the Godfather became engrossed in the story.

Spedino suddenly snarled, "You are a fool, Enrique. Do you know who Nicole Farber is? She is my consigliere. Do you know what that means?"

"Yes, sir," he stammered. "Yes . . . she is your second-in-command, your confidante, your advisor. I didn't know she was your consigliere, Godfather. You must believe me."

"Of course I believe you, 'Tomas Rodriguez.' I named Nicole Farber my consigliere only a day ago. If she had been my consigliere before you kidnapped her I doubt you and I would be having this conversation. Do you know what I mean?"

"Yes . . . yes, Godfather. I apologize if I offended you, sir."

"You didn't offend me, Enrique. You shamed one of my friends. You cast your lecherous eyes on the body of Nicole Farber. You allowed yourself to lust after her. Now first I want you to tell me how you and your contact on the expedition communicate by phone. Do you call or does that person? How exactly does it work?"

John Spedino learned everything he needed to know. They drove silently back to the airport. Spedino got out and told Rafael what to do next. Rafael's eyes widened slightly as he heard what was planned for Enrique Costa but he averted them. The Godfather didn't need to see his alarm. Twenty minutes later his bound prisoner was in the cargo area of the SUV and Rafael himself was driving away from Guatemala City.

Within six hours the mining camp in the Montanas Mayas was active once again. Since Nicole Farber's escape it had been deserted but now there was a new prisoner.

Enrique Costa, the man who called himself Tomas Rodriguez, was stripped naked and tied firmly to the four corners of the metal table, the very place where Nicole herself had been spread-eagled by

ANCIENT

Enrique. Rafael carefully repaired the corner post that Nicole had broken, affixing it to the table with wire. It was very secure. He was certain that there would be no escaping this table a second time.

Taking his time, Rafael removed the netting that still hung over the table. It had protected Nicole from animals or bugs that might fall through the roof hole or the open windows. There was no need for that protection any more.

Rafael put no grease on the legs. That precaution had been taken to ensure small insects or even snakes couldn't make their way up to the tabletop and get to the prisoner. The Godfather had told Rafael to skip that step.

"Well, Enrique," Rafael said at last, "it is time for me to go. It will be dark soon. I trust you will have a good evening. I will not be back and no one will come to let you loose, so if you can free yourself it would probably be a good thing to do quickly. Oh yes, there's one more thing I was told to do before I left."

Rafael walked to the doorway where he had dropped a sack on the way in. He opened it and set a bottle on the table next to Enrique.

Enrique began to moan. "Oh God, no! You can't do this. For the love of God, Rafael. No!"

"You must have really made Mr. Spedino angry, Enrique. That was not smart of you." He unscrewed the lid of a jar of honey and poured the thick liquid liberally over Enrique's genitals. "This is for your lust. Now you had better close your eyes. This will be sticky." He took his finger, dipped it in the honey and smeared the gooey substance over Costa's closed eyelids. "That is for watching the girl. Goodbye, Enrique. I hope a jaguar happens to come by and kill you. That would be better, I think, than the insects eating you alive." He turned and left the room. The prisoner lay on the table fighting mightily against the tight ropes that bound his hands and feet. Nothing worked. He prayed for a merciful quick death. That would also not happen.

BILL THOMPSON

By late afternoon the Gulfstream was winging its way eastward. John Spedino had a light lunch then retired to the bedroom. It was a three-hour flight and he wanted to be in top form when he arrived so he decided to take a short nap. He hung his clothes neatly in the closet and lay on the bed in his shorts and t-shirt. Before he slept he looked at Enrique Costa's phone. He saw a text message that had been sent from Lynne Parker's phone the night before. It said, "We found the temple. Captain Jack's wife is dying."

He put off his nap for another twenty minutes. There was a call he needed to make; once that was done he drifted into the slumber of a man with few cares.

ANCIENT

CHAPTER TWENTY-FOUR

The excitement was palpable as the group moved through the crouching jaguar statues into the first room of the Temple of the Sanctuary. Every wall of the room was lined with shelves reaching about eight feet from floor to ceiling. Every shelf was empty - a layer of dust several inches thick lay both on the shelves and on the floor in front of them. "Sadly, that dust is the remains of codices that have disintegrated in this humidity," Lynne observed. "It's sad to see but I really didn't expect to find even one book in decent condition. In five hundred years it's obvious nothing survived."

Brian walked into the second room, then a third. Each was the same as the first, containing a window on each side wall. The rooms had remains of wooden furniture lying in a heap in the center. He commented, "All this history, all the combined knowledge of the Mayan people, either burned by Bishop Landa five hundred years ago or crumbled to dust right here in this building. It's just tragic."

A final room led to the rear of the building. This time not only was a pile of wood on the floor denoting where the table had been but a human skull also lay in the pile, grinning up at the explorers. "This has to be the guide who brought Cortes here," Lynne said quietly. "And then Cortes executed him."

BILL THOMPSON

"And here," Sam said with a flourish, gesturing toward the back wall of the room, "is the thing you've all been waiting for. What's behind door number three?"

A door about three feet wide and six feet high was clearly outlined in the wall. It appeared that mud had been used to seal it on all sides. Dozens of glyphs had been drawn into the mud while it was still wet – most were clearly visible although a few had begun to flake off.

Brian strode to the door, reaching out his hand. "Don't touch it!" Lynne screamed, his fingers millimeters away from the dried mud.

Brian jerked his hand back. "What the hell?" he yelled.

"That stuff will slough off in a second if you touch it, Brian. Don't even get close enough for your breath to hit it."

Duly restrained, Brian said, "According to the letter Alvarado thought Cortes might have returned and taken the gold. Do you think this seal is intact? It looks broken to me."

Lynne stood a foot from the Mayan pictographs and looked at them closely. "It's been opened, I think. See the thin line down the middle of the seal that outlines the door? I think it's been opened but we can only hope Cortes didn't come back and take everything that was inside.

"This is as far as we can go for today. We have a lot of work ahead and we must do our duty as discoverers. I have to thoroughly document this door and its markings before we open it and go into the room beyond. This is unprecedented. I'm not aware that anything like this has ever been seen before. We're the Howard Carters of the Mayan world," Lynne said, referring to the man who discovered the tomb of King Tutankhamen in Egypt in 1922.

"Remember what Howard Carter said when Lord Carnarvon asked him what he saw in the next room?" Sam laughed. "'Wonderful things,' he replied. I hope we can say the same thing when we open that door."

ANCIENT

Brian said, "Alfredo, how about you guys set up camp? We shouldn't stay inside this structure; there's no reason for us to damage anything we don't have to. Lynne, are you going to start now on your documentation?"

"Yep. I'll need you two to help me." From her pack she took out her camera and two stainless steel plates. "These will function as mirrors. It's better to use natural light than a flash or strobe so you guys position yourselves. Sam, stand next to the window and direct the sunlight to Brian's mirror. Brian, pick up where he directs and shine it over here on the glyphs, one by one as I direct you. I'll photograph them first and then I'll draw each one."

Sam complained, "My God, Lynne. There must be a hundred. How long's that going to take?"

"We have to be patient. We're on the verge of something enormous. I can feel it. Even if there's nothing in the room beyond this door these glyphs are priceless artifacts, incredibly rare. We have to do this right."

"Agreed," Brian said. "As much as we want to finish this we have to ensure we document it properly. We would be no better than the Spanish conquistadors if we contributed to the destruction of the heritage of this civilization."

They focused mirrors and watched Lynne work until the sun dropped behind the mountains. The Belizean men had set up camp, begun preparing dinner and at Sam's direction they pulled out the last of the rum to celebrate. She had managed to photograph and draw about thirty glyphs comprising all of one side of the door by the time they had to stop because of the failing light.

"I can read most of the glyphs," Lynne advised the group. "They honor a Mayan ruler – Jasaw Chan K'awill. He reigned in the late ninth century and died around 890 A.D. I figure he must have been the one who was ruler of this city."

"Are there any curses?" Sam laughed. "I heard King Tut's curse killed most of the people who were there when Tut's tomb was found."

BILL THOMPSON

"I really don't believe in curses," she replied. "There actually is one though. In the upper right corner where the horizontal glyphs on the lintel stop and begin moving vertically down the right side of the door there's a curse that roughly says, 'Death awaits those who enter here.'"

Brian laughed. "In reality death awaits all of us – not just the ones who go through that door."

They talked more about the glyphs then Sam asked Lynne to check the signal on her phone. "Check the battery too," Brian said. "Where does it stand?"

She turned the phone on. "Looks like 44% and one bar."

"Why's the phone losing power so fast? No one's using the phone that we don't know about – right? I'm asking everyone – has anyone else used this phone?" He got negative responses from everyone, workmen included.

Lynne said, "You know, it could be losing power because of heat and humidity or just how long since we've charged it. Who knows? IPhones are strange, as anyone who has one knows! I don't think there's a mysterious conspiracy going on. I think it's just a natural phenomenon."

Sam took the phone. "I'm going to try to call." He attempted to get the call to go through several times to no avail. "OK, maybe tomorrow."

"Hey guys, if no one minds, can I guard the phone for tonight?" Brian asked.

Lynne shrugged and handed it to him. "Here, Sherlock Holmes. Let me know when you've solved The Mystery of the Dying Phone Battery." Brian laughed and put the phone just inside his tent flap.

The rum was warm but the celebration was no less happy as a result. Everyone felt a sense of euphoria – they were on the verge of a major discovery and each person went to bed wondering what might lie behind the ancient door.

At midnight a hand reached through Brian's tent flap and felt around until its fingers wrapped around the cell phone. No call was made - after a

ANCIENT

phone number was entered two sentences of text were written. "We found the temple. Captain Jack's wife is dying." A whooshing sound confirmed the text had been sent. Then the text was deleted.

The hand quietly replaced the phone inside Brian's tent. As it withdrew Brian grabbed the wrist tightly, threw back the tent flap and looked directly into the face of the person who had put it there.

"We need to talk," he said grimly to Lynne Parker.

BILL THOMPSON

ANCIENT

CHAPTER TWENTY-FIVE

Arrangements had been made for John Spedino's arrival at Flamingo Airport on the sleepy island of Bonaire in the Dutch Caribbean. Customs was a cursory document check and the godfather was soon seated in the back of a black Audi that the Cardinale Casino had sent to the airport.

Upon his arrival the casino manager, an impeccably dressed man in his thirties, came to the car, opened the door and said in English with a distinct Dutch accent, "Welcome, Mr. Spedino. It's been too long since we last saw you. Thank you for advising us you were coming. I have your suite ready."

"I'm glad it was available on such short notice."

"Ah, sir, it is always available. We never rent your suite to others. It is always ready should you choose to visit us. After all, if you decide on a whim to come check on your investments in Bonaire we should be ready for you, am I not right?"

"I'm not sure what you mean about my investments. I just know I enjoy this beautiful island resort from time to time." Spedino made a mental note that this man talked too much. And whoever had told him that John Spedino had investments in Bonaire had spoken out of turn, to put it mildly. That would be corrected later.

An hour later John Spedino was sitting in the living room of his suite. The doorbell rang and he answered it. "You must be Arthur Borland. Come in."

Borland entered the room and sat where Spedino gestured. "I know you're wondering why I called you here. First, do you know who I am?"

"I've heard your name."

"*You've heard my name?* I am the Godfather. Do you know that?" he roared.

Borland averted his eyes from Spedino's face and nodded.

"Good. I can be your friend or I can be your worst enemy. That's your choice. Now to business. It seems we have some mutual acquaintances – do you know Tomas Rodriguez or Enrique Costa?"

"Those names don't ring a bell, I'm sorry. May I ask what this is about?"

"Patience, Lord Borland. Indulge an old man. You'll soon learn the purpose of my wanting to see you."

The godfather continued. "A few days ago you received a phone call from a man who gave you a deadline – ten days to finish looking for the Ancient Library. Do you know the name of the man who called you?"

"No. I presume he works for Jorge Arocha."

"Ah, there's another name. So you know Mr. Arocha?"

"I don't know him well. He and I are in a couple of business transactions together. That's all. With all due respect Mr. Spedino, I'm not going to talk further until you tell me what's going on."

Spedino was unaccustomed to receiving orders; he was far better at giving them. In this case he merely smiled and said, "Jorge is your partner in the funding of your drug and gambling addictions – is that what you mean?"

Lord Borland blanched. He swallowed hard and stammered, "I . . . I have no idea what you're talking about."

Picking up a piece of paper from the end table next to his chair, Spedino said, "Twenty minutes ago my people whisked you from your chair at the blackjack table to come see me. At that time you were in debt to the Cardinale Casino $213,000. Additionally, you buy your cocaine by the quarter pound – you must have quite a craving. You've bought $15,000 in cocaine just since you came to Bonaire, not to mention over $100,000 you owe to your dealers in New York and London. And if you owe dealers in New York and London, you owe me, Lord Borland. You owe the Godfather. You're in a bit of a fix, I'd say."

"Please. Everything will work out. Jorge Arocha is my friend. I told him I'm good for everything. Once my luck turns around I'll pay everything I owe. He knows I'll pay. Plus I have another deal working that will make everyone rich."

"I'm sad to report that your friend Jorge has departed this earth. He had a misfortune in Guatemala earlier today. I uttered a single word, one command, Arthur, and Jorge Arocha got a bullet to the head."

Borland looked down at the floor, terrified. "I . . . uh . . . what do you want with me, sir?"

"I know what you owe for drugs because Jorge told me. I know what you owe this casino because I own it. This place belongs to me, Arthur. You're dealing with me. Your 'other deal' that's working – I presume you are referring to the expedition on which Brian Sadler is looking for your father, but also for gold.

"Speaking of family, I'm so sorry to hear your mother is dying. You are many thousands of miles from her bedside – this seems like a strange place to wait out her last days. Is she anxious to learn what happened to her husband, your father Jack Borland?"

"Yes . . . yes, my wife is caring for Mother now. I just wanted to be closer to the search for Captain Jack."

"You wanted to be closer to the search for your father and so you came to a casino on an island? You just made a big mistake, my Lord. You're an idiot. Don't ever lie to me again. I have no time to suffer fools like you and I do *not* have time for lies. Your mother isn't dying, Lord Borland. She's over seventy years old and fit as a horse. She lives in a retirement center near Oxford. Half an hour ago she finished a good dinner and was preparing to play a game of bridge. She doesn't know anything about Jack Borland because they were divorced thirty years ago. The staff at the center doesn't recall her ever mentioning his name."

"All right," Borland said quietly. "What do you want?"

"I am in charge of your life from this moment forward. You will do anything I say, exactly when I want it done. Right now I want you to go to your room, pack your bags and come with me."

"And if I refuse?"

John Spedino laughed heartily. "If you *refuse*? I just told you more about your mother than you knew yourself. I know all about your wife too. What's precious to you, Lord Borland? Your family? Your good name and reputation? Your ability to gamble on other people's money whenever you wish? Let's just say this. In life I have learned that the best leverage is in knowing your opponent's weaknesses. And you have so many - I just named a few of them. You won't refuse. You have far too much to lose."

"What do I do about my place at the blackjack table? They're expecting me back."

"Actually they're not. They have already cashed in the tiny stash of chips you had left and applied it against your markers. No one will challenge your leaving and you don't even have to check out. I'm taking care of you, Lord Borland. You're mine in every sense of the word from now on."

"What's in this for you?"

Spedino laughed. "Now it wouldn't be fair if I told you everything, would it?"

They flew without incident to Guatemala City and went directly to the Rosales Hotel and Casino on the fashionable Avenida Reforma. John Spedino was shown to a two-bedroom suite. "This is your room,"

ANCIENT

he pointed to a door on one side of the expansive living room. "Here's ten thousand dollars. Don't spend it all, my addicted friend. I may not be so generous next time. You may snort your cocaine; you may gamble in the hotel. But you may not leave the premises for any reason. If you attempt to do so my people will detain you. For once in your miserable life, be smart about this. Do as I say."

"If I may ask, what are we doing here in Guatemala City?"

"We're waiting."

BILL THOMPSON

ANCIENT

CHAPTER TWENTY-SIX

Lynne and Brian sat by the dying fire. The Belizean man on watch sat ten feet away from them, smoking.

"What do you think you're doing? Who the hell are you communicating with?" He whispered furious words.

Lynne responded quietly. "Calm down. I have one motive, one goal. My goal is to make a name for myself. Lynne Parker is going down in history for finding a previously unknown Mayan city. I learned a long time ago that no one was going to do anything for me. I had to use every angle to further my own agenda. And I'm tired of being an associate professor with no tenure, no recognition, nothing except approving glances at my physique. How about my brain? How about what I can contribute to the knowledge of the Mayan civilization? So I communicate with Tomas. So what? He's not even here – he can't hurt us."

"Tomas? That's who you're texting? My God, Lynne. Are you nuts? Do you think he can't hurt us? Is that what you really believe? Since he knows we've found the temple he now assumes there's gold. What if we get finished and head down to find that Tomas has killed your friend Lucky at Jaguar's Call? Then he kills all of us too, except you of course. To further your 'own agenda' you have to stay alive so you can lead him back up the mountain to the gold he intends to take for himself and his boss, whoever that is. And after we're all dead I'm sure Tomas will send you off with a nice pat on the back and a wish for luck. Really, Lynne? Do you think Tomas will cut you in on anything? You won't be alive long enough to take credit for finding the Ancient Library. He tied my girlfriend naked to a table and left her in the jungle. Do you think a man like that isn't furthering *his* own agenda?"

For nearly twenty minutes they talked. Brian told her how dangerous this whole situation was including his fear that once they came back down the mountain they might be captured by Tomas once again. "We have to all be on the same side, Lynne. If I can't trust you I have to cut you loose regardless of how valuable your training is to this expedition."

She hung her head. "What you say makes sense. I was just trying to make sure I had every angle covered. If things went one way I had you. If they went the other I had him."

He was furious. "What the hell were you thinking? You don't *have* me. And unless you're totally nuts you have to know you don't have him either. He isn't afraid to kidnap people, to torture and lie to them. I can't believe you of all people are working with Tomas, the man who not only kidnapped Nicole, but Sam, Alfredo and me too. For God's sake, do we mean nothing to you?"

Tears streamed down Lynne's cheeks. "I understand. I was wrong – so wrong. Please believe me. What I did was stupid and selfish. I've worked so hard for so many years and gotten nowhere in academia. I just decided this was my last chance for fame. Fortune too, I guess. But fame for sure. I'm done with Tomas. I promise. Keep the phone with you from now on and Brian, I have a gun in my pack, a .38 pistol Lucky told me to bring along. I'm going to give it to you so you have it if anything happens." She walked to her tent and returned quickly, handing him the revolver.

Brian made a quick decision. "I'm taking a chance. I'm going to believe you but I swear we're going to watch you like a hawk. If you betray me again you'll be a prisoner yourself – my prisoner until we can get you back down the mountain. And if that happens you can kiss your career goodbye. Treachery and double-dealing aren't how you get ahead in life. Keep this up and you'll be banned from every academic job in America, if I have anything to say about it. End all this now and we'll put it behind us."

"You can trust me, Brian, I swear it. From this moment forward I'm on your team. One hundred percent. Please forgive me."

BILL THOMPSON

ANCIENT

CHAPTER TWENTY-SEVEN

Lynne spent all of the next day photographing and cataloging the glyphs in her notebook. Brian and Sam held mirrors while Alfredo and the workers lounged around the camp. In the afternoon one of the men carved a long stick with a very sharp point and ventured into the forest. There was a commotion and a high-pitched shriek. "Estas bien, Fernando?" Alfredo called out. *Are you OK?*

"Si." The man came out dragging a twenty-pound animal three feet long behind him.

"Que es un tapir!" he cried.

"What is it?" Brian asked.

"It's a tapir. Its meat is prized and is incredibly delicious. You'll think it's pork. Are we having fresh meat for dinner tonight?" he called to Alfredo.

"Yes we are. I'll prepare it myself."

The prospect of eating something besides packaged meals meant everyone was starving by sunset. They lounged by the campfire as Alfredo cooked the meat on a spit. It smelled delicious.

"I've finished the cataloging," Lynne said. "Tomorrow we open the door."

At five Sam tried to call Odette but the call dropped. He tried a second time with no success. "Third time's the charm," he said. The call went through.

BILL THOMPSON

Odette answered on the first ring. They talked briefly for five minutes then he disconnected. Walking over to Brian Sam said, "Nicole emailed Odette. Said to tell you she loves you very much and things are all fine in Dallas. Nicole also checked with Collette and everything is under control at the New York and London galleries. So just finish up here and have a good time. That was her message to you."

"Did you tell Odette what we've found?"

"Yes. She was really excited. I have to tell you, I am too. I can hardly wait to see what's behind that door. I've been in Belize for decades; I've found a few things on the ground when I was walking around like pottery and stuff, but I've never been a part of what could be something really big."

Sam continued. "I also told her to contact Collette so she can reach Lord Borland and tell him we're at the site but have nothing to report yet."

"That was a good idea. He needs to know where we stand. I know he's worried about his mother so maybe this news will cheer him up."

The roasted tapir dinner was wonderful. They all ate until they were stuffed. Alfredo cleaned up the area and put all the trash into a baggie in his backpack. Brian pulled out a cigar and offered one to Lynne and Sam. "I'll give it a shot," she said.

Brian enjoyed the smoke and had to laugh as Lynne inhaled a big puff, resulting in an extended coughing spell.

"I'd skip the inhaling part," he suggested. "They're plenty strong without it."

"Hell, I've never been very good at smoking. I tried cigarettes in college but that didn't work either. I'll just let this go out and you can smoke it later."

In the middle of the night Brian heard the cell phone ding. He reached in his pack and looked at the screen. "Have you found the gold?"

Brian typed back, "Doesn't look like the right place. More later." Tomas would think the response was from Lynne and perhaps they could stave off his enthusiasm. Brian didn't know that Tomas had been left in the jungle to die. Instead,

ANCIENT

John Spedino read his text. The Godfather might not use modern cell technology but he could adapt when it was required. This was one of those times.

By daybreak everyone was up, each one anxious to get the day started. Lynne took a small chisel and a hammer from her pack. "It's time to open the door. We can use the chisel if we need to but like you said, it looks like someone already opened the door before we got here."

"How do we open this massive door?" Sam asked. "It looks like a solid piece of rock and it must weigh a ton. Literally."

"The Maya knew the science of balance and counterweights," Lynne replied. "I saw a door in a temple in the Yucatan that swung on crude hinges. The trick here is going to be finding what makes it swing open. There has to be a lock somewhere."

She instructed everyone to run his hands up and down the walls. "Stay away from the glyphs. I don't want them damaged any more than we have to."

They felt every square inch of the wall that contained the doorway. They pushed and prodded but nothing happened. "Let's take a break while I think about this." She stood in front of the wall for ten minutes looking it over closely.

"I want to try something," Lynne said at last. "Look up there in the corner where the glyph with the curse is. That set of pictures says 'Death to all who enter here.' It's the only thing on the entire wall that refers to entering." Standing on tiptoe she ran her hand lightly across the glyphs themselves. In the seam between two of them was a round rock. She pressed on it and the door slowly began to move inwards.

"Oh my God! Oh my God!" Lynne cried. She stepped back – when the door had opened a few inches the Belizean worker Juan rushed up and shouted, "Yo primero!" *Me first!*

"No!" Alfredo yelled, trying to stop him as the small man slipped through into the darkness.

Suddenly the door swung shut and they heard a bloodcurdling scream.

"Open the door!" Brian shouted. "Hurry!"

Lynne pressed again but the door wouldn't move. "It may have to reset itself," she yelled. "I'll keep pressing but we have to be careful!"

Sam and Alfredo ran outside and brought a large oblong rock into the room and laid it by the door. "We'll prop it open with this," Sam said. "Hurry!"

Lynne's fingers found the round rock again and she pressed hard. The door swung open and Sam moved the rock to wedge the door. There was a two foot opening and darkness beyond. When the door attempted to close again, it was stopped. The wedge held it open.

"Don't stick your head through the opening until we know what happened to Juan," Sam warned. They grabbed flashlights and aimed them through the narrow aperture.

There was room for only a couple of people at once so Brian stood back as Lynne and Sam took the first turn. "What do you see?" he asked.

"Hard to tell in the darkness," Lynne replied. "I see Juan for sure. Looks like a large stone fell on his back. He's not moving. I . . . I think he's dead, guys."

Lynne spoke more softly. "There's another person in there too. I can't see very well but it looks like Juan may have fallen on another body. The room's pretty big and there's an intact table in the middle. My eyes are getting adjusted now. I also think there may be . . ."

"Codices," Sam finished. "There's at least one shelf with books or scrolls on it, far as I can tell. Guys, we have to get this door open wider so we can check on Juan."

They quickly crafted a plan. They found a longer rock that two men could still carry. They made ready as Lynne pressed the mechanism again. The door first attempted to swing shut but then it swung open further as Alfredo and Brian wedged in

ANCIENT

the second rock. They heard a loud thunk. The door started to shut again but the wedge held fast. The opening was now four feet wide and some light was shining into the room.

Sam said, "Your turn to look, Brian." Lynne continued to peer into the room as Brian moved over to the door. He turned his light upwards.

"Look Lynne, there's some kind of primitive mechanism affixed to the ceiling."

"Yep. It's a trap. Looks like the little side slot on a pinball machine where the ball goes. There are a bunch of round stones. When the door opens a certain distance one of the balls drops. That was the noise we heard when we wedged the door wider. Another of the balls fell."

They shined the lights on the large rock balls. They were spherical and looked as though they weighed about fifty or sixty pounds each. "That must have killed him instantly," Lynne murmured, looking at Juan's body on the ground two feet away. She grieved inside for her fallen comrade.

"Do we feel it's safe to go inside?" Brian finally asked.

"Just watch your step. There may be more traps. And one of us has to stay outside all the time. If the door happens to break the wedge and shut again we have to have someone to open it back up."

"I'll stay for now," Alfredo volunteered. "Go, Brian." In Spanish he turned to the other guide. "You go in too, Fernando." Recalling that Fernando's brother had accompanied Captain Jack, they all feared what he would find.

Brian stepped over the two wedged rocks and shone his light carefully on the floor, walls and ceiling. Carefully he put his full weight down on the stone floor. Nothing happened and he was now standing inside the room.

Lynne followed him in. Fernando stood just behind him in the opening. The room they were in was about ten feet wide and twenty long. It had a large stone table in the middle. Lying on the floor just in front of them was Juan's body, partially covering that of another person. The lower one must have been dead for some time, trapped inside the room with a booby-trapped door.

From outside, Alfredo told them he and Fernando wanted to retrieve Juan's body. Alfredo crept inside - they lifted Juan carefully off the other corpse and took him into the anteroom where they laid his body carefully on the floor.

"Wonder how long this guy's been there?" Brian asked. He leaned down and turned the body over. There was a patina that looked like soot or mold covering the face and hands but it was clear to see that the man was fair-skinned. Brian felt the man's shirt pocket, reached in and pulled out a small notebook and a folded piece of paper.

He opened the first page of the note pad, read it and said, "Well, we've solved the mystery of Jack Borland's disappearance. And I'd bet money what this is." He unfolded the paper and found the map Arthur Borland had described.

"Hi, Captain Jack," Brian said softly. "Looks like you died the way you lived, having an adventure. I bet you'd rather have had it this way than sitting in a rest home playing checkers from your rocking chair. And you found your ancient library. You did it. Arthur will be proud of you."

"So his body's been here over a year," Lynne said. "The way this room is sealed, there's almost no humidity in here. Smell how stale the air is? I doubt you could live in here very long if the door shut and sealed itself. Speaking of that, if those are actually Mayan codices sitting on that shelf on the left they'll turn to dust in a few hours just like the ones in the other rooms did. Air is the worst enemy for them. And they are codices, I'm sure. We need to make this fast, guys."

Lynne asked the guys outside to get some smaller rocks, maybe five pounds each. They passed them inside one by one and she told Brian to throw them on the floor, hitting various stones. "I watched enough Indiana Jones movies that I want to see if there's a booby trap that activates when you step in the wrong place."

Nothing happened. She ventured three feet further into the room and walked to the left. Finally she stood in front of the shelf filled with codices. Turning back to him at the open entrance she said, "Brian, these are priceless manuscripts. There were only four in existence until now. There must be fifty here. Oh my God . . ." she suddenly put her hand to her mouth.

"What is it?" Brian shouted. "What's wrong?"

To Brian's left the door stood open. From Lynne's vantage point she could see behind it. "There are three more bodies behind the door, Brian."

"I figured they were somewhere," he responded quietly.

"How . . . how did you figure that?"

"We know that Captain Jack had three Belizean men with him. The party hasn't been heard from in over a year. We just found the entire expedition. They probably opened the door, everyone rushed in and it all happened in a matter of seconds. The falling stone killed Jack immediately just like Juan a few minutes ago. His three guides were trapped when the door shut and they died either of asphyxiation or starvation. Except for Jack I'm sure it took a long time for everyone to die."

They stepped out and explained to Alfredo what they had found. He and Fernando went inside and they heard muffled sobs from the man who had at long last found his brother.

Fernando came out of the room and sat on the ground, crossing himself and uttering a prayer in Spanish. Everyone in turn offered condolences and they held hands for a group prayer for the brother who had lost his life. Leaving Fernando to mourn his sibling they continued to work.

Sam and Alfredo went into the sealed room and used the five-pound stones to continue checking the floor for traps. They ended up on the other side of the table. "Holy shit, Brian! There's a whole lot of the gold sheets stacked neatly in piles over here,"

Sam yelled out. "Maybe a couple hundred. Maybe more. They have the same glyphs on them that Arthur's two sheets have."

Everyone got a chance to see what was in the room. After fifteen minutes Lynne said, "That's it. We all need to get out, guys. We must let the door seal back to save the codices. Then we need to formulate a plan." They pulled away the stones that blocked the door's closure and it swung tightly shut.

As they ate the rest of the tapir meat for lunch Lynne offered a suggestion. "There's no way we can carry this stuff down and at this point we're really required to get the Guatemalan government involved. For a find like this they won't wait very long to show up, I guarantee it. This is maybe the biggest find in Mayan history. I can't think of anything to top it."

Brian responded, "So what do you suggest?"

"My vote would be to seal one of the codices in plastic wrap and take it and two of the gold sheets. This gives us something to show the authorities. We can notify Arthur Borland of the whereabouts of his father and tell the people in San Ignacio where the three guides ended up. At least there's an ending to the puzzle even if it's tragic. We would leave everything else and post Fernando to guard the site. We have enough food and water for him to stay a week. If something happened to us and someone doesn't show up by then he just walks down the mountain to Jaguar's Call."

The group agreed. Alfredo said, "We can't leave Juan's body out here. An animal will eat him. What should we do?"

After discussion it seemed that the best way to preserve Juan's body until his family could be notified and make a decision was to place it back into the room where Captain Jack and his three guides lay. The room was almost airtight and it would be a safe resting place.

That afternoon Lynne and Brian reentered the sealed room while Sam and Alfredo moved Juan's body, reverently placing it on the ground next to Captain Jack.

ANCIENT

"Let's make this as fast as possible," Lynne said. "I want to keep the air out of here as much as we can." She went straight to the shelf of codices, looked carefully at them and selected one. She immediately put it into a 2-gallon plastic storage bag, expelled all the air and sealed it tightly.

Brian was behind the table. He picked up the first two gold sheets and put them into a canvas bag. "Ready when you are." All told, they had been in the room less than three minutes.

"Me too. Let's go."

They removed the rock wedges and let the door seal itself tightly shut.

Since it was early afternoon, they decided to break camp and start down. Lynne offered, "We can hike until five then get up tomorrow morning at dawn. If everything goes well we'll be back at Jaguar's Call tomorrow afternoon. It took several days to get up here but it will only take maybe a day and a half to get back down. Much easier going and no new trails to blaze."

They left Fernando at the site armed with the pistol Lucky had given Lynne and almost all the food and water they had left. He pitched a tent and was smoking a cigarette as they started their descent.

That night Brian took Sam aside and told him what Brian had learned. He said that Lynne had regularly called Tomas with updates on their progress including notifying him that they had found the temple. "He replied asking if we found the gold and I told him no but I doubt that's going to put him off. We need to think of what's next. Once we leave Jaguar's Call we have to go down to the main highway. How are we going to get back to Belize from there? I don't have my passport – do you?"

"As a matter of fact, I do," Sam replied. "In all this adventure I'd forgotten that I pulled my passport out of the hotel safe when we left for the cave that morning. You never know if you're in Belize or Guatemala out there in the jungle and I find it's always good to carry it just in case."

BILL THOMPSON

"Think I should call Nicole and get her boss to help me get out of Guatemala?"

"I have a plan that's way easier than that, Brian. How about I call Odette when we get to Jaguar's Call? She can get your passport out of the safe and meet us at the bottom of the mountain. The only thing your passport won't have is an exit stamp for Belize and an entry stamp for Guatemala. She can call that Embassy guy in Belmopan and enlist his help – the same guy who rescued Nicole."

"Works for me."

The trek down the mountain the next morning was as easy as Lynne had predicted. They made good time and walked into Jaguar's Call at 3:30.

"Anybody home?" Lynne yelled.

"Hey, it's good to see you," Lucky came out of the office and hugged her tightly. "How did it go? Where are the other two men?"

An hour later Lucky had been told everything. They showed him the Mayan codex but Lynne wouldn't let anyone unwrap it. "This has to be opened in a controlled environment to avoid having it turn to dust," she cautioned.

Lucky held the gold sheets in his hands and gazed at them. "You say there are a lot more of these up there? My God, Lynne. You'll all be famous. You'll all be rich. It's incredible. A lost city – the Ancient Library of the Maya. People have wondered about this for centuries. But you guys found it."

They discussed how much should be revealed when Sam made his call to Odette. Brian said, "I have to call Arthur tonight. I'm OK with telling Odette what we found and I'd like for her to contact Nicole too – she can then call Collette so everyone's in the loop. We need to tell them to keep it quiet though. Before we notify the authorities we sure don't want looters coming around. They'd do anything to get hold of what's up there. I'm sure the life of our guard would be worth nothing if they came for the gold."

ANCIENT

Lynne's phone had been on a charger since they arrived. At five Brian turned it on and placed a call to Arthur Borland.

"I have important information for you," he said in a voicemail. "I'll call you again tomorrow at this same time."

Brian handed the phone to Sam who placed a call to the San Ignacio Inn. Odette answered and they talked for nearly fifteen minutes. Sam told her what they had found but asked her to say nothing to anyone except Nicole, who in turn was to call Collette and confidentially advise her. Odette promised to get Brian's passport and contact the Deputy Ambassador's office.

"I'm sure they can work everything out," she said in her usual optimistic tone. "And I'm so happy for your discovery, Sam. This is just incredible!"

As soon as the call ended Odette dutifully called Nicole, passing along the information along with the admonition to keep it under wraps. Nicole promised to call Collette. When they hung up she first dialed Randall Carter's office.

"Good news, Mr. Carter. After all you've done to help me I wanted you to be among the first to know what's happened in Guatemala. Brian and his party have made a discovery. They've found a lost city and they've located the Ancient Library of the Maya. Gold, codex books, even Captain Jack Borland's body. They've found it all." She asked him to keep it totally confidential and he assured her that was no problem.

And he did except for one phone call. "Have you heard the news?"

"No. What news is that?"

Randall Carter related everything he had been told by Nicole in confidence. "Looks like they're coming back down the mountain the day after tomorrow. I thought you would want to know all of this."

"Oh yes. This is very important information. Thanks, Randall. I owe you one."

BILL THOMPSON

Randall Carter sat back in his chair, wondering if being owed a favor by this man was worth the price one had to pay. Was he being seduced by the temptation of the fast life, limos and jets, money beyond imagination? Carter already had it all – why did Spedino's power enthrall him so much? What was it worth to sell your soul?

ANCIENT

CHAPTER TWENTY-EIGHT

Late the next afternoon Brian, Sam and Alfredo were camped halfway between Jaguar's Call and the highway at the bottom of the mountain. Lynne came along too so she could retrieve her phone from Brian once they met up with Odette.

Brian called Arthur Borland but his phone again went to voicemail. *That's odd,* he thought, leaving another message for Arthur to call him at his earliest convenience.

There was an air of anticipation as the four cooked their last dinner on the mountain. Lucky had replenished their provisions so they had beef jerky and canned potatoes. Coffee followed, and Brian smoked his last cigar. Pumped by excitement, no one slept much that night – they took turns on three-hour watches and each of them was already awake when it was time for the shift to change.

They packed everything for one final morning and started downhill. Around noon they reached the highway. Sam saw his pickup parked on the side of the road and ran to embrace Odette. They introduced her to Lynne then Odette steered everyone to the back of the truck. She opened a cooler and handed each of them an ice-cold Gallo, the local Guatemalan beer. "I'm not sure anything has ever tasted so good in my life," Brian said.

"How'd Brian's passport work out?" Sam asked Odette.

BILL THOMPSON

"All good. I ran it down to the Embassy in Belmopan yesterday and they stamped some things and issued a letter to Guatemala. This morning when I came through the border station I presented the letter and got it stamped here too. Brian, I'm pleased to say that you're free to come back to Belize!" She handed him the passport and the stamped paperwork.

The group stood and talked by the side of the two-lane highway as an occasional car sped by. In a few minutes a black four-door sedan approached, slowed and pulled in behind Sam's truck. They all looked at it as the back door opened and a man got out.

"Who's that?" Sam asked quietly.

Brian smiled. "That's Arthur Borland!"

"Arthur! Am I glad to see you! I have news for you. Did you get my messages?" As he thought through it, Brian began to wonder. "How'd you know to come here?"

When he got closer Brian saw that Arthur's countenance was grim. He was shaking and his eyes darted left and right. "Uh, Brian . . ." he stammered. "Did you find the gold . . . uh, and my father, of course? What did you find?"

"What's going on, Arthur? Why are you so nervous?"

The driver of the sedan got out and walked to the back. He opened the door and a man stepped out. He was impeccably dressed in a grey suit, white shirt and tie, despite the temperature and humidity.

"Hello, Brian. It's been a long time."

"What the hell are you doing here?" Brian's anger overflowed.

Sam came over. "Is something wrong, Brian? Do you need some help?"

"No, Mr. Adams. He doesn't need any help. Aren't you going to introduce me to your friends, Brian?" He turned to Sam and said, "I'm John Spedino."

Sam was shocked when he heard the name. He recognized it immediately. But what was this mob boss doing here in the jungle? And how did he and Brian even know each other?

Spedino asked to talk to Brian alone. They got into the back seat of the car. As much as Sam and Lynne wanted to know what John Spedino's connection was to Brian they felt they had to tell him about Captain Jack. They said they had found his father's body along with his three guides. Borland's head dropped as he heard the news and their explanation of what had likely happened.

"I was afraid it would turn out like this since it had been so long."

Lynne and Sam offered their condolences.

"Thanks. He was a real adventurer," Arthur said. "He would have wanted to go this way."

They discussed the find. "Did you find gold?" Arthur asked.

"Until we find out more about why you and John Spedino are hanging out together, I think we'll stop talking for now about what we found."

Arthur fidgeted, his hands never still. "It's all right. I can't talk right now but you'll learn everything shortly."

In a few minutes John Spedino and Brian Sadler emerged from the sedan.

"Brian's riding back with me," Spedino said.

"Right," Brian replied impassively. "I need to talk to him. We'll meet you all at the hotel."

Sam asked, "Brian, are you OK? What's going on? How do you two know each other?"

Brian looked at his friend. "Trust me, Sam. I'll tell you everything soon. I'm good tor now."

He handed Lynne her phone. She hugged him and said, "Well done, Mr. Amateur Archaeologist. Quite a discovery we have on our hands. I think you've joined the big leagues!"

"Thanks. We couldn't have done it without you, Lynne. Literally. I'll be in touch to let you know what's next."

"OK, call me and let's talk about how to handle everything. We have to get our man back down from up there. And the bodies."

Spedino said, "Brian will be in touch once we have our plans finalized."

"*Our* plans?" Sam was shocked. "Brian, what the hell is this guy talking about? What does he have to do with this? And why does *he* have plans?"

"I suggest you stop now before you say more than you should, Mr. Adams. Brian and I will meet you at the hotel. He can explain everything then. Rest assured my interest in this matter is the same as yours. The outcome will be positive for everyone. Gather your things, Brian. I have a lot to tell you."

Brian said, "Sam, just trust me. You've known me for years. Trust me."

Arthur climbed in the front seat of Spedino's sedan as Brian threw his backpack into the trunk after retrieving his passport and the paperwork. He and John Spedino got in the back and the car drove away.

"What the hell was that all about?" Lynne said to Sam.

"I'm not sure. Do you know who that guy John Spedino is?"

"Nope. Is he a movie star or something?"

"Not exactly. He's called 'Teflon Two.' He's a mobster. He's head of the Mafia in the U.S.– some people say he may even be the Godfather worldwide."

"Are you serious?" Lynne was shocked. "So Brian's in bed with the mob? What's this going to mean to our discovery?"

"I trust Brian. I have to believe he's not in bed with this guy. Brian's a good man. I know that. Something's going on and I'm not going to jump to conclusions. Obviously he knows this guy but he sure wasn't happy when he saw Spedino get out of the car. I promise I'll call you the second I find out anything about what's going on."

ANCIENT

CHAPTER TWENTY-NINE

The border crossing was uneventful for John Spedino and his passengers. At Melchor de Mencos they were all required to exit the vehicle and go through the Guatemalan exit procedures while the driver pulled the car to an inspection area. Brian and the others walked through a narrow hallway, cleared Guatemalan immigration without a hitch then walked outdoors fifty feet to another building which bore a large sign that said, "Welcome to Belize." Customs and immigration on that side took five minutes and they were soon reunited with their driver.

On the Belizean side of the border the town became Benque Viejo del Carmen, or just Benque to the locals. At Spedino's instruction the driver parked at an outdoor café situated along the Mopan River. Spedino said, "We're going to have a coffee, men, while we finish our conversation and allow Brian's friends to get back to the hotel before we arrive."

An hour later the sedan pulled up at the San Ignacio Inn.

Sam had stood in the front window for a half hour watching for Brian. He saw the car pull up and observed Brian as he exited the back seat. His friend's jaw was set and his face showed his anger. The driver popped the trunk and Brian pulled out his pack. He said something through the car window to whoever was in the back seat then he walked inside as the car pulled away.

Odette welcomed him back. "I can't tell you how good it is to have you two safely back here!"

He hugged her and said, "I need to talk to Nicole. Where can I use a phone?"

"Oh, you just reminded me!" Odette ran behind the front desk and grabbed a package. "This came from Nicole this morning. I think it's a new iPhone – she told me she was sending you one by Fedex."

He tore open the package and was pleased to see a new phone programmed with his number and all the old contact information already transferred. It was ready to go – she had even charged the battery. "Excuse me for a few minutes," he said as Odette handed him his key. He walked up the stairs to his room, shut the door and dialed the number.

Ryan Coleman answered Nicole's office line.

"Put Nicole on," Brian said curtly.

"She's not in the office. She's at a deposition downtown but said she'd call you this evening if you're back in Belize." Brian affirmed that he would be waiting for her call then stripped off his clothes and spent ten minutes in the hottest shower he could stand.

As Brian walked downstairs he saw Odette and Sam on the patio. She had ordered up snacks from the kitchen. As Brian sat down he saw Leo, the man whom he had dubbed the best bartender in Belize, coming through the lobby with a freshly prepared XO vodka martini in his hand. "Mr. Brian, welcome back. We're all happy to have you safely in San Ignacio."

"Leo," Brian said earnestly, "seeing you walk through the lobby with that martini was one of the best sights I've seen in weeks."

As soon as Leo had left and they were alone Sam Adams jumped right in. "So tell me what's going on. What's the deal with John Spedino? Why is he here?"

ANCIENT

"Here's what I can tell you at the moment. I'll know more when I talk to Nicole – apparently she's representing him as his attorney at the request of the senior partner in her law firm. She's very good at criminal law so I'm really not too surprised he would want her on his team. But Spedino told me she is going to be acting on his behalf going forward in some other arrangement. There's more, Sam. There's some stuff that I don't want to talk about right now. There are things I need to hear from her, not from that asshole. I have to talk to her. Hopefully I can tell you more after that."

Brian explained his prior association with John Spedino and the mobster's involvement with The Bethlehem Scroll, one of the world's priceless artifacts. Sam felt better once he understood that Brian detested Spedino but was likewise gravely concerned about Nicole's potential involvement with him.

"Arthur Borland apparently owes the mob a lot of money. Something about a gambling addiction, maybe drugs too. I don't know about all that but I'm going to try to reach Arthur and talk to him when Spedino's not around. He has wormed his way into our discovery through Arthur. Spedino wants a cut – not just to settle what Arthur owes him, but a big piece of our deal. He wants fifty percent ownership of the codices and the gold and says the rest of us can do whatever we want. Makes him no difference."

Brian said that Spedino intended to play a behind-the-scenes role with hidden ownership so no one would know he was involved. "He says that'll be better for the four of us, but in reality his public ownership of anything would bring up many more questions than it did answers. He's way too high profile to own something in his own name and he's used to doing everything in secret anyway. This would be no different."

"By God, we aren't going to let this bastard weasel his way into this deal, are we? What would he do with the gold and the books anyway?"

BILL THOMPSON

"Whatever he does with the things we found, you can bet they won't end up benefitting anybody but him. He wants everything brought to the USA any way we can, legally or not. He says he's going to send a plane to fly the stuff back if we can get the codices properly preserved to make the flight. I told him I wouldn't be a party to smuggling."

"What did he say to that?"

"He just laughed and said, 'Talk to Nicole. She'll come up with a solution.'"

"What the hell did that mean?"

Brian shrugged, his eyes angry. "I don't know. I don't know what he's done to Nicole or what hold he thinks he has over her but I'll kill the bastard if he hurts her. I'm going to talk to her this evening. That's all I can say for now." He clenched his fists tightly in anger.

Sam said, "The truth of the matter is that Lynne has undoubtedly already contacted the Guatemalan archaeological authorities so the idea of whisking the codices and gold out of the country just won't happen. It's probably out of our hands already."

"That alone gives me some comfort but you have to realize that a guy like John Spedino never plays by the rules. He'll come into Guatemala and spread money around to buy off some people and next thing you know some or all of the stuff we found will just turn up missing."

"That really couldn't happen, could it?" Odette asked.

"In the USA, not so much. In a third world country, absolutely. Payoffs are common in many small countries and I'm afraid he's going to take control of this stuff either with our help or without it. This is the most important Mayan find in history. We can't let him do this. But at the moment I don't have enough information. I have to talk to Nicole."

ANCIENT

CHAPTER THIRTY

They ate an early dinner. Brian excused himself and was back in his room by seven. Ten minutes later his phone rang.

"Hey there, baby," Nicole said brightly. "Are you safely back in San Ignacio?"

"Cut the shit, Nicole. I just spent the afternoon with a friend of yours – a really close friend. Do you need three guesses who he is? Anything you need to get off your chest?" His voice was short, abrupt.

She started to cry. "Brian, I promise you I was going to tell you everything before you had to ask me. How did John find you? I didn't tell him anything about you. I swear Brian, I wouldn't do anything to hurt you, ever."

"'John', as you call him now that you're on a first-name basis, tells me you're his new right hand man. He tells me the new relationship he has with you is far more than attorney-client. He says you're his consigliere, Nicole, and his personal little consigliere too. He showed me the video. He showed me. I saw you. I saw what you did. Tell me the truth – can you still tell the truth now that you've literally slept with the devil? What have you done? What the hell have you done?"

She told him everything. She started with the lunch at the Petroleum Club where Randall Carter introduced her to John Spedino. She told of her fear that Carter was enamored with Spedino but she also said how easily that could happen given the charming demeanor of this ruthless mobster. She told Brian how they had met for drinks after a long day of work and she had gone to the restroom, returned and had a second cocktail, remembering nothing after that.

Sobbing, she continued. "Brian, I swear to you I wouldn't do this. But I did. He drugged me – it had to be some kind of date-rape drug – and he recorded me. I was naked and so was he. We were in my bed. I did things to him, Brian. But I don't remember, I swear. When I went with him to the airport he showed me the video then he made me perform sex on him in the back seat of the limo. And I did it because I was terrified. I'm so sorry. I'm so incredibly sorry. I know you probably can't forgive me – I don't know if I can forgive myself – but he drugged me. I swear to God."

She continued, telling him that Spedino intended to make her his consigliere, his closest advisor. He would blackmail her and ruin her career if she refused. "But listen to me. I've already done something about it. It won't erase the things that have happened, but it will clear my conscience that I've taken every measure I can to stop this monster." She explained what she meant.

At last she stopped talking. There was no response. "Sweetie, please say something," she said, tears streaming down her face. "Please don't cut me off."

He took a deep breath. "Nicole, I hear your story and I understand your version of what happened. Now that I've heard both sides, I want to believe you. I don't think the truth matters one iota to John Spedino. I want your story to be the true one. I also think what you're doing now is the proper move to begin to make things right. But you need to understand something. At this point I need some time to think about where we go from here – you and I. Regardless of your motives or your memory this son of a bitch has had sex with my girlfriend, the

ANCIENT

woman I love, and you've done things to him that are the most intimate of all. Things you and I did."

As he continued all he could hear was sobbing on the other end. "Right now I have to figure out my feelings and see whether they can survive this or not. Are you the same person you were? Am I? I just don't know. I'll call you later." He hung up.

BILL THOMPSON

ANCIENT

CHAPTER THIRTY-ONE

After dropping Brian at the hotel John Spedino and Arthur Borland had headed back to the border. The crossing into Guatemala was again uneventful. The driver steered the car through the vehicle lane while the men walked through Belizean immigration, had their passports stamped then walked to the building that said, "Welcome to Guatemala" in both English and Spanish.

Once inside they stood in a short line. Arthur presented his passport to a sleepy clerk who stamped it and waved him through without a glance. John Spedino laid his passport on the desk and the inspector took it from him. Looking up into his face the inspector said, "Welcome back to Guatemala, Senor Spedino. I hope you have a good trip!" He smiled broadly, stamped the passport and waved him through. As soon as John Spedino had exited the building the inspector picked up the phone next to his desk and said, "He just entered the country."

Spedino had spoken to his pilot earlier, ordering the Gulfstream to fly to the town of Flores fifty miles from the border. It was a small airport and saved them an hour of driving. The godfather was ready to get in the air and out of Guatemala. Things had gone very well and once he disposed of the sniveling idiot in the car with him he would be very happy indeed.

BILL THOMPSON

The men sat in silence as they drove to Flores. The car pulled into the airport and drove toward a hodgepodge of hangars in which small airplanes were parked. The Gulfstream sat prominently in front of one of the buildings and the driver went directly to it.

As he exited the car John Spedino was surprised to see no security people around his plane. That was standard operating procedure and he made a mental note to deal with the pilot about this error once they were back in New York. A uniformed officer strode out of the terminal building and stood at the foot of the stairs while Arthur Borland entered the plane, followed by Spedino. The officer came on board and remained at the back of the cabin while Spedino and Borland sat down.

The door to the cockpit opened and a man in a suit walked out. John Spedino looked at him, a flash of anger on his face. "Who the hell are you? Where's my pilot?"

"Mr. Spedino, I'm James Ruskin, and I can't tell you how glad I am to see you."

"You're American? What's going on? Get off my plane."

"I'm afraid that's not possible, sir. In fact, there are two of us on here who are going to arm-wrestle later on to figure out which one of us gets this gorgeous jet of yours!"

Spedino angrily looked at the man. "Get out of my plane," he said curtly. "You have no idea who you're dealing with."

The man seemed extraordinarily happy. "Au contraire, Mr. Spedino. I know exactly who you are. That's why we're so glad you're here! I need to dispense with a couple of formalities before I explain everything. As I said, I'm James Ruskin. And yes, I am an American. I'm in charge of the Drug Enforcement Administration's field operations team in Guatemala. First I want to let you know that you are under arrest for the murder of Jorge Arocha. The gentleman behind you is from the Guatemala City Police Department and he is here to take you into custody."

ANCIENT

Spedino moved to put his hand inside his jacket. "No, Senor," the man behind him said as he pulled a pistol from his holster. "Raise your hands in the air now."

Ruskin walked to Spedino, reached inside the godfather's coat and withdrew a gun.

"Stand up," the Guatemala policeman said. He frisked him thoroughly then pulled Spedino's hands behind his back, cuffed him and pushed him back into his seat.

"I'm not quite through, Godfather," the American said, smiling ear to ear. "That's what you call yourself, correct? I want to use respectful terminology. Mr. Spedino, you've become a worldwide sensation! In addition to your problem here in Guatemala you're charged with drug trafficking in the United States and other charges are pending in London and the Dutch Netherlands Antilles, specifically the island of Bonaire."

"I have no idea what you're talking about."

"Let me read you your Miranda rights and I'll explain everything." He pulled a card from his shirt pocket and began to read. At the end he said, "Do you understand your rights and do you wish an attorney at this time?"

"I understand my rights. I don't want an attorney at this time," Spedino replied. "What the hell is this about? You people are making a huge mistake. Enormous. You have nothing on me."

The American rapped once on the cockpit door, a signal to the pilot. Momentarily over the cabin intercom system Spedino's cruel voice could clearly be heard. "I'm sad to report that your friend Jorge has departed this earth. He had a misfortune in Guatemala earlier today. I uttered a single word, one command, Arthur, and Jorge Arocha got a bullet to the head."

"You little prick!" Spedino spat words furiously at Arthur Borland. "You wore a wire. Your life isn't worth five cents . . ."

""Uh oh," the American officer said, still beaming. "Better not make things worse, Godfather.

BILL THOMPSON

Let me return to my explanation. Your popularity has created a problem for us, sir. Everyone wants you. They are going to detain you here in Guatemala for murder. I want you extradited to the States for drug trafficking."

"Drug trafficking?" Spedino snarled. "You have nothing on me."

"Let's see, what was it you said to Lord Borland? 'If you owe dealers in New York or London, you owe me, the Godfather,'" the drug agent recited from memory. "And your airplane – well, my Guatemalan friend here thinks the millions Guatemala can get from selling your plane will supplement the police force's budget nicely. I of course would like to have the DEA get those funds. But we'll decide that later - right, Antonio?" The Guatemalan policeman laughed heartily.

"Excuse me for digressing, Godfather. I know your time is valuable. I was explaining that Guatemala wants you, London wants you for drugs, Bonaire for secret money laundering and casino ownership without proper licensing and of course we want you back in the good old U.S. of A. for that little drug trafficking thing you admitted to on the tape.

"The good news is if you agree to be extradited and Guatemala goes along we might get you back into the States within a month or two. If everything goes well here in Guatemala, that is. And as you probably know since you're a big international businessman, sometimes these little countries are slow to act, sometimes not. I hope for your sake things go fast because you're going to be sitting in a nasty jail cell in Guatemala City until either they decide to prosecute you or we get you back."

Spedino sat back and said, "I want an attorney."

"Of course you do and you need one badly I think," the American officer said. "We'll make sure you get to make that phone call just as soon as you're booked in Guatemala City."

"I can do it from here on my phone."

ANCIENT

"Sorry, Senor," the Guatemalan police officer said. "That is not allowed. You will do things my way now. You are the big shot in some places but here it will be different. Here you may find that some of our prisoners are not so partial toward Americans. We will of course do our best to keep you safe and secure." He laughed again.

BILL THOMPSON

ANCIENT

CHAPTER THIRTY-TWO
The Mansion on Turtle Creek, Dallas
Six months later

Brian tapped his glass with a spoon. The guests at the long table stopped their conversations and looked expectantly to the head of the table.

"I'd like to start by saying how thrilled I am to have all of you here with Nicole and me in Dallas. I hope you enjoyed the wonderful dinner – I think the Mansion on Turtle Creek and our servers are due some recognition for the fantastic service tonight. Come in, ladies and gentlemen!"

The door at the end of the private dining room opened and the men and women who had attended them paraded inside to enthusiastic applause from the seven people at the table.

Once dishes were cleared he continued. "Thanks to the efforts of the people in this room we made the most fascinating discovery in Mayan history. For years to come scholars will be working on translating the seventy-two codices we found. The work they've done so far has already given the world amazing insight into this ancient civilization whose history was shrouded in mystery. And there are many codices left to translate - they've barely scratched the surface."

He reached into an envelope that had been next to his place setting and pulled out one of the gleaming gold sheets the expedition had found in

BILL THOMPSON

Guatemala. Holding it up for the assemblage to see, he said, "We found three hundred and six gold sheets. The world wonders what the value of this hoard is. In fact, every single one is priceless. Before the Mayan ruler of the lost city ordered them removed, they and many others covered the outside of the building in which we found them. It was part of a golden city shining in the clouds high above the rain forest. Most of the sheets of gold were transported to Hernan Cortes in order to ransom the king of the Mayans. But obviously the ruler hid these particular sheets to keep them safe.

"The gold sheets have given us dramatic insight into the writing and history of the Mayan people from which they came. Like the codices this project will take years to complete. And six months from now we'll be featured on national TV when Discovery presents its four-hour documentary on our expedition."

Brian stopped talking and paused to look at each of the guests individually. "I know that everyone here knows everyone else but I want to go around the table and acknowledge the contribution each of you has made." He turned to his right and looked at Nicole. "You I am saving for last!"

The group laughed as he turned the other direction and said, "Odette Adams. You were our communications link. Your messages were passed to critical people at critical times and it was crucial that we had your help. And you gave moral support to Sam. I know he thought of you often as he trudged up that mountain with us. Thank you." Applause.

"Sam Adams, I've known you since I was five years old. We grew up together and remained friends even when you moved far, far away and became a charter boat captain and hotel owner in paradise!" Laughter. "I thank you for being my friend and for being the person I could lean on in our expedition when I needed support. I thank you for going every step of the way with me. Many people thank you for the work you and Lucky did to retrieve the bodies of the people who died in the ancient city – Jack

ANCIENT

Borland, his three men and our comrade Juan. You and Lucky gave your time, selflessly leading a group of men back up to the top to bring the fallen down to their families for a proper burial. You're the best and I will never forget it." Applause.

"Lynne Parker. Lynne Parker. The vixen of the jungle who will do anything to further her goals. What can I say?" Laughter, not terribly sincere from Nicole. "We had a few ups and downs but what counts is that we made it. We found what you knew in your heart was up there. You've come a long way in the six months since we found the Ancient Library. You're now a full tenured professor at UCLA with a major discovery under your belt. And it was *your* discovery. Your knowledge kept us on track and your perseverance brought us to the previously unknown Maya city we found. It truly wouldn't have happened without you even though you were on the wrong track for awhile. Now you're going to be a TV personality as the narrator of the upcoming documentary. I salute you, Professor Parker!" Applause.

There was an empty seat next to Lynne with a place setting in front of it. Gesturing to the chair, Brian said, "Ralph 'Lucky' Buncombe. Proprietor of the Jaguar's Call on a remote mountain in Guatemala. I wish you were here tonight, Lucky, but you're here in spirit. Thanks to you we found out what Jack Borland knew, we had food and water . . . a little rum and a little warm beer . . ." Laughter. " . . . and from your jumping off spot we made it five thousand more feet to the top. To a lost city. Thank you, Lucky, for being there for Lynne and for us." Applause.

He continued around the table. "Alfredo Rivera. The man who wanted nothing more than to show me a new cave he had found!" Laughter. "The man who never came back to rescue me, allowing me to learn that I was man enough to climb out of that damned hole by myself!" More laughter. "Alfredo, you were the strength on our expedition. You were the man who kept our workers on track and who toiled alongside them every step of the way. You were the man who had to leave one of your countrymen in a ruined building on a Mayan mountain. You are a man among men. Thank you for everything you did to make our expedition a success." Applause.

"Arthur Borland, stand up please." Lord Borland pushed his chair back and stood, holding his hands in the air as if to ask why he was being singled out. "This man had perhaps the hardest role of all. A British Lord, a member of the aristocracy who took on another personality entirely to bring to justice one of the most dangerous men in the world. Without regard to the reputation and safety of himself or his family, Arthur created the fiction and assumed the character of a drug and gambling addict. I hope I don't embarrass you – everyone who knows you has seen your chronic nervous condition – your shaking hands. But in your role as an addict that manifestation was a big help. You made a great addict but I'm really glad it was all an act." Applause. "I'm not quite finished with Arthur but you may be seated, my Lord. After all, you're considerably older than I am." Laughter.

"Your father Captain Jack Borland never wavered from his belief that there was a treasure to be found. He spent his life and his fortune seeking it and I choose to believe before he died he laid his eyes on what he sought – the codices of the ancient Maya. Jack Borland is an inspiration to us all. There's a little bit of Captain Jack – a tiny bit of adventurer – in every human being. And he will be prominently featured in our television documentary – the ancient city is as much his discovery as it is ours. Tonight I salute your father, Captain Jack Borland, along with you." A toast and applause.

"Finally Lord Borland, thanks to your courage and your foresight in knowing exactly what might trap John Spedino, you singlehandedly brought him to justice. And for any of you who might have been lost in the jungle the last couple of months and missed the news, I'm pleased to say that the godfather was sentenced to life in prison not here in

America, but in Guatemala. We're optimistic that his money won't buy him happiness there and the United States Government has promised to help keep an eye on his incarceration. If things begin to get too cushy they'll attempt to seek extradition to bring him back here for more justice. Arthur, my sincerest gratitude goes to you. There is absolutely no telling where this would have gone without your courage and selfless service." Loud applause.

Two more empty chairs were next. "Those chairs represent Juan and Fernando, our two Belizean workers and our friends. Juan gave his life on our expedition and Fernando found his brother, a member of Captain Jack's team who died with Jack. Fernando remained alone to guard our site until the authorities and Lynne could get back to work on cataloging everything. These two men were tireless workers and an integral part of our team. Juan will be missed by his family and by all of us as well. Fernando, although you are not here tonight we salute you and your brother!" A toast followed by applause.

"Saving the best for last, as they say. Now I want to say a few words about Nicole Farber. Here's a person who signed up for a little bit and ended up with a whole lot. Like Alfredo, she was along for the ride – a visit to an unexplored cave on the third day of our trip to Belize. She wasn't going into the jungle with me. She was going to hang around at the hotel and have a little vacation then jet back here to Dallas to wait for my return. My *prompt* return." Laughter.

"And what happened instead? She was kidnapped, treated cruelly and inhumanely by a crazed man driven by the desire for gold. She escaped by herself . . ." enthusiastic applause. " . . . made it across the border with no papers and no passport, got back to Dallas and found herself in the clutches of the Godfather himself. Sadly, that was my fault. If Nicole had never met me she would never have met John Spedino.

"So the Godfather threatens to blackmail her after drugging her. He appoints her his right-hand person, his consigliere, and what does Nicole do? She courageously goes straight to the FBI and volunteers to bring him down. Risking her stellar career at Carter and Wells, she talks to the senior partner at the firm and tells him everything. It turns out Spedino's cast his web of crime around Randall Carter too. Impressed by Nicole's action in the face of danger, he chooses the high road as well. Her boss goes to the IRS and provides proof that John Spedino is the secret owner of one of the largest mortgage brokers in the southwest, funneling millions of dollars a year in profits through a series of foreign corporations to avoid taxation. So now John Spedino has also been charged with income tax evasion but he can't defend himself. He's off enjoying the Federal penitentiary in Guatemala City! So that charge will have to wait until Spedino gets to come home, if that ever happens.

"Nicole, my partner and my best friend, I salute you for your help. You may have done our country the greatest service it's seen in awhile – the ridding of a festering maggot named John Spedino." Everyone stood, applauding wildly.

"In conclusion I thank you all for making the trip here . . ."

Nicole stood. "One moment, Brian. We've omitted one person from the honors tonight."

"Really, sweetie? Who's that?" Brian looked at her, genuinely puzzled.

"You! Now sit down." As he sat Nicole did too, gesturing to Odette.

One by one the people at the table stood, paying their respects to a man who had faced danger, handled adversity admirably, fought for what was right and survived an ordeal most people would hope to never face. Each of them told what Brian Sadler meant to them personally until at last it came back to Nicole.

She stood and turned to face him. "Brian, you've stood by me personally through all this. You've proven your love for me in a way I hope I can prove to you over many more years together. In addition you've been part of an expedition that gave Central America and the world a new treasure, a previously lost city and the only collection of Maya codices in existence. The millions of dollars of value in gold pales in significance to the historic value of the books your group found.

"To recognize your contribution, Randall Carter and I have pledged one million dollars each to build a new museum at Tikal, Guatemala's most well known and most visited archaeological site. We have received approval from the government to house the codices there. A complete laboratory will be created to study and catalog the manuscripts and we'll have an exhibition room displaying them, much as the Dead Sea Scrolls have been exhibited in the United States and Israel. Hundreds of the gold sheets you found will be displayed too and the government is considering an auction of others in the future to benefit archaeological efforts in Guatemala.

"Lord Borland, I'm pleased to announce that the part of the building dedicated to the ancient city they discovered will be known as the Captain Jack Borland Hall. It will be a lasting tribute to him." She turned back to Brian. "Brian, it's my honor to name our new structure the Sadler Museum of the Maya."

Thunderous applause and a standing ovation. And for once, a speechless Brian Sadler.

BILL THOMPSON

ANCIENT

EPILOGUE
Pavon Prison
Fraijanes, Guatemala

John Spedino sat in the room where he had lived for six months. As is the case in many third world jails, money could buy something close to happiness at Pavon Prison. Word and dollars traveled fast in the small town of Fraijanes near Guatemala City. It had taken less than six hours after his arrival for the godfather to be housed in a room that wasn't created to be a cell at all but instead had been a guard station for one of the cellblocks. It was quite large by prison standards, almost eleven feet square, and Spedino's money had bought a regular bed with mattress and box springs, a table and chair. He even had a lock on the door, this one on the inside where he was in control of it instead of the guards.

The godfather had finally joined the technology of the twenty-first century. He had bought a cell phone rather than standing in line to use the pay telephone which worked only sporadically anyway. Rafael, the man who had served Spedino well in Guatemala, visited him every third day unless the godfather summoned him sooner for something specific. Rafael was such a regular by now that he was admitted with a wave and skipped the usual pat-down and frisking for contraband. After all, with the godfather's money there was really no such thing as contraband while he was incarcerated at Pavon Prison.

The United States Embassy kept a close eye on Spedino's incarceration. They knew his dollars had bought him comfort but the officials were determined not to let him go free. Guatemala had insisted on keeping Spedino for itself. It was a major coup for a small country to have a high-ranking U.S. Mafia chieftain – the highest, in fact – and the Guatemalan government created a media heyday with the story.

Thanks to the U.S. Embassy, extradition papers had been placed on file with the courts in the capital, to be activated in the event anything resulted in a potential release of the godfather. The United States Ambassador himself had had a quiet conversation with the Attorney General of Guatemala, stating in no uncertain terms that it would be considered a direct insult to the American government if Guatemala failed to keep this man imprisoned.

The Attorney General stopped by Pavon Prison one morning on an unscheduled visit as he did from time to time when he had business in the area. Over coffee in the warden's office he mentioned that he would like to see John Spedino so that he could report back to the United States Embassy that things were going well.

The men passed through several checkpoints and lockdown facilities before they reached the area where Spedino was incarcerated. The warden walked to Spedino's room and knocked on the door. There was no answer and when the Attorney General tried the knob he found the door was locked. A guard was called and the warden learned that no second key to this room existed. The guard took a few minutes to jimmy the lock with a small pick and the door was finally opened.

John Spedino's room was neat and tidy. The bed was made but there was no sign of the godfather.

ANCIENT

"Where is he?" the warden angrily asked the guard, who shrugged his shoulders. This was embarrassing, in front of the nation's highest legal official.

"You know that we do not control his movements within the prison," the guard responded.

The penitentiary was placed on lockdown. As the warden and the Attorney General waited in the administration area, the guards did a headcount. They were off by more than twenty inmates – a situation that apparently wasn't that rare in this third-world prison environment. One of the men who was missing was the godfather, John Spedino. Upon being questioned none of the guards could recall having seen him for at least two weeks.

BILL THOMPSON

Thank you!

Thanks for reading *Ancient*. If you liked it and have a few minutes **I'd really appreciate a brief review on Amazon, Goodreads or both.** Even a line or two makes a tremendous difference so thanks in advance for your help!

To get advance notice about upcoming books, please sign up at billthompsonbooks.com.

Please join me on:

Facebook
http://on.fb.me/187NRRP

Twitter
@BThompsonBooks

Books by Bill Thompson

The Crypt Trilogy

THE RELIC OF THE KING
THE CRYPT OF THE ANCIENTS
GHOST TRAIN: THE LOST GOLD OF THE NAZIS

Brian Sadler Archaeological Mystery Series

THE BETHLEHEM SCROLL
ANCIENT:
A SEARCH FOR THE LOST CITY OF THE MAYAS
THE STRANGEST THING
THE BONES IN THE PIT
ORDER OF SUCCESSION

Middle Grade Fiction

THE LEGEND OF GUNNERS COVE

Made in the USA
Columbia, SC
27 October 2023